I0626284

Dallas Shadows 2

By: L.R. Claude

If you ever doubt yourself,
you may never truly find out how amazing you can
be.
If you ever question yourself,
you may never realize how amazing you already are.

Cover Design:
Heidi Hobde Dailey

Cover Model:
R.M.Foor

CONTENTS

I am considered many things by many people, beautiful, strong, poetic, athletic, threatening, stubborn, and sometimes even vulgar. I consider myself independent and strong, I'm also downright adorable. I am not passive and certainly not a submissive girl. I am a cute queen, I've never needed to be rescued nor do I need to be saved, I can do that on my own. I am not a "woe is me" darling nor a "do it for me" kinda gal. I am not some sit and stay puppy, and I am certainly not a stand quietly and turn an ignorant eye to a problem sort of girl either. I'm a walking threat to douche bags, depots, and oppressors. Even when I am unarmed, I'm still very dangerous. Three days ago I was bagged and dragged out of a mold slimed rotten prison cell somewhere in bunghole Mexico only to wake up on the dusty streets back in the U.S.

I was still very defensive when a phone *r-r-rang* to wake me up in a hotel, I smell clean linens, my throat is dry and my head has a slight hangover throb. In the blur of my sight I see white, a lot of white, and I feel naked. The warmth of bed sheets pressed against my entire body, the gentle cradling is a stark difference than anything I have felt in a very long time. I'm still in Deep South of Florida, so south I can damn near smell Cuba. Images of last night are slowly coming back to me, as are some of the stiff and sore muscles as reminders that I am a jerk to myself sometimes.

The ringing echoed in my weary head, I hadn't requested a wakeup call but the curtains were orange with the rising sun so I began to muster a little. It was early and already I was pissed off. I felt soft linen sheets against my skin, my entire body was enclosed with clean white sheets that smelled like freshly washed heaven, and felt even more caressing to my body. My eyes felt heavy and my head was slow to put the pieces together as to why I was naked and in a hotel room but at least I was alone, a quick double take of the rest of the room reassured me that I was in fact, *alone*.

"*Lu*?" I jerked the receiver from the base hoping my mom was on the other end; my throat itched and I sounded like Louie Armstrong in my head. It was the same woman's voice I heard through the phone in prison; "Sorry biking beauty, its check out time I need you in Philadelphia by night after tomorrow, it's time we meet, I'll buy you a latte" the female voice on the other end instructed. "Sorry unknown buzz kill lady, I have my spa appointment at nine and I'm not wearing anything but the robe on the door that makes love to my skin until at least lunch. I'm not worrying about anything today but the level of my drink, and perhaps getting some sun, my skin needs to be spoiled and I need a me day." I retorted to the same voice that apparently sprung me from the Mexican prison and also encouraged me to come to the prepuce of Florida only to get beaten up along the way, and all to end up disappointed. "Not happening dick" I growled as I hung the phone back up. Yes I sometimes call girls "dicks," after all sometimes you are what you eat. I could already feel my blood pressure going up in the early hours. My body ached from three long physically abusive days between waking up on a sidewalk in Arizona to now waking up in a hotel in south Florida, at least my bedding choices have improved.

Lifting my head from the super soft fluffy white comforter ended my slumber. I laid half under the comforter with the air slightly blowing on my skin to keep me cool as I slept, the indent in my bedding was deeply inlaid into the plush comforter and the thought of having to leave just sucked. "NO" I said aloud to myself, I was not convinced enough to leave my bed. I spent months sleeping on a cement slab with only a few minutes of cold, moldy smelling water to wash my hoo-ha with each day. I hated myself for hating the idea of getting up and there was no way in this near tropical land I was about to pass up my spa appointment. I was getting waxed, trimmed, cut, shaped and lotioned and frankly I'd rather lay naked with a fat guy hopped up on Viagra and laxatives than even consider missing it.

R-R-R-Ring the phone blared out another banshee like scream in my ear. "Bite...MY...ASS" I bellowed back into the receiver before slamming it back down. I cocked my hand back and stared at my reddened and cracked knuckles, I lotioned last night preemptively but in all honesty my body was long overdue for many levels of hygiene and repair. I slapped the phone off the nightstand and onto the floor and swore if it rang again I was going to throw it from the window. My arms were sore and my shoulders felt frozen as I pried them under me in order to lift myself from my warm imprint in the pillow top. I spent a moment on all fours taking stock of my body; the cool breeze whipped under me and left me with a whole body shiver. I couldn't find any part of my body that didn't hurt even a little.

With a slight sway left and then right to loosen up my throbbing thighs and shoulders I gained enough momentum to move to the side of the bed, it was time to pee. Looking around on the burgundy carpeting there was no sign of my clothes, my boots were on the bathroom floor as I sat down for my business. There was a bottle of Jameson that was empty and still in the tub, there were some empty lotion bottles strewn around the bathroom also. I still felt dry despite nearly sliding off the toilet seat from being greasy from all the lotion. I dropped my head into my hands and tried to rub the extremely tired and weary from my head as I sat in the quiet and brightly lit bathroom. I haven't had one night for me since I left prison three days ago, I've ridden for almost the entire time and also killed four people, interrupted an international human sex trafficking ring while hand delivering it to the feds, and all the while desperately needing a mani-pedi and a shower. I'm neither La Femme Nikita, nor Wonder-woman and I'm in desperate need of some recovery and pronto.

I robed up and scanned my room again, recalling more of my previous evening. Last night I ordered a bottle of Jameson to cuddle me to sleep and spent most of the late hours with it while soaking in the tub till it was gone before dropping to bed to sleep. I snagged my room key off the corner of the temporary dresser that doubled as a TV stand and tucked into my pocket. I rolled the bottom drawer out to ensure that my leather jacket was still where I shoved it. I pulled few of the hundred dollar bills from the left pocket for spending money for my morning. The room was small but functional, I wanted so many things when I entered last night after I finished my salad at the Hogfish, a few more drinks were at the top of my to do list. I booked a massive salon spa package when I checked in, the portly fella behind the counter wore a faded blazer and yellowed dress shirt underneath and was easily dissuaded from asking many questions when I paid in cash for my room.

I thought about calling Lu with the hotel phone but it was blocked from calling anywhere outside of the hotel and even though I missed her tremendously, I figured I'd just pick up a disposable phone later in the day. I flicked some channels on the TV while the tub filled but once it was full of hot clean water, I slid in and left my clothes hanging in a garment bag on the front door knob for room service to dry clean and slid into the tub with my Jameson. Watching the sudsy water slowly cover over my body as I eased into the hot water was euphoric. Each inch of me that disappeared beneath the bubbles seemed to finally relax and begin to loosen up from months of knots and tension. There was a distantly familiar feeling that came over me when I was finally fully submerged into the tub, a tingling that crept through me and made me a little antsy at first. With several tall glasses of water mixed with my drink of choice and the realization that I was alone, it was time for some self-loving and enjoyment in the tub to enjoy my freedom.

I was slow moving as I left my room, the carpet felt amazing under my feet in my room but it was distasteful to wander the halls barefoot so I decided to use the el-cheapo single ply sandals that were tucked into the plush white robe. The spa was on the second floor so I made my way down the elevator. I enjoyed the solitude of the bare and quiet hallways; no loud out of control kids running off their leashes causing hell for other guests because they had weak or ignorant parents, it was peaceful. I was anxious for the salon because It had raised canopies for individual little corrals for patrons to sunbath in in privacy. The extended canopy was away from the main building and offers complete privacy for European style sunbathing, my skin needed the sun. I figured sunning in a small cubicle on the roof was a good place to hide for an hour before my spa appointment since I was up and my stalker was already creeping on me. The Desk of the spa was light brown with gold trim, the man behind the desk looked Haitian in his white polo with light blue horizontal stripes, his name was "Shay."

With a hefty lisp and very effeminate nature Shay welcomed me to the Key Spa; his big smile flashed some bright white teeth with his morning greeting. "Dallas Griffin" I forced out with exasperation to the wide eyed receptionist. Shay stared up at me, he wasn't as well adapted to hiding that he was looking at my bruised face but I was too tired to care. "Can you be my best friend and put me in a sun booth out on the deck and order me something green tea and banana based, I need some work" I asked Shay, he began typing with a smile and said; "Dorothy, I can be your Toto." Shay stood up to walk me to a sun booth; he wore bright white sneakers with short white cloth shorts. Shay had a lot of energy in his step as he walked; he was nearly hopping. I felt bad for hardly hearing much of what Shay had to say but my head ached and only a third of his fast lisp laden speaking made sense in my head, I just tried to follow his feet under the bright light above.

Shay had his tight curly hair pointed on top of his head to create an afro-hawk of sorts with zigzags buzzed into the sides of his head all the way around. There were half a dozen oblong booths on the deck; each one had a tall wall and enough room inside to let in plenty of sun and no peeping eyes. "Hunny you're signed up with Kelly at nine, you have her for a while, mmm aren't you just spoiling yourself" he began to pry a little as he led me to my private stall. "I spent eight months in prison and then rode a motorcycle from Arizona to here and only got to nap on the ground one night and then in the back of a cab for an hour until I arrived last night and all in three days, I need to recharge" I warned him with a bit of sass as I turned to walk into my booth. "Gur-r-r-l-l-l, fo real?" Shay let out with a wide eyed look, his eyes screamed pity but his mouth smirked a little with slight disbelief sided with curiosity. I handed Shay a hundred and told him to make sure that I had the second masseuse for later with Kelly and also pleaded for the thickest health smoothie he could find. I thanked Shay for his help and also warned him that he was now going to be my Jiminy Cricket and then nodded with thanks before shutting the booth.

The sun felt warm against my skin as I dropped my robe, the long chair was topped with a thick blue foam pad and clean white linen lay on top, my body craved spreading out on the pad to soak in the sun rays to continue to rejuvenate. I could hardly stand from exhaustion and being depleted of energy. I stood in the sun for a moment to look around; I couldn't see any of the guest rooms or distant windows above me. I was clear from any prying eyes, it was a comfort as I stood in nothing but a dropped robe wrapped around my ankles. I locked the door to the booth behind me and laid back onto the padding and let my body continue to loosen up. I felt the bulge in my lower back from hoisting up the gas station robber before I slammed him to the floor; it was tense just above my hips in my back making lying flat a slow process. I felt the rough skin of my elbows from prison grind on the sheet below me, and I felt the sun against my right swollen cheek bone from Putty Nuts punching me, what kind of shaft knob punches a girl in the face? He tried to kidnap me so I kidnapped him back, and won.

The sun slowly warmed my whole body, I spread my ankles apart to air dry some light sweat, the booths didn't offer much in the ways for a breeze in the warming Florida sun, but it felt amazing. Through a crack in my eyelids I looked down at my body beginning to glisten in the sun, some of the black in my tattoos looked like they were beginning to fade a little before but were coming back to life in the sun, not nearly as bright as they once were which is a sure sign that I need moisturizer and pampering. I thought back to my monthly pampering when I modeled bikes, I was almost ashamed that I was modeling back at the motorbike store with long roots and my weary body not being as luscious and sexy as I was at my peak a year before but that was before prison and, oh well. I tried to expose as much of myself to the sun coming up from above as I could, I needed the vitamin D and to be warmed all the way through, prison was endlessly chilly all the time. I hated being cold and with no towel to dry off with after the short bum baths I had to take, having to air dry or dry with my dirty t-shirt meant I was cold all of the time.

Knock Knock Knock I rose my tired head from my laying back; my body was warmed on top but still very weary. I felt a tad behind, like mentally, most likely from the drinking but I was slow to move. I pulled my robe back up and wrapped it around me and opened the door. Shay was standing with his left leg crossed over his right and his heels together, I couldn't tell if the ballet stance was of habit or him being cute but it made me exhale in a puff with the bit of humor, he had his wide smile and deep dark dimples as he Vanna White displayed my big thick green smoothie on a shiny small tray. Shay had my change arranged on the tray next to the large glass with a straw and little Pina Colada umbrella sticking out from the top. I pocketed a twenty leaving him with the rest. As I began to shut the door Shay spoke up; "Miss Griffin, you have a message" his whole demeanor changed as he slouched his shoulders and cleared his smile. "A lady on the phone said to tell you: "Philadelphia, three days" she sounded pretty serious." All I could do was pause and then drop my head.

I rolled my eyes and continued to close the door on Shay I dropped my robe and returned to basking in my glory. I laid face down in order to sun up by backside and also slowly slurp down my smoothie. The cold gooey concoction was a relief to my sore throat as I tried to find enjoyment in the quiet of the surroundings, something about the silence was unsettling for some reason though. The pressure of the pad was gentle, the lack of weight on any one particular area helped to ease the tough muscles that had become dense during the ride and the bare air on my tail bone was almost a tickle. I laid out in the sun and sipped my smoothie; bits of ice soothed my throat as the thickness coated the passage to my stomach. The antioxidants flowed through me and I was slowly beginning to feel cleansed and replenished. *Knock Knock* Shay gave out a loud and obnoxious throat clear as he rapped on the door again. I shouted without even moving from my position: "I loved you the moment I saw you, but your being adorable won't keep me from causing you great bodily harm if you bother me one more time."

I closed my eyes and let the sun sooth me to sleep, I awoke to Shay tapping lightly and telling me in his heavy speech impediment; "ith pamper tuyme mith Gurlll" his tongue roll on the end of *girl* was thick and once again made me smile, disarming me a little. I let out a groan as I gathered my strength to push myself from my new best friend: the foam pad. I picked up my robe from the ground and worked it back over me again, wrapping it and tying it up to remain covered. Shay stood a bit further away from the door and bent over at the waist and peering at me with his left hand near his face, peering between his parted fingers, he was looking pretty defensive against my threat. I dropped my head and raised the rest of my smoothie to my lips, sucking on the straw. "Really, prison" Shay asked once I broke passed the doorway of the private booth, I only had the gumption to nod and then began to follow.

A tall slender brother named Omar cut and styled my hair. Omar wore black skinny jeans with white dock shoes paired with a light blue dress shirt and white suspenders that matched his whit cabana hat. Shay sat right next to me trying to get me to join in his chats with Omar by bringing up prison as well as prodding about some of my ink (tattoos). Shay and Omar seemed very flirty with each other, they were cute but I had enough stresses to deal with. Omar flipped and snipped away lots of my hair, the length gave way to a lighter feel, the light hairs on the back of my neck tickled a little as I moved. I hadn't had my hair so short of in a very long while; it was sexy and very Victoria Beckham. Omar focused on his tasks as Shay flipped magazine pages loudly to be provocative and playfully irritating, really just passing the time until I opened up and told him more about prison while Lindsey Stirling and Bond played overhead. I told Shay very little but did inform him about some of the guards I had assaulted a little, especially about squeezing the man's gonads until I felt his warm blood in my hand; causing both men to shift uncomfortably.

Omar gave me a short bob which was much easier to deal with despite that I would miss my longer hair, at least the bleached tips were long gone and I was looking cute again. Shay led me back from the small salon to my massage room and that was where I met Kelly finally. Kelly was a fit woman in her late thirties, maybe early forties; it was hard to really tell. Kelly wore a white visor and her hair in a ponytail that bobbed and bounced out of the top. I was still chuckling to myself at Shay and Omar and their eccentric squabbling back and forth over some of the latest celeb gossip in Shay's magazine. Kelly squinted an eye at me as I smirked, I assured her it wasn't about my pending massage with wraps and whatever else I signed up for when I was drinking but rather the two goofy guys that had doted on me during my haircut. Kelly began mixing a bunch of green ingredients into a bucket and mixing it all with a long wooden spoon and began to warm mineral oil, the concoction looked much like the one I drank earlier.

Shay lead me into the main spa room, each room was private and tranquil with a small running fountain on a small towel table in the corner. I was shown a small shower room just off to the side behind a rice paper door and a table covered in plush white towels in the middle of the room. Shay still walked with a spring in his step, he was adorable but beginning to teeter on the edge of my last exhausted nerve. I felt guilty that he had no idea but he was cute about it. The room was warmed but I felt a bit of a chill because it wasn't as warm as it was outside in the sun but I was looking forward to being pampered. I was long overdue for some attention. Shay instructed me to hit the shower and rinse off, he suggested that he get more hands on deck because he got another looming call that I was due in Philadelphia...ASAP, I waved my hand to hush him about the topic before he could even finish his sentence.

I rinsed really fast and as I was finishing I heard "hello, I'm Yasmine" a lady with a slight eastern European accent spoke up. I toweled off and wrapped up and stepped back into the next room. Yasmine had her hair tied back also and had set up the small table near the far wall from where I stood, she waved me over while smiling and then informed me that she was there to do some grooming. Yasmine and I spoke about my requests and with the help of two other girls; I was waxed, buffed, painted and cleaned up and ready for the next round of attention. Everyone at the spa was nice and seemed really focused on what they were doing. One heavier set lady pencil thinned my eyebrows while Yasmine took care of everything else south of the border, I felt like I was shedding weight and being scrubbed of the prison once and for all.

Kelly handed me a pair if small cotton undies and suggested I hop into them and disrobe, leaving a towel wrapped around my waist and to lay down on the table as she turned her back for a moment. I was a little concerned that the table might shift and buckle underneath me if I shuffled so I stepped down to suit up. I bent down to slip my feet into the foot holes of the panties and tugged them up under my robe and then with my back to Kelly, I wrapped a towel from the table around my waist and then tossed my robe to a small seat on the wall near the rice paper door to the shower. I was exposed and a little leery about it, Kelly was quick to assure me that the undies were to keep most of the cleansing goop out of the more intimate of areas underneath. Kelly seemed nice and nothing about her set me uneasy but I kept in the back of my mind that the voice knew where I was and was hounding me already in the morning. Kelly flexed her arm muscles as she stirred the bucket, the mixture got thicker and thicker inside and the room took on a slight smell of the pungent mixture. I asked Kelly to call for Shay, she let me know that she intended to holler for her second set of hands to massage me and she'd call for him momentarily.

I dragged the table ninety degrees so that I could keep an eye on the door rather than it be directly behind me, it was a comfort thing. I was naked other than a small air of undies and it was alarming. Kelly eyed many of my tattoos as she asked me why I was so adamant about moving the table. "It's better for my chakras" I replied, the look on her face wasn't one of having been convinced but I stuck to my story. I was slightly irritated from being waxed and it made climbing back onto the table a bit strenuous. I hadn't had proper pampering in a very long time and things get sensitive to certain abuses and primping methods I reminded myself as I laid back onto the table. Kelly hit a red call button on a small speaker in the wall near the door, "I'm ready" she called into and with a squeak it was silent. Kelly cracked the door for a moment and let in a younger girl, also wearing a white visor and tight yellow top. "I'm Laura" the girl introduced herself with a head nod. Laura took over stirring the big bucket of green glop while Kelly shook her arm for a moment and then pulled out a box of gloves.

Shay knocked on the door as Kelly and Laura began to scoop mounds of the green mud onto my bare back, I nodded him in and asked him a big favor; "I need you to pack me up, can you find my dry cleaning and bring it to me, then gather up the rest of my things" I pleaded. Shay dropped his shoulders in a huff and rolled his eyes upwards, Kelly and Laura both chuckled at him and his antics. Shay took three large Joker like steps towards me; he halted my girls from glopping more mud on me and began to pull at some of the skin on my arms to get a better view of most of the tattoos on my left arm and back. I kicked my foot into the air to shoo him away and to put some hustle in his ass to go do my bidding. I told Shay to grab my key from the pocket of my robe on the chair and to go run my errands. I felt I was running out of time for my morning spa. Shay jumped like a startled cat when I flailed my foot at him and his loudly white sneakers bounced back and forth with his feet as he jumped and let out a "*whoo.*"

Shay left the room with a huff and a slam of the door signaled both Kelly and Laura to begin their task of rubbing me down with a green tea kelp wrap that wasn't too far off from smooshy peas, it felt like warmed baby food as they began to work the goop into my skin. Kelly and Laura both stood on opposite sides of the table I laid on and rubbed mat, scooping more and more of the warm muck onto my body. The girls used their small fingers to work the mixture deep into my skin, working out kinks, knots and bruises. Once I was fairly coated above the waist and looking like the Jolly Green Giant had his way with me, the ladies unwrapped my towel and continued to smear it elsewhere there was exposed skin. I understood the point of the skimpy undies as I was worried about the mud seeping into my more intimate areas. I felt nimble fingers rub the coarse fibers out of my muscle tissues; some of the rubbing nearly hurt and caused me to grunt a few times. My feet were gooped and rubbed; spasms ran halfway up to my legs causing twitches. I fought my best no to wiggle and laugh out loud as some of the massaging tickled.

Just as Kelly instructed me to begin to turn over, Shay knocked again. Laura stood to keep my barely clad backside from being exposed to the doorway as Shay let himself in; he carried a small plastic bag with my folded items inside. Shay looked at me with despair, he looked as if someone kicked his puppy and for a moment my heart dropped. "What?" I asked. "Riding pants, really? And a black bathing suit? This isn't dry cleaning, this is half of an afternoon on Daytona Beach gurl" he piped up. I rolled my eyes in disbelief that he was judging me; he was the one with a faux afro Mohawk after all. I waved a green mud covered elbow at my robe for him to drop my stuff and then instructed him to grab my boots and where to grab my jacket. I assured Shay that I was trusting him and that I would kill him if he blew it. Shay cocked his head with a very sassy attitude and propped his hand on his hip as he shifted his weight to further give me attitude back before he spun on his toe in a half pirouette and left the room again.

Kelly and Laura continued to make small talk; they asked if I was down in the area for vacation or for work. I had mostly seen just the small touristy town in the Caribbean atmosphere; "what kind of work could I be here for" I prodded. It clicked to me that the spa and salon were both pretty quiet. At first I suspected that maybe the spa was quiet because it was early in the day when I entered and then sat out in the nude sun rooms. I didn't notice the serenity because I was tired and maybe a little hung-over, plus I had my new bestest girlfriend-man Shay to keep me annoyed enough not to notice. I felt the room narrow in around me as Laura began to scoop handfuls of green masking mud onto my stomach and chest while Kelly finished rubbing down my legs. I tried to keep my head clear as both woman hummed to themselves and focused on the parts of my body they were massaging. I felt warm but also sticky, the exfoliate in the mixture was gritty and covering me from toes to hairline.

I did my best to keep my eyes trained on the ceiling while Laura asked a few times what I had been up to in the area, what I had done for work and if I perhaps had a boat in the marina or something. I snarked a little at the thought of looking like the snobby yacht type then politely assured her that I was not. I stuck to the story of just being in the area for vacation and some relaxation but was enlightened to the fact that on the other side of the highway was a military base. I began to wonder if either lady thought I might be down with a spouse or visiting a boyfriend, I felt at ease for the moment when I assumed that both women were merely making idle chit chat until Shay hurried back into the room. I jumped a little when the door flipped open, Laura jumped away from me after I jumped from being startled, Kelly spoke sternly to Shay about how he should have knocked.

"Girl what are you into" Shay asked, he had my boots and jacket in hand, I felt a little more relaxed after seeing the rest of my clothes. "Dude chill, what has your manties in a bind?" Before I even finished my sentence Shay cut in with: "No manties, no binding...she hulk" as he gave a catwalk spin to show that his rear end was panty-line free. I coaxed Shay to relax and talk to me more calmly. He set my stuff down and pushed his hands against his sides and ran them down to his legs. Kelly and Laura both slowed as they rubbed more of the sludge onto my chest and near my neck, the Anna Kendrick looking Laura hardly watched what she was doing as she rubbed up upper chest, she was distracted by Shay and his wild hand gestures as he tried to calm himself down. "Right after I got your things and as I neared the elevator, I saw two men, a cute one with dark jeans and a cute blazer that looked like a Spanish Taylor Kinney and an older one that sorta looked like Nick Nolte both stepped to your door, I slowly walked into the elevator as I watched them swipe a key to open your door and let themselves in, that was when the cuter one pulled out a gun!!" Shay waved his hand to fan his face a little as he let his knees wobble a little while holding himself up with the wall. Laure spun her head around to look down at me and make eye contact, her green eyes opened widely.

Kelly snapped off her gloves and raised her hands a little as she began to step back from me. Laura let her hands linger on my chest for a moment until I pulled on the table underneath me and began to sit up. I began to question Shay and his certainty of what he saw, he repeated over and over how sure he was and with utter disbelief. Kelly backed towards the corner of the room while Laura stared at me face to face as I sat up. "Can you lay out some towels down for me dear, I'd like to rinse off and find out what the hell" I said to Laura as I began to slide off the table. The temporary undies I was wearing felt full of that green mud, I was certain I had an ass crack full of kiwi green tea exfoliating mud and whatever other funkiness that they poured into the bucket before slathering me head to toe. My ass slid down off the table, I could see the mound of green crud on the edge of the table after having been scraped off of me on my way to the floor. Laura backed away from me as she laid down a few towels to make a path to the shower. I thanked both ladies and asked them to excuse me for a few minutes and that I'd be out after my shower. I instructed Shay "tip them" suggesting he hand them both a hundred dollar bill from the wad he scavenged from my robe.

I nodded to Shay to lock the door after both ladies left and to stay inside and stand guard for me as I cranked the shower nozzle on. I told Shay that I'd tell him everything but that I needed his help, he was still fanning his face and doing Lamaze breathing to keep from passing out. I didn't wait for the shower to warm up; I hadn't the time as I slid into the stream of crazy cold water. I didn't pull the rice paper door shut in order to wash, I knew Shay was only a few feet from me but I also didn't want any surprises while I was deafened by the noise of the shower. I ran my hands around my body as fast as I could to scrape off the thick layers of expensive jolly green jizz. The mud plopped to the floor of the shower in large clumps and slowly broke up in the warming running water before making small green streams that headed to the drain. I told Shay to listen up and to relax; I *had* the vagina but he was the one *being* one, he was almost impossible to communicate with his huffing and puffing, it was frustrating. I soaped and washed over and over, the water grew warmer and it made the mud run down me with ease. Shay stood with his back leaning on the wall next to the shower as I washed frantically.

I told Shay the fastest summation of my earlier three days as I could, I spoke about my dealings and what I had done in Atlanta, which was why I suspected I was being sought after by some sort of agents. I washed as fast as I could move my hands, the mud was everywhere, and I mean EVERYWHERE. I instructed Shay to pull the rest of my clothes out of the clear garment bag he picked up for me from the in-house launderer and to grab me a towel Shay was whimpering and on the verge of getting head-butted but I tried to keep my head. As I stepped out of the shower stall Shay was knelt down trying to rip open the small plastic bag, he was trembling so badly I began to feel badly for barking at him so crudely. I toweled off with panic in my hands, I moved as fast as I could to dry as best as possible. I stood completely bare in the shower stall before moving out to see Shay hunched over my garment bag on the floor, luckily he was focused on that and not on the naked girl stepping up behind him. I moved Shay aside and ripped the bag from his hands to pry out my clothes from within.

I yanked my bathing suit bottoms up and my leathers were close behind, my damp skin made it a struggle to get my pants on quickly but a little leg kicking helped. I didn't bother with my bathing suit top I just worked my shirt over my head and shoved my arms through the holes and tied up my boots. I had only known about the agents for five minutes or so but figured they knew where I was and couldn't be far behind now. I slapped Shay on his shoulder with my hand and jerked him up from the ground by his collar. I pulled a few hundred bucks from my coat pocket, I instructed him to give one to Laura and another to Kelly.

As for Shay; I told him to keep the other two bills, and to trust that I wasn't a bad bitch, well not a criminal type of bitch at least. Shay's hands trembled and shook as I tried to force him to look at me, he was truly scared and I felt bad for that but he was going to be fine. "I love you" I called out to Shay to disarm him right before *Slap*. I landed a mild open hand to the left side if his face, the slap was followed with a really feminine "Ugh" on his part but he shook his head and stood up straighter and looked at me with amazement; it worked well enough to encourage him to toughen up.

I demanded to know where the back way was to get out of here and to the east parking lot where my bike was. Shay pointed that I should go right out of the room rather than left towards the main salon waiting room. I grabbed Shay and yanked him out of the room and apologized as I shoved him to the left, barking orders to the frightened man-boy to tell them I hit you and was still in the room. I felt clumsy as I tripped and fumbled my way out of the door, colliding with the door frame as I hurried. I made it to the back stairs, the door was rigged with an alarm if it opened; I had no other way out.

Down the hall I heard some men's voices, I felt the hot breathe of the devil on my neck and I began to run down the rest of the hallway towards the windows. There was a window that was partially open, the problem was that the opening was hardly big enough to squeeze through and I'd have to pry back the small rectangle that opened inwards and even then, squeezing out was going to suck. The small sitting area by the window only had two chairs and a fake tree plant thing, neither had the fortune of being a crow bar. I thought about swinging a chair to break the glass but hotels put in thick enough glass to keep people from jumping out, and being Florida, the window glass is thick enough to stand up to flying debris from storms and what not so breaking the glass wasn't happening, not without a gun or like a tank.

I grabbed the long fake tree plant, often times they are just crappy fiberglass but the better ones have a long piece of iron rebar inside. Sure enough, swinging the plant by the top let the base slam into the smaller pull open window in the middle of the glass. The base of the plant sent fake Spanish moss into the air and sent dark plastic wicker shattering to the ground. The red and gold woven carpet looked like it belonged back in Persia or some Aladdin crap as fake plant bits rained down on it. I felt my heart begin to beat frantically in my chest as I pulled the fake tree back again to bust the hinge off of the window. The crash screamed in my ears, I was certain I was hemmed up and any moment the two agents would come barreling down the hallway at me. The right side of the window hinge bent enough that with two more hearty kicks sideway I was able to bend the hinge arm away. I shoved the fake tree through the opening in the glass to bust the screen out.

I was staring at a pretty tight fit if I was to make it through the opening, I wasn't even sure my hips would fit. I thought I could roll my shoulders to make myself fit but the rest was a gamble. I used the fake tree to pry some of the metal to open more of the window, I bought myself a little more room but that was only the beginning. I was still eighteen feet up from a thin corrugated metal canopy that hung over a side entrance, I was screwed out of options; desperation was now my guardian angel. I turned around and began to feed my legs through the open window, the hard edge of the frame nicked against my shin bones as I wriggled and walked my hands backwards. I tugged on the leaves of the fake tree to keep it with me as I worked side to side to wedge my hips out the window.

Once I got my stomach resting on the window frame I wriggled my feet side to side to find a small bit of a toehold, there was hardly half an inch worth of edge to ease some of my weight off my stomach. I didn't hear any voices down the hall just yet but it was only a matter of time. I had to wriggle side to side to get my hips passed the window frame; if I was any bigger I might not have fit at all so here's to being slender. Looking out I realized I was a lot higher up than I thought. I pulled my torso out of the window and pulled the fake tree out with me, except for the remainder of the shattered base.

I felt my eyes tear up and the wind blow a little, making me even more uncomfortable as I hooked the bit of fake tree in the corner of the window frame. I held on with my life with one hand to the frame of the window and tried to kneel down on the half inch ledge that I was standing on, my just massaged muscles were all tense and full of knots again and my smoothie was trying to make a comeback up my throat. Tears welled up in my eyes as I wrapped the dark green leaf around my left hand and slowly tried to ease myself down enough to use my right hand to grasp the small ledge to lower myself down with even more. I had about fifteen feet below my feet to the corrugated metal awning, my legs already hated me for what was about to *SNAP* the fake leaf broke. I was suspended in the air for the longest second or two imaginable. "Trapt" began to play in my head as I free fell to the off-white metal awning below me. The air rushed up my shirt and cooled my sweaty torso, my arms hung above my head as they followed my body downward. I was gravity's bitch.

I had always been taught how to fall and so on with martial arts, if you exhale with a shout as you land on your back it'll reduce how hard you get the wind knocked out of you. If you fall from ten feet or so and use your legs like springs and bounce a little into a tucked roll it'll also soften some of the blow to your body. I was deep fried no matter what and when I say deep fried I mean like a Twinkie at a fatty fair. The raised portions of the roof threated that I might roll my ankle if I didn't place my feet right when I landed. I worried about breaking an ankle or knee or even hip. I contemplated my life and how horribly it was about to end when I landed, I thought about all of it as I fell. I tried to position my feet to land on the flat sides of the canopy. I anticipated the thud of hitting and I was going to slow my decent and let my ass drop down and then spring back into a roll.

As the canopy came rushing up to me I felt my hands get clammy, my mouth go dry and I began to feel dizzy. My feet touched (thud thud my heart beat) the souls of my feet felt like they had been beaten with bamboo poles. The pain immediately seared up my legs and through my hips as I focused on all of my joints bending together to slow how fast I was falling so my tailbone didn't crash into the canopy also. I felt my muscles get tight with tension so I sprung back aiming to summersault along the long side of the canopy. It all happened so fast. I threw my body forward to roll and suddenly I felt weight under my right shoulder, but not my left. I rolled off the edge of the canopy. I continued pleading and bargaining with karma as I began to fall again. The first free fall made me knot up in my stomach, the second was wildly out of control and unplanned and and and, and SHIT.

I unraveled once I left the metal canopy; a whole new and unexpected shock filled my body. I tried to force my eyes open to get my bearings as I fell but I only saw some evergreen shrubs fly passed me right before I collided with the ground. My left thigh and ass attacked the ground first; the rest of me hit and fell limp to the grass next to the evergreen shrubs I flew passed. I felt my body sob two or three times, every ounce of me wanted to unleash and continue crying, it felt good and I needed the cry, I really did. My entire left side hurt. I flexed my right toes and then calf muscles, once I had some feeling besides paralyzing pain, I felt grateful that I was merely hurt and not injured. I didn't feel broken anywhere just hurting like a pair of torqued ovaries. I tried to roll to my right a little to sneak under the canopy and out of view from the window I just plummeted from, my left leg sent fluxing pain surging through me and it made me short of breath for a moment.

I don't know if I hit my head, or my ass. Maybe I hit my head on my ass or my ass to my head. I've been threatened to have my ass kicked up between my ears before; OH GOD did that happen? Did I break my head and my ass? Both ends of me hurt and the ruckus I made must have echoed through the whole hotel that I collided with that canopy. Oh my ass is killing me, and so is my head. My entire body is numb, am I paralyzed, oh shit did I really just drop from a third story hotel window only to bounce off a stupid metal canopy and then fall again to the stupid ground? My anger picked up as my contorted body slowly began to get feeling back. I was getting riddled with sharp pains coursing all through me, each pain grew more and more intense and some of the pains took my breath away.

The cement was cooler in the shade of the metal canopy overhead, my hands trembling and shaking as I rubbed my legs, feeling for any breaks. I laid back and tried to pull my body straight, my left hip was rife with intense pain as I pushed into the crease of my pelvis. As I looked above me at the canopy I tried to massage the knot out of my hip, I saw the indent that I made when I landed. Little ole me made one heck of a dent in the metal roof, I forced out a tear covered smile because I was impressed. I sat in limbo of wanting to cry and having to hurry and pick myself up, I just wanted for everything to be over, god my body hurts.

I had half a mind to write the hotel and inform them that when numbering a building that the ground floor is the first floor, not that the first floor should start at the first floor above the ground, what kind of asshole would screw up a numbering system like that?

After I got my hip to work (I worried I might have dislocated it until I twisted it back into place) I rolled to slowly get into a child's pose before downward dog pose then pushing back onto all fours to rock backwards and then slowly to my feet. As I was rising up and still wondering if I broke my ass a lady came out of the doors at me, she looked a lot like Elizabeth Shue but with short bouncy blonde hair and light freckles across her cheeks. I scanned the woman in search of a weapon or body manner that might suggest that I was about to get my ass kicked. I thought about how pretty the girl was until she opened her mouth and George W came bumbling out. "You okay missus" she stammered, completely unaware of what had just happened. "There's two men after me, I think they're on their way down here, can you call the cops? There's an old guy and a younger guy and they're wearing blazers and jeans" I told the girl with exaggerated fear in my voice as I fought back tears of pain not fear.

The girl turned and hurried back inside, leaving me to limp as quickly as I could towards my bike. My left leg dragged behind me but with a steady grip on my pant leg I grunted the sixty yards to my bike. My leg nearly gave out from underneath me as I swung my right leg over the top of my bike, the pain was unbearable but I had no other choice. Sitting on my bike shot pain through my ass and up my back but I started up my bike and headed back towards the highway to get clear from the hotel. I tried my best to watch around me to see if I was being followed but the pain in my hip was intense and I just wanted to zig and zag through cars for a while and haul ass up the scenic ocean highway and in the opposite direction of the iron gates of the military base that was only a few hundred yards from the hotel I stayed at. I needed to get to a place I could hide out and recover a little better, the massage was wonderful but unfortunately it was interrupted horrible and my tension was up even more because of it. I white knuckled the throttle until I got off the ocean highway 1 and veered off the course I came down on.

The four hour ride to Miami Beach was nerve racking, my hip hurt like a bastard and trying to straighten it while riding was a near death attempt each time, plus at the wrong angle it cramped up and made the tears flood back to my eyes. I watched behind me while riding and at gas stations for any cars or trucks that might have been following me. I limped into gas stations and quickly back out to keep my eye on things and to avoid any unwanted surprises. I wished Pickle or Dexa were with me, it was always nice riding with friends. I'd been mostly alone for months in prison before the random voice of "Jake" showed up late one night. I was so devoid that just his gravelly voice in the late hours vibrating through me was enough to entice me to near pleasure. When "Jake" first started talking I was so overwhelmed with happiness to hear a fellow American I wouldn't have cared who he was, I would have held on tightly and cried with my arms wrapped around him, he really helped to save my mentality. I was growing bitter and withdrawn before he showed up; I wonder what became of him.

Each time I had to splash water on my tattered body in prison it always came at a cost, usually it was because the guards watched. If the water wasn't cold the air drying afterwards was and it was always miserable. I tried to picture myself in a shower or some cool water waterfall fed by a cool stream in the deep remote woods where I was alone to just bask in nature alone a delusion at best but it was all I had. I was always on the slender side of body types until I started squatting to strengthen my legs to upright a bike with. The thicker girls were always jealous of my "thigh gap" (which is a term for having slimmer thighs resulting in a small gap in between my legs) and they would point out my chicken legs in the locker room even though it was apparent that they were husky and jealous about it. I often responded that not having a space in your thighs was a turn off for guys because they wouldn't want to shove their face in a fat cramped sweat box; that usually ended the conversation pretty quickly.

With each stop for gas and stretching time my hip slowly loosened up bit by bit. At the first stop I grabbed a diet Pepsi and a few hundred milligrams of pain killers, they may have slowly kicked in and helped to unknot my left pelvis, but there was still a lot of throbbing from my hip both down to my knee and up to my mid back so it was hard to tell. That fall kicked my ass and I was miserable having to deal with it. Many bikers have gone to some the wild parties of Daytona Beach, I went when I was eighteen and despite being under the legal drinking age, it wasn't a hard task to find some frat guys or fellow riders to offer up plenty when you walk around in a bikini for them to gawk at.

There aren't enough guys that can see a scantily clad woman and retain some intelligence, like trying to get your dog to perform tricks when they are in a room of other dogs and kids with treats, it just isn't happening. I didn't realize much in my teens in regards to what I was doing with my body, it was fun to jiggle and shake a bit with a walk for stares and the loud exhale as cute guys passed by. When I really learned what I could do with a confident strut that was when I also realized just how dumb so many guys are for a tight ass or a perky chest. I found that my true power was hidden in confidence and loving myself. A girls' true beauty comes from loving herself, not from someone else. I didn't need or want any drama in my life but life comes with a certain amount anyways, there is just no way to avoid it.

I chose to run and hide out for a night in Miami Beach. I needed to know what the hell was going on and why I had agents after me. Sure I did some crappy things but to be honest it was all for the better good. I wasn't sticking around to voice my case until long after I had ample time to figure out what was going on. After the first hour of riding I was near the main land, I made sure to snake out of the way off the highway each time I filled up on gas to make sure I wasn't being followed because if you see a similar car a few times you learn to grow suspicious. With the lady voice on the phone being certain of what I had been up too while riding with Melanie and then some, she must have reviewed cameras of what I had done who knows what else.

I grew more curious as to what I was caught up in the more I thought about everything. I wanted to head home and be with my mom and friends and get away from this mess, but I was trapped. My feeling of gratitude for my father's case worker brought me from that sidewalk in Arizona and across the damn continent down to the tip of Florida, but now I didn't know why I had stayed as long as I did. The thought of a massage and day at a salon was enticing enough to take the gamble and stick around for a bit, boy I sure lost that gamble at the hotel. I tried to think about all of the exchanges between random voice lady and me, I mentioned the spa but it was her that called me at the hotel, was it because of proximity to our meeting place or was she tracking me? I paid cash for the hotel room so it wasn't like she could have monitored ATM use or something government like that.

Most of the gas stations I stopped in at I made it a point to be in and out, I tried to keep my face down in each one to avoid any video identification, I paid cash quickly and then I rolled out just as quickly. I felt like a paranoid person, I wonder if Dexa felt this paranoid all the time or if maybe he was so deep that maybe he didn't realize it. I remember one night Chips and Dexa came out for one of the football games I was cheering at; Cheryl had to work and even though Dexa was terrified in crowds, he promised me he'd go to a game to support me, and he did. Dexa and Chips were good guys, they were like uncles to me and they meant a lot in all that they did. After the game I snuck up behind the guys to let them know that I wasn't going to shower but instead just ride back with them and they wouldn't have to wait for me.

As I crept up on them, I heard them talking about a "Claire." It was hard to sneak up on Dexa, the man learned to grow eyes in the back of his head. Dexa spun around to nearly catch my hand as I reached up to snap Chips in the back of the ear with a flick to mess with him. Dexa hardly stopped moving his eyes side to side sweeping around to keep an eye out for any potential threats. Dexa taught me many things, especially cheap and easy alarms like an empty pop can sitting on a door handle so if it moves much it'll fall and make noise. Dexa was very withdrawn most of the time and having him leave his comfort zone behind him to come out and watch me cheer really meant a lot to me. Chips was much more open and during my cheers he was almost as loud as us girls when we cheered, he was adorable with his wife and an all-around great guy. It took me several weeks of pestering in the garage before Chips finally gave in and told me more about Claire.

Claire was a bright eyed young girl that met Digger at the medical center he had his appointments at. Digger and Lu had been divorced and apart but still managing to put Waylon County on the map, literally. Digger still had follow up appointments for some of the burn scars on his left arm and because he was a veteran, his place of care was a Veteran's hospital. Clair and Digger hit it off apparently; she rode on the back of his bike for a few dates before they decided to go steady. Once Claire had become comfortable with Digger and the idea that he was beginning to build a city with his ex-wife and their small biker club, she was around more and more. I was in high school when I first heard about my dad's girlfriend but she was before I was born, so what. Claire was the one that first turned Dexa to some of the meds he still takes to handle is mild PTSD and paranoia. I was surprised that I hadn't heard of Claire, not by any of the members that hung around, even seventeen years later or anything. I spent a school year with Pickle and even after his mother passed and so on, he never once mentioned her.

I lived with Pickle the year after I lived with Otis and Trish but I moved back home for the summer in between. Both Otis and Trish were club members but chose to move out to Gilbert to retire. I liked Trish; she was a bubble popping lady that walked around in high heels and leopard print *everything*. Trish was funny; she would snark at Otis and then drool over the pool boys. During the school year at Gilbert I was educated to many things about the origin of the club but Claire was still left out, it wasn't until I moved back to Waylon before my junior year that I first overheard Dexa and Chips talking about her. According to Chips she was never brought up because she was a sore spot for both Digger and Lu. I suspected that maybe Lu wasn't over pops when he brought the girl around or maybe there might have been some other beef so I never gave it much never mind.

With each gas station I put behind me I thought about how I might be better off if I disappeared again, stopped running these state to state rides and hit a boat. Perhaps flee to Europe or back to South America, just much further south than 'ol Mexico this time. The lady on the phone said she was covering my ass about the path I left behind me but I sure wasn't feeling it with two agents storming my room and nearly chasing me out of a hotel window three stories high. About an hour into my ride my neck was sore from constantly looking over my shoulder that was about when I began to question my sanity about everything, what if Shay just had it wrong about the room? I still drove further into the cities to fill up my tank and found different routes back to the highway make sure I wasn't being followed, I was as cautious as I could be. Maybe I'm a little paranoid after all.

I reached Miami beach city limits, I was almost cramped in the sitting position from my hip hurting but I wanted to put a little more distance behind me as well as get to a city well equipped to hide out in. Miami Beach always has a ton of foot traffic, biker traffic and college student traffic; it was perfect to blend into. With my bandana tied over my head for my whole journey, it shouldn't be very hard to walk around with my new haircut and avoid being spotted just in case I am being hunted down. If I had more time it would be worth getting a call out to Dexa and having him send me something to help me relax, but since I'm out here my options are limited. My arms were still tired from the heavy bulky sleeves of my jacket, I tried to alternate which ones I kept lifted as I rode so they didn't get all that tired but it only worked for a short period. Heading down one of the main strips that line the beach I knew that a majority of the college tourists stayed right on the beach, I thought about doing the same but I also thought about just ducking to one of the darker side streets and tucking away within the shadows of a large hotel to help hide me away.

Down Willis road there is a dingy little Conquistador Hotel, it was two stories and much like the one I happened into when I first got back into the states. The building was mostly grown over with Ivy and even in the daylight, it sat mostly in the shadows.

The neon sign out front only had "Con" flashing while the rest of the letters remained dark, coincidental I hoped. I was sure that the only reason this place remained open was from over charging drunken college idiots and bikers during the peak touristy times. I decided that the Conquistador was good enough, there was broken glass littered on the ground and the white painted bricks were poorly painted over the graffiti all over the place. I felt more comfortable with the establishment when I couldn't find any security cameras after looking around a bit. Through the hallway that seemed to head to a courtyard I could see two or three people laying out, based on the size of the two hats, I guess they were ladies.

I parked my bike and worked myself off, my hip was so knotted up that standing was next to impossible for a moment. I squeezed and worked my hands into my side to release the tight muscles in my hip and ass from my fall. Each spasm of pain caused me to wince and grit my teeth as I took large strides to stretch the muscles out. All I could think about was how stupid it was to jump from a friggin building higher than I am tall, "brave but damn stupid Dallas" I said out loud. This will be a story for Chips when I get back home I thought with a chuckle. I kept my eyes over my shoulder to make sure I wasn't trailed into the motel parking lot, the entrance was wedged between two larger buildings and there were some more hotels down the street but I needed the shady one that would take cash and not ask questions. The amount of used condoms in the bushes gave me the notion that maybe there were some tricks turned in this vomit pile of a motel and that was probably how they were still open, but pimps and hookers don't like cops either.

The manager's office was a bullet proof window that looked like it was or is part of a bedroom, gross. The man sitting at a desk on the other side was a portly fella with a massive amount of stains on his hole filled red shirt. The manager looked like he smelled as he scooped large clumps of noodles caught with a rusty looking fork into his scraggly unshaven face. I almost vurped (vomit/burped) into my mouth when the man opened his patchily bearded face to reveal half crusted greenish nubs that were once teeth as he took his bite. The floor behind the man was littered with trash and wrappers and assorted nudie mags. I assumed the issue of "Folds & Cuckolds" on the desk wasn't for the articulate writings on interior design.

The man didn't bother to kick his feet down from his desk or avert his eyes from what the computer monitor was playing; it looked to be some weird Asian squid porn something I think. I could tell the man smelled just by looking at him; he glanced to me and then wedged himself further back into his seat before acknowledging my presence. I told the man I needed a clean room for a night and slid a fifty under the small slot under the window. Without saying a word the man reached behind him without looked and molested a peg board for a random key and tossed it at the window to land in the same tray that the cash was sitting in. The heavy set man leaned forward and showed me an intimate shot of his cleavage as he moved in his chair; his brownish hair was greasy and matted. As he reached for the money I caught sight of his ratty sharpied nametag; "Carl." Carl looked like the kind of guy that got off while watching himself in the reflection of the toilet water beneath him while he took a dump. I was beginning to worry that maybe I hadn't seen any video cameras outside because they were all in the showers in the rooms.

Carl didn't even bother to point in the direction I was supposed to head, I did my best to pinch on my hip to dull some of the pain as I walked to find the room to squat in for the night. I took stock of my surroundings: questionable hallway leading to the parking lots, two hookers lying poolside, one of them well past the age that she should be hooking, serial rapist and fetish masturbator managing the slums and more different DNA on the ground than in all of West Virginia, but I had most of my health I suppose. Room 197 was back in the corner, it looked like the ivy was on the verge of covering over the main door. I suspected that there was probably no back window that I could see out of because of the foliage but it was tucked away. The older of the two ladies tanning must have been in her late forties, and not nearly attractive, she was heaved into a one piece bathing suit that was probably left behind along with some dignity by some sorority girl over spring break.

The second gal I suspected of prostituting was wearing green and white bottoms and a black floppy brimmed hat, yeah, just that, and she was staring across an empty hot tub quarter filled with a green goop that looked like my massage mud. The younger of the two must still have been in her mid to late twenties, she was very tan in skin and wore bright red lipstick, even to sun (in the shade) next to an empty hot tub. The man sitting near the far wall was as shady as you'd suspect, he wore bright yellow short swimming shorts and his bright colored Bermuda shirt was unbuttoned and failing to hold back his feral silver chest hair that seemed mangled in a wad of gold chains. His mostly gray hair was sleeked back on his head as he leaned back in his chair a little.

The older Italian looking guy was very vigilant, I suspected that he was watching me through the dark tint on his gold rimmed glasses but he lifted his head from his newspaper and made it a point to follow me with his head to assure me that I knew I was being watched as I neared my room. The older guy had three gold bracelets on his left hand and even the stereotypical douche pinky ring, something about him made me want to knock his teeth in just for staring at me. I kept my head held high; I wasn't going to let some geriatric stare me down anyways. I decided not to stare back but keep my head straight ahead to prevent him from getting the smart idea of messing with my bike and besides, my hip hurt enough to avoid a confrontation for the time being. My key was spotted with rust and dangling from an old school plastic key chain, I wondered how long it had been since the locks were changed around this place and how many keys were out there floating around. Every motel/hotel kidnap rape movie began playing through my head and the notion of sleeping soundly was beginning to become an illusion rather than possibility.

I jammed the key into the keyhole but tried to keep the key-chain from juggling so I could hear if there were any footsteps coming up behind me. I braced myself against the door in order to push backwards if necessary but the old guy didn't leave his seat. The room reminded me of my old prison cell, it was dark and musty but the bed was made and I couldn't see many signs of rodents or bugs to crawl on my face as I slept. The bed was sunken in in the middle, the cover was green with blue and gold, it looked very eighties but it hid whatever hooker stains were probably underneath so I accepted it. There wasn't much to the room, a small table with some chairs in the corner, a small two drawer nightstand and small half sink next to a door that hid away a toilet and bathtub. It didn't smell great but it didn't smell like I'd find a dead hooker under the covers with either so it was a draw.

I was terrified to look into the toilet so I used my foot to flush before I had to drop off the watchtower to the neighbor, an inside joke with Lu (about those stupid shit flyers that always show up wedged into the front door) when it came to pooping. The tub looked like it was used to wash a bunch of messy dogs.

The ring on the tub was crusted and hardened, I hoped it was mud and not dried sewage. Seeing the tub looking like a nasty butt was where my heart really sank, I just wanted to sit it in a hot bath and soak until my left hip stopped throbbing but that wasn't happening and the hot tub outside looked like a giant dip-spit cup.

I removed my jacket but thought twice about removing my shirt, there was one light bulb in the lamp bolted to the wall but I wasn't taking the comfort that I wasn't on camera for Carl to whack off to. I forgot I shoved my bathing suit top into one of my jacket pockets so I removed it and began to tie it around my waist before pulling it up and into place under my shirt. I scanned the carpet for razors or needles before sitting on the bed to bend down to undo my boots. My body felt better on a softer seat and without the weight of my jacket.

My prison cell was much worse and since I hadn't caught tetanus in Mexico, I hoped that my luck would hold up and I wouldn't catch some airborne ghonna-herpa-syphil-aid or some other nastiness that might rot my crotch out. I began to stretch and work the sore knots out of my hip. The pain sucked of course but it slowly began to ease up with some mediocre yoga. Between leg stretches and side bends I continued to monitor the old pimp sitting out in the courtyard, I felt uneasy about him and couldn't figure out why, perhaps he was just monitoring his property or scouting for more girls, either way I was skeptical. I was willing to bet that all three of them lived here somewhere and I didn't suspect that they paid money to do so; I bet Carl took all sort of kinky payments, even from the old guy.

After half an hour of deep tissue massaging I pulled my pants down to take better look at how bruised I was, sure enough my whole left ass cheek was beginning to speckle with red spots and turn different shades of purple, and of course is hurt like a bastard to push on and massage but I had to break up the blood clot to speed up the healing. I pulled my bottoms to the side to further inspect my bruising, man the guys back home would be proud of this one, it began running down the back of my leg and up my back. I didn't see an ice machine or any niceties of the most basic motel courtesy so I was stuck for a bit. I ran some of the water until it went cold and soaked a hand towel to press against my skin for a bit of a quick chill but it hardly mattered.

I hated the notion of being stuck and immobile, I hated the notion that a mere fall from three stories could put me out but I also hated the notion of not walking with my head held high anywhere I might go. I am generally a tough chic, at least when I'm not trying to spar with the ground using my left butt cheek (and losing). I like that I can be as tough as a uterus but I'm also cute and dainty when I'm not limping like a kicked puppy. I know who I am, and what I am, and frankly, there isn't a guy out there that is going to make me feel any different, especially not any less than worthy of everything I could ever want. The biggest problem is that my bruise on my ass was what was hindering me a little, yes I was the one that was kicked my ass but I'm the only one that can. Girls are all tough and strong, the biggest issue Is that not enough of them know it and they let schmucks and dill-holes tell them otherwise and they believe it. I have scars, I have tattoos, I have kickass stories behind all of it and I'm still young and have plenty of life left to live.

I wiggled and jiggled to get my pants back up, the pain coursed through me as I squeezed back into my pants, the tightness helped a little with the swelling but it also made my walk a little funny, it gave me a slight limp. I forced out a few squats with my hand holding tightly to the bed to keep from falling over. I was on the verge of tears as I forced my muscles to push away some of the throbbing but it wasn't working. I grabbed my jacket and put my key in my back pocket and headed back out of the door to cross the courtyard and the old timey Mafioso with his old ass parked in a plastic chair. I can't say I haven't been hurt, heck, even within the last few hours since I had plunged into a metal canopy only to fly off and land somehow on my ass and almost into a bunch of damn shrubs. I am a girl and I am as tough as many others but we still get hurt. The biggest difference between me and most other girls is that I'm aware of my potential and I refuse to listen when guy or even other catty bitches get to groaning about male superiority or girls being weak in one way or the other, what a croc of shit!

I rolled my shoulders back and despite the agony going on with my left hip I was going to strut across the eerie courtyard and back to my bike. The older lady laid back in her chair, the younger one eyed me a little as I walked, neither were a threat even in my slightly dented state. I kept my ears tuned for squeaks in their chairs or the rustle of skin if they moved enough to become an opponent just in case though. The younger lady just sat there topless and kept working on her even tan. The topless chick kept her head laid back, I admired her not for her job but for the confidence and good self-esteem she had about herself enough to let them ta-ta's breathe.

A few years back I met a guy named Hudson, he was poorly shaven but cleanly groomed, he rode a sweet white hard-tail and was a writer and photographer for some magazine for which he wrote on a per-diem basis which let him travel. Hudson and I met on a DC rally for wounded Vets and the piss poor care they get when they need it. Hudson was covering more of the rally rather than the rights that our Vets were being screwed out of but we met nonetheless. I rode out to DC with Pickle and a few of the other guys that could go, it was always Digger's dream that his club would ride for what was right for Vets and servicemen and women that deserved admiration. I did my best to always join up riding groups that rode for honor and for our military family, home or abroad.

Hudson and I hit it off and hung out for the weekend rally, I admired that he made most of his living riding and that urged for me to glorify him a bit, his strong jaw and brad shoulders made me lust for him too. It was nice to be hugged on and doted on by Hudson and even though I'm a motorcycle rider, it doesn't mean I don't like to be romanced. Hudson and I were in the midst of a group of rowdier riders when one of them grabbed my butt, not uncommon but still uninvited. Hudson made a chivalrous attempt to defend my honor and turned to land a solid fist to the gray bearded chin of a fat guy wearing small sunglasses. The old man had his head knocked back but he did not drop and when his head returned to back on to his shoulders, his right arm came up from nowhere and hit Hudson in the chest. Hudson caved a little with the hit and then began to stumble backwards for a step or two.

I cocked my body to the side and as fast as I could I rapid punched the burly man in the throat to raise his hands. As soon as he grasped his neck, it was prime to swing my heavy boot covered foot to his groin. The heavy set man bent enough for me to pull his head down to meet my knee as I swung my knee up a second time. I felt the bones in the man's face crunch when I connected with it. The heavy guy sent blood spurting out and over my knee as he let out a groan. I hoped the man would have stayed standing long enough to deliver another solid blow but squeezing him down onto his big gut made him spring backwards and to the ground. Win or lose I know to stand toe to toe for myself, I have had men willing to defend me but rarely have I ever needed it. Hudson tried to defend me and was nearly punched in the throat and that made me feel bad. Towards the end of the trip I realized that Hudson was just a soft guy on a hot bike, he was a photographer more than a rider, it was just his transportation. I liked Hudson for the few days but it was more to pass the time I suppose.

I checked my pockets to make sure I had my keys and belongings I brought with me and then swept my eyes around the room to clear it of anything I might have left behind before I yanking open the door to head back out. I saw the old Guido still wedged into his wobbly plastic lawn chair and his older of two ladies still sitting topless across from the stagnant defunct hot tub, I'm not sure if she was relaxing or advertising, either way it didn't look all that successful. The leaves on the ground had merely blown to the edges and the ivy on the wall had become grown, but no one seemed to care much about maintenance. I let my boot heels thunk to the ground as I walked, I didn't step as lightly as I often did out of courtesy, I wanted to make my presence known and walked with my shoulders back, head up and my fists clenched.

It took some prompting to get my leg swung over my bike, my ass muscle was a tense knot and I was certainly stiff and sore from my fall still. The beach was rife with sun-bunnies and old perv's scoping out the young bronzed bodies. The northern beaches of Florida are where all the trashy tourists end up, the ones from Jersey and what not that show up to weather the winter and litter the beach with their poor manners and talking with food in their mouths and so on, just nasty. The lower end on the Atlantic side is often where you'll find the younger crowd and the Gulf side is primarily for the snowbirds over the winter. I needed to load up with supplies if I was going anywhere, starting with sports rubs mixed with aspirin to break down this gnarly butt bruise, a working favorite of Dexa taught to me to deal with post jujitsu sparring bruises.

The vibration of my bike helped to diffuse some of the pain, but not enough. Leaning into turns hurts like a bastard with a knotted up lower back and left hip so I kept a lookout down the distance for shops on the right rather than the left as I rode. I decided to stop in one of those beach stores that had neon beach towels hanging in the window. Last time I stopped in at one of the hippie-dippy granola stores I think was for a Daytona bike week or something, either way it was for stupid crap but I knew I could browse t-shirts and bathing suits. I had to make a real fast stop in and then an even faster out through a drug store, they are much more likely to have video cameras so I had to keep my bandana on and my head down to get some ridiculously strong sports rub along with more painkillers, I am a mess and I need to start making some fixes or I won't hold up.

I stepped into the fairly empty beach bum store I caught glimpse of one other browser pecking through store racks when I entered. There were pathetically distasteful shirts about blow jobs and other low-life gear mostly pot-heads would spend their money on for amusement, as well as hermit crabs and racks upon racks of tie-dyed sundresses. The place stank of patchouli; it made me nauseas from the start. There was a white girl with dreads sitting behind the counter; she didn't even look up to greet me.

The girl could have been fairly cute had she showered and maybe even put a bra on. The girls' hair was sandy blonde and poorly tucked into a knitted Rasta cap with a few strands hanging out of the sides. I nodded to acknowledge the mumbled greeting as I quickly browsed some of the garments bulging from the racks. I had a bag in my pocket from the pharmacy and I was aching to get my ointment rubbed into my thigh and begin to ease most of my pain, but I also wanted a new shirt and some socks before going to change. Since I was here it would only make sense to swap out bathing suits as well.

The hemp rags on the walls and stoner band posters were all shameful and just pathetic but not my scene and not my problem. I had a backbone for life and was in a bit of a hurry to get myself patched up and mobile again. Many of the shirts were boasting Rasta colored happy faces and dumbness but what would I expect from such a place. I browsed racks until I found a black tank-top and a new bathing suit. I paid the grungy gal for my clothes and stepped into the changing room to get to work, she still hardly looked up from her phone to take my money before I scurried off to a change. I opened the jar of muscle rub and began to crush plenty of aspirin to mix in with it and began to massage it into my aching muscles. I stood in front of the body length mirror, most girls hate mirrors, especially ones that seem to expose faults and flaws. Women hate bumps and nicks and scrapes and scars, me, I keep tabs on things that I've lived through and I don't see them as ugly; they are my metals of honor.

Most woman take a beating in scars and stretch marks, our bodies burst forward when puberty hits; our hips spread and boobs grow quickly and coordination sometimes goes out the window, almost overnight. I was pretty self-conscious when I first started noticing I was changing, some of my favorite pants grew tighter at the hips and I could slowly tell that I was getting more three dimensional. Lu educated me about lotions and how to keep some of the scars to a minimum and I tried my best but I was not without them. Girls need to learn how to be confident with themselves, it's hard being an awkward teen and when they start ganging up on one another it's downright vicious now a days. Girls have no need to fight for a guy, if a guy truly loves you then there won't have to be a fight, if only women would teach their daughters that then the world might begin to be a comfortable place to grow up in.

As I stand bare in the mirror and look at how beat to crap I feel, I saw that I still had globs of green mud caked in some parts of me; it made me smirk a little. I wish I would have had longer to have showered before having had to jump out of a hotel window. I thought to myself about how tired I looked but that I was a badass as I smiled and continued eyeing my body standing in that mirror. I kept my lean look as I withered away in prison, I was still grayish and a little pale but I looked better than I did three days ago in the motel room. Strangely at that exact moment I thought about Melanie and her cute little hips and us dipping in the pool and how nice it was to have half a night of fun rather than the gauntlet of chaos that ensued after I left her behind.

My ass hurt all the way up my back as I scooped the menthol heavy cream from my knees to my shoulders. The coldness burned and riddled me with goose-pimples, the played out nineties erection softening music overhead hummed in the background as the goo squished from the container into my hands. I watched myself in the mirror as I rubbed the cream harshly into my skin, the grit from the aspirin stung in small bits as I ground it in. The pain was welcomed as it meant that soon enough my muscles would loosen up and work properly again.

The scars on my back were older and faded but as I twisted over my left hip to see more of my backside in the mirror, the stretching of the skin makes it look plastic like. Each time I see the scar it brings me back to my motorcycle accident when I was younger, another box-step dance with death and I came out on top and still standing tall. Sometimes it helps to look at the scar and remember that even when I was scared, hurt, broken and bleeding, that the time passed and I healed. The idea that time heals all wounds is bull-crap, the scars and wounds never go away but you learn to accept them, embrace them, and hold them like a badge of honor, proof I weathered the winds of life and continue sailing.

Bending over to pull up my bottoms and my pants my backside was already feeling better. I still felt stiff and rigid as I slid my jacket back on, the padded forearms were a little constricting and a bit difficult to slide into but I managed. My eyes watered from the menthol but so be it, there wasn't much I could do but slide out of the small changing room and get on my way. I was spooked by the silence of the store, the crappy nineties music still played overhead and I found myself the only person in the store. My steps eased and I walked with bent knees to crouch a little as I crept between the aisles, I couldn't find anyone or any movement. I was ready for another fight or to run and save myself if I had to. I planned to ask the grungy girl behind the counter if she had any maps of the area but I couldn't see her as I rounded the hippy sun-shirt rack, she wasn't behind the counter where I left her. My blood pressure began to rise, I wondered if maybe the two guys that tried to attack me back at the hotel had caught up with me as I hid out in Miami beach and maybe followed me here so I kept my hands clenched and my eyes towards the exit .

I stepped one foot over the other, I tried to remain silent but the strength of the menthol on my skin was certain to give me away long before I could be seen. My knuckles were reddened with bruises and cuts from boxing with Putty Nuts in the box truck, my cheek bone still hurt from his punch and now my ass was half broken from falling on it after climbing out of a hotel window. With each silent stalking step some of my life's choices came back to me in my mind, flashes of laying down a motorcycle, falling from the canopy and everything else, I really need a new way of entertaining myself. I heard some muffled squirming coming from behind the counter, movies now flashed through my mind, movies where some young helpless girl was tied up somewhere and then all the bad guys pop out. I'm sure as hell not some helpless girl but I might be about to get my ass kicked by ninjas or something.

I ducked down a little further and tried to eye down the slim rows of the aisles behind me. I looked for shoes or even toes at the bases of the clothing stands to make sure I wasn't about to be ambushed from my blind spots. Dexa taught me at an early age how to keep an eye out for predators, he wasn't talking about the occasional coyote or mountain lion in the mountains, he was talking about those sick ass grown men that like little girls. Dexa used to have to go on patrols with his squad mates around in the outskirt cities to search for enemy combatants; he found it unnerving because his squad members were the ones that stood out, not the enemies.

Dexa always told me that if I felt like I was being watched, to yawn. Yawning isn't necessarily contagious but seeing it does in fact make you yawn so if someone is watching you long enough or with enough intent, then they'll yawn and you'll know they were watching you without letting them know that you know. Dexa was mildly paranoid about most people and public places but he had good ideas. Another thing to watch out for are toes, often times when people are interested in you, they'll point their toes towards you subconsciously, that trick has come in handy when getting hit on at bars and in clubs, if you watch out for toes pointed at you despite someone facing you or not, you can figure out if you have a tail. Dexa was good at reading people; he adapted his skills while surrounded by small Kurdish cities where most of the residents wore long shirts and garb that concealed most of their bodies. Dexa learned to watch hands for nervous twitching, eyes for fleeting movements of paranoia and to watch for the one person sweating more than the guy next to him. You watch for toes pointed at you because you are being watched or followed and he learned the yawn thing that saved him several times while in the midst of crowds.

I knelt down to peer under the racks of clothes looking for feet or movement that would let me know I was being flanked but I couldn't see anything. I heard a slight moaning or heavy breathing sound just a few feet away and it made me nervous. I couldn't see where it came from so I kept moving towards it. I crept around the side of the checkout counter; it was a glass case full of head shop bullshit; glass smoking crap and other useless junk. My hands were still sore from fighting hand to hand but that couldn't stop me from doing it all over again if I had to. I duck walked slowly and took a deep breath in anticipation for what I was about to find, I tensed all of my muscles and slowly peered around the edge.

The menthol on my skin made my nose burn, the squatting made my butt burn and my hands shook with the surge or adrenaline. My thighs were sore and tight as I did one last duck step around the corner to finally place my eyes on the source of the squirming sounds. As I kept tight to the counter display case I held my breath, the pounding in my ears made it hard to tell what I was getting ready to see, I just flexed my muscles and readied for another fight. The first thing that came into view was a wild mop of nasty dreaded hair on the floor, I stepped a little more and readied to pounce when I noticed that the guy on top of the clerk girl was feeling her up because they were making out on the damn floor. The guy jumped up and in doing so he pushed back on the girl causing her to hit her head on the floor. The boys' jumping back caused me to jump back from being startled and ready to defend myself while the girl yelped in response to the screeching as she scurried to cover her hands across her bare chest.

The boy stumbled backwards to get away from me before he realized I was no threat per-say. The shock sent my heart beating wildly and ready to start fighting again but luckily I didn't have to. The girl spun around to look and see what had caused all of the commotion and why she bumped her head backwards to the floor, her brown eyes met mine and her cheeks instantly blushed. I noticed that the boy and girl rolling around on the floor together both had bloodshot eyes; stupid kids were stoned and forgot I was in the changing room, for *five minutes*. The boy was wearing green skinny jeans and a stained hemp shirt, if he was listening to Phish he would have completed the whole grungy nasty persona, she was definitely his equal. The girl apologized over and over for forgetting I was there as she hurried to pull her shirt down over her head to cover up. The boy was weakly and insisted how sorry he was to both me and the girl, his whiny tone made me feel like I was his dad and had just caught him beating off in the woodshed or something, all I could do was roll my eyes and make my way out to the door to leave. I was just appalled at the level of stupidity in the world more than I was anything else.

Cautiously I stepped back out the door; I put my new sunglasses on and looked up and down the street for anyone that looked like a tail or anything shady, of course I didn't see anyone. I decided that it was time to put some food in my system and enjoy a nice meal for the afternoon. I had been nonstop running and with almost five hours of riding behind me, I was plum tired and wanted a place with quiet music to sit and eat in peace. I decided to find a nice salad restaurant, the cars in the parking lot were upscale and that assured me that I could eat in a nice setting. I pulled a few bills from the wad in my left pocket and put them in my right, I was always brought up to not keep your money all in one pocket just in case something happens, it sure beats dropping more than some or getting robbed of it all. The restaurant was quaint, there were white walls with light gray stripes in a herringbone pattern, the music was orchestra based and light on the violin, oh so very soothing.

I tipped the maître d to put me in a quiet corner booth towards the back of the restaurant so I could watch over the room as well as eat without having to watch my back. I had grown accustomed to being on edge, that was where I lived and it didn't often get to me but lately has been very different. I wasn't a teenager living on sushi and Pepsi all summer long and still able to look adorable anymore. As an adult I need to work on eating cleaner and with all the abuse, I need to do a better job of taking care of myself. I felt the stress manifest into a greasy forehead and dry skin, it didn't feel nearly as clean as I wanted it to. I was in my twenties now and this was no way to live, but leaps better than prison. I thought about how rough it was to try the whole office job with Chips' sister Evelyn and how it ended pretty poorly. In prison I spent most of my time thinking about getting through each day, which guards might try to run in and rape me when I changed or used the restroom, which guards watched me pee or might have been trying to take pictures of me while I slept. I didn't really spend all that much time thinking about my future because I didn't really think I had one.

I ordered a mandarin salad with fresh Bluefin California rolls to accompany it, the long few days has really left me needing more than just the salad, I needed protein. Plus all of my time in prison has left me feeling gross and depleted of energy so the greens would be good for me. I watched as the sun reflected off of windows of cars passing by, I thought about any possible job I could do for the next thirty years of my life or even close but each time my mind came up blank.

I thought about Melanie, she was fun to ride with and I thought about the first night we camped out along the highway in the fog next to the bike. I smirked recalling Melanie chasing the muscly guy down the motel hallway we snuck into to go swimming so we could cool off in New Orleans also. I had been locked away for eight months and she really helped to calm my anxieties about being out. I wondered what Melanie was up to as I sat and enjoyed my salad. I felt somber at the way the last few days panned out, I wondered how the voice on the other end of the phone knew I was in prison and then again how in the world she knew I was at that hotel on that small ass island. My head was starting to pound again with a slight headache; the pain was originating from my right cheek.

I nursed a diet Pepsi along with my Bluefin rolls, the tuna was fresh and frankly, it is the only kind of fish I happen to like. I was hesitant to go back to the hotel so I thought about getting back out into the city to search around. I had been down in the area a few years back but wasn't old enough to actually enjoy the club scene much, not the ones you could drink at anyways. I wanted to go and dance and figured it would be a good distraction from my day and a good way to hide out until I figured out what the hell was going on. I decided to go and cruise the strip that faced the ocean. Once the sun began to lower over the buildings the nightclubs should start hopping. My body was tensing up to the idea of going out and forcing my way between sweaty bodies at a club, especially after watching Melanie get snagged in a crowd back in New Orleans. I was in my riding pants and a bikini top under a tank-top under my riding jacket and a purple bandana keeping my hair back, I wasn't dressing in a sexy short skirt or cute outfit. I debated on even going for half a second, but then decided that I could hide away for a little while and watch a bunch of sexy bodies writhe all over one another to some good music and finally enjoy a bourbon.

I decided to stop off real quick to a phone store and pick up a cheap throwaway phone, I missed Lu and my friends and it's been a few days since I left a fairly frantic voice-mail with her and I really need to explain where I've been. The throw away phone I bought came with one hour of talk time, I had to call the gas station to talk to Lu because it wasn't late enough to catch up with her at Car13 (the bar). Lu had a million questions and I fielded them as best as I could to summarize what the hell has been going on for the last year. Le was worried sick when I left the last voice-mail three days ago and I really couldn't apologize sincerely enough for it because I was in a hurry when the phone I had died. Lu poked and pried for every little detail about the strange voice on the phone, she fell silent when I mentioned Mexican prison and she hardly responded too much in between. I tried to ask about the guys but she kept reverting the conversation back to me and where I was.

Lu seemed to have pressing matters distracting her and I couldn't figure it out, some of the silences in our conversation were weird interruptions and it further prodded my suspicions about being followed or something. I avoided saying exactly where I was with much certainty; I just mentioned I was in Florida and near the beach. Lu was nonspecific about how the guys were and the shop was, just that things were "fine" and that was the majority of her responses, she was also fairly vague. I was running low on minutes when I ended my conversation with Lu, I told her I wanted to see her soon and would be on my way, I avoided speaking about any of the things that happened between Arizona and when I finally called her, including climbing out of and falling from a hotel window further down state.

I sat back and watched the waves roll into the beach, there were plenty of people strolling along the board walk as I leaned back on a cement bench and focused on hearing Lu while keeping my eyes on the random lives wandering about. I came to realize early in life that I was the only person that could ever really stand in my way of becoming anything I ever wanted to be. I grasped the notion of physical strength when I began working out but it was earlier than that when I began pushing myself harder and harder with my jujitsu when I learned what real strength was, it was continuing to get back up no matter how many times I had been knocked down. I sat and let the warm cement bench warm my tushy and contemplated what might happen, *when* I got up, not *if* I got back up.

When I was growing up I always called Lu "ma" when it was just us, but when we were at the gas station or the bar, or anywhere else for that matter, she insisted on calling her "Lu" which was short for Eluna, or Luna, it made it easier to find her in a crowd rather than shouting out "mom" or something that would get thirty people to turn and look. Lu was always careful not to use my real name in public when I was younger also; she also always called me "Dolly" rather than Dallas so that if some strange perv wanted to take off with me, then they'd have to prove it by knowing my real name, smart move on her part. The sun was setting but still warm, I was full of clean healthy food and still recovering after some long months capped with a long few days of hard riding and rough situations while pushing myself to derail the messed up human trafficking ring thing that Fred and Putty Nuts had going on out of New Orleans . Putty Nuts tried to kidnap some girls including me so I ended up kidnapping him back and his Sasquatch sized friend tried to kill me so I killed him first. I wasn't certain I was all A-OK with taking their lives but they deserved it and I wasn't going to let what happened dampen my strong spirit about myself, I am a strong woman and a survivor, and I'm surviving.

I am strong enough to be alone, I am not one of those girls that always has to have someone around. In high school there were always enough girls around that always had to have some form of attention or another, that crap is exhausting and it made it hard to have girl friends. I always found that guys were much easier to get along with, they needed less drama to fuel them, although when you are friends with some guys they are less filtered to scope out chicks and make eye opening comments, inventive albeit crude sometimes. I love myself enough and am smart enough to be able to be content with who I am, even in the dead silence for days of solitude.

I needed a few vacation days to kick it on the beach and soak up more sun; my body and mood crave it. I enjoyed light sunbathing on my roof back in Waylon and even this morning at the spa for a short while. I was enjoying my green tea smoothie and wrap and was about to be rid of lots of free radicals and oxidants until I took that tumble off the canopy I dented with my landing and refilled myself with radicals and oxidants all over again. The air was warm and salty, the gulls soared on the late afternoon air and I felt my body let up and my blood pressure calm back down, I felt peace trying to warm over me and it was weirdly making me worry. Staring out into the ocean I thought more about what I might think about doing for a living. I had two sleeves full of cash and my bike, I could take up college somewhere down where it was warm and had nice roads and take up a degree for some career or something. I just didn't know yet and I have no idea why the topic was on my mind, probably to dissuade me from panicking about everything else that was going on.

I have always thrived well on trauma and intense situations, martial arts helped to prepare me to think more clearly when I've got hands flying at my head and being a girl I am not squeamish around blood so maybe I could take up being a doctor, or a nurse or something. I've crossed paths with many dimwitted doctors so if they just studied and passed exams to make fat money, I could easily do that too. I thought about nursing for just a few minutes, the notion of purposefully keeping people alive that didn't want to be or dealing with asshole families and extremely rude and inconsiderate people…. PASS. One week after Esther passed away Pickle was having some chest pain; I was really worried about him when his face began to turn blue so I hurried to call an ambulance. The two paramedics loaded him to a stretcher and we hauled ass to the hospital.

I waited around the emergency room for hours while he underwent tests and probing to find out what was wrong with him, I wasn't his daughter so they argued about letting me back to hang with him to keep him company so I just waited. Pickle was told that his stress levels were too high and it coupled with being overweight. I was grateful that he was alright but walking around the emergency room I dealt with loud ass families, irate patients waiting to score meds because "they forgot their scripts" and a slew of trashy idiots that have no respect for a healthcare facility, and there were plenty of them. I was miserable dealing with douche-bags complaining about dying of pain but their faces let up and they seemed to magically feel just fine to hit on me right in the waiting room, sicko's. People are extremely inconsiderate and it bugs me to my core. Besides, there are too many shriveled wrinkled penises to deal with when it comes to nursing.

I considered the amount of schooling required to be a doctor, I didn't have the drive to sit and smile next to so many jagoffs to become one of them. Many doctors I've crossed paths with seemed to have sticks up their asses; many have that air of superiority because they are doctors. When you look at the grand picture there are hundreds of thousands of other doctors and most have to put their finger in a butthole on command so that's not for me. I sat and thought about trolling back and forth across some random college campus with hopes of validating myself in the eyes of society and so on; it didn't tickle me in the least.

I sat with my arms outstretched and began to contemplate the vastness of the world, my life and choices, the things I had done and places I had seen and how tired I was of plenty of it. I began to think about maybe becoming a paralegal and helping more people that needed it when suddenly the phone in my pocket began to ring. I had just bought it to make one phone call to Lu and when it was almost out of minutes when I hung up, why the hell was it ringing. I dug into my pocket and began to work the small phone out, my tired body fought with the pocket liner for a moment and I nearly ripped my coat when I finally pried the phone out.

"*Lu?*" I answered. "Still no sweetheart, you should be on your way to Philadelphia, not strolling the beach with the golden oldies over there" the same woman's voice broke through, the same voice that woke me up earlier in the morning. "Didn't /tell you to bite *my* ass?" I snorted out. I thought about her saying "over there" and it made the hair on the back of my neck stand up, I couldn't help but to immediately begin to look around me. "You may have mentioned it, but since you missed our first date you're now putting our second one in jeopardy, I decided to give you a call and motivate you" the lady responded. I thought about letting her talk some more and try to figure out what she was all about, she was elusive and obviously connected further south but I wasn't sure about here.

Now I had only had this throw away phone for an hour and she already had her hand in my butt like I was a puppet. I considered she must be pretty connected to be able to reach out and get my new number so quickly. "So his parole officer tracks people down now huh" I asked hoping to keep her talking. "I said case worker, but nice try sweetheart" she rebutted. I tried to scan the beach and see if I could spot anyone on a phone that might be on the other end of my conversation but I couldn't find what I was looking for, it seemed like everybody was on their phone and I couldn't hear any seagulls in the background noises on her end either.

The depths of depravity of the guards in prison were endless and cruel, the journey since then has left me without fully feeling like myself. I felt numb after the gauntlet of bull crap, the barrage of people trying to kill me and the unlimited number of bad people that needed to have their asses kicked. I felt like I was recharging as Kelly and Laura began to work out all of the knots as they my muscles while slathering the refreshing green tea mud mix all over me except that sliver of a nice moment of peace was cut short and not ten minutes later I was tumbling from a hotel window three stories up. I just didn't know if I could take anymore let alone how much. "Hmmmm" I buzzed as I let out a deep lung filling breath of exhaustion. "Dallas it's rather important that you come and find me, you might be surprised to find out what you can learn." I was growing tired of the cat and mouse game of chasing a phantom voice. I stopped taking orders before I graduated high school so I wasn't about to roll over and beg on command now. I swished my lips back and forth and gave deep thought about what I had already been through trying to find out what this lady had in store for me, I couldn't find the motivation to go through it all again.

"Yeah I don't know there phone lady, you've found me impressively enough but anymore screwing me and you might just have to propose." I could hear the voice sink slightly with impatience; just the reaction I was seeking with my insubordination. I felt myself smile a little now that I seemed to gain a bit of ground. I don't like anything but an even playing field and I've had the disadvantage since I first picked up that nasty ass phone in prison. I refuse to back down when someone thinks they have an upper hand or advantage over me, in fact it pisses me off. I decided to test some nerves and take some of the power back by defiantly sitting and enjoying a warm cement bench on the shores of Miami Beach for a bit longer. The moment of silence hung on the air like seagulls above, I waited for the lady on the other hand to change her tone or break the silence. "I left in order to clean up your disaster at the airport, plus with the mess you left behind you and your little friend between Arizona and where you are now, you aren't totally off the hook for any of that don't forget" the woman opened up and took all the upper hand back. The dick played a pretty beefy trump card, I wouldn't expect to get away with murder but those jackasses dying was a result of me defending myself, it wasn't cold blooded murder or anything. I quickly went from queen to pawn.

I was doing my best to keep my voice calm, I felt my fingers twitch a little with my anxiety as I stood my ground and waited to see how the conversation transpired. I learned in middle school that once someone can really piss you off, they then take away all of your power. Often times when someone grows furious they begin to lose their thinking abilities, and when you can stay calm and defend yourself verbally, it becomes easier (and mildly amusing) when someone else loses their shit, unless they happen to be some goat rapist that throws acid up on somebody of course. People feel threatened by things that are true or that can hurt them, and those threats become scary and frightening. I look at things logically and for what they are, I am not easily backed down therefore I am not easily threatened which translates to not having anything to be afraid of, not even some voice on the phone threatening to leave me out to dry for things I in fact did do.

I stopped a gas station robbery and in doing so, the robber passed away from a head injury that I caused trying to defend myself and two innocent ladies. I stole a motorcycle to elude possible incarceration for who knows what; okay, my bad. I stopped a human trafficking ring in New Orleans and in the process one man died from suffocating in his hoodie, not my fault, just circumstantial. And as far as anyone knows ole Putty Nuts was the one that shot Fred in the van or the giant that died on the ground in the park, still none of it was really my fault. I was just saving some asses, starting with my own. I have no complaint with being held accountable for my actions, but when my actions are a reaction to some gritty situations; that's just Newtonian. I will own up to my mistakes, I spent my time in prison defending my womanhood from animals but not once did I think to myself that I didn't deserve being in jail for helping to part out stolen bikes, even if I didn't know they were stolen until after I was busted.

I loved cheerleading, I loved having a plan as your tosses' hoisted you into the air and then your rehearsed plan was set into motion and the rush was upon you. I loved having a radio with Blink182 or Metallica growling out speed riffs while we practiced, the soundtracks to keep your heart beating only made the rush more intense. I missed back when things were easy and your actions were scissor kicks or back hand-springs, not having to rip some heavy set gunman from the floor to pile drop him to the tile and crack his head open in the process. Being an adult sucks, I guess I ran to Mexico to escape having to face down the adult life and all the accountability that came with it.

"You already ruined my spa appointment this morning, I was stark naked and being royally massaged with the cleanest gooiest mud that my skin could have ever asked for and by two of the nicest ladies I have spoken with today. I was making another budding friendship with soft linens until your call woke me up. The days' momentum turned into two guys chasing me out of a hotel and I had to run like a rapper at a paternity test." I laid into the lady voice on the phone, I was growing tired of the mystery and was trying to debate if it really was worth the hassle of getting back on my bike and hauling leathered ass up along the coast. I just wanted my day in the nice weather and time to slowly digest my amazing salad with peace and the beach warmth. With my legs outstretched on the pavement and right arm laid out across the back of the bench my body was enjoying the tensionless state of relaxation, even with an unknown stranger stalking me and calling me on the phone, I was feeling pretty peaceful.

"You have no identification, no money, and calling home puts a lot of people on a radar that they don't want, stop being a prissy brat and do as you're told" she grew stern with her words before finally hanging up the phone. (Looking at the call time on the phone in my hand) almost sixteen minutes for the duration of the call, strange seeing's how I had less than five remaining after an all too short call to Lu back home. I wanted to head home, I wanted to turn around and go back to my friends and forget about this week, but I had a bad feeling that I couldn't. I was pretty tired of the drama of the last three days, but at least I was out of the prison. I was in fact grateful that I was enjoying a beach; I had taken in a little bit of sun over the last few days even though my pale skin didn't really show it yet. I was emotionally spent, exhausted and worn out, I just wanted to tilt to my right and lie out on the bench in the cooling breeze and fall asleep.

Pickle once told me that it isn't crying that makes someone weak, sometimes it takes strength to let yourself have that emotion, it's the weak that let those emotions control them though, especially anger. Pickle once reminded me that the strong wipe off the tears and keep going; he did add that it was always a smart to fix your mascara though. Growing up around bikers and vets there wasn't much outwards emotion, even from Lu so I often pushed down the small bits of scared and pretended things didn't bother me. Pickle helped me to understand that crying was OK if you were so overwhelmed with hate and anger or sad and despair, the matter of fact was more so about not letting it show in front of someone that hurt you so they don't get the satisfaction. I cried plenty at night under my blankets only so I could smile at school the next day.

I refused to cry in prison, I didn't want to be the cliché that refused to cry but broke down and let the entire place see that I was weak or easily taken over. I did knuckle push-ups to remain in control of my emotions and mental faculties however. I thought about some of the letters I got from Digger while he was locked away from me. Digger and I corresponded plenty and as most children would; I asked him tons of questions about all sorts of things, including his time in the army and getting shipped out. I remember one letter when I was young; he spoke about when he first left for the military. Digger was eighteen, he wanted to serve his country proudly and to honor the memory of his father so he found an army recruiter just a few days after he graduated high school and was shipped out for basic within the week. Digger spoke about being a gung-ho teen with endless angst to serve coursing through his veins, he felt indestructible and immortal as he boarded a large greyhound bus and headed to Missouri for his training.

Digger spent a dizzying two days in processing with hundreds of other men in the same situation as him, each just as young and naïve as the man next to him, and none with any answers or ideas about their futures. The days of drilling were loud, devoid of any real direction and seemed to only have chaos as the organization. The nights were a vastly different story, quiet and almost lifeless as most recruits slept or lied still trying to sleep. Digger found himself lonely during these times, he was in a room with one-hundred other men, but he was alone.

Digger missed his friends and family and was hundreds of miles from any of them and he questioned his own purpose and if he had the strength to maintain his head. Some quiet dark nights you could make out some sobbing in the hue of the red lights they used as night lights but once the blinding white florescent lights exploded with their light overhead, nobody spoke of the night sobbing, everyone just continued to grunt and jeer through their days. Digger spent most of his days worrying about the day at hand, looking back only reminded him of someone he once was and people he once knew, he didn't want to look too far ahead because the notion of the long future ahead was also intimidating and frightening, it was easier just to worry about the day he was in.

Thirteen weeks of living day to day had changed Digger, he reminisced about the days he left behind and the people he once knew but he knew that he would never really return to who he once was, and the people he once knew were never going to be those people again either. I sometimes found myself angry about everything that Digger was missing, he missed the Daddy-Daughter dances, he missed me jumping from couch to couch as a small child and he missed my entire life, and I missed him. It pained me that I had to describe my life to him on paper. I had most of memories of talking to him through bulletproof glass after half an hour of getting my belongings searched and my privacy invaded in the prison entrance once a month.

The entrance process to inmate visitation wasn't as demoralizing as a kid but I noticed plenty of lingering hands as I developed in my teen years. I often squirmed while being groped, the wincing of my eyes showed Lu the level of disgust I faced as some scumbag without self-control felt me up as a young teen girl, I hated it and those are the memories I have of my father, not playing princess or dress up. I know I am still bitter about my lacking father and so on but the last twenty-four years are behind me and my father is mostly just a random postcard in the mail. I can't say my life had been all terrible, quite to opposite in fact, I have had some of the coolest uncles from the Squad and I have had an upbringing that movie producers would make a fortune off of, it's my childhood and it is all I've known.

My favorite tea party I can remember was with Lu when I was five or six, I had four Barbie's set out and she joined me for grape tea and Zots (a sour candy I loved). I had a GI. Joe set up for dad because he couldn't make it. Cheryl had planned to stop by with Chips for some light yard work as a favor. Pickle showed up to help Chips drag some hedges from the ground in front of the house, both Chips and Pickle saw Lu and I propped up at the table in matching camo tiara's enjoying our tea. Pickle made some peanut butter and jelly sandwiches and quartered them while Chips placed the napkins and utensils for a proper tea party. Both Pickle and Chips played waiters for us ladies as we sipped my imaginary grape tea and ate our fancy crumpet sandwiches. I remember Pickle whistling as he robotically turned the plate over and over to cut each sandwich, I still couldn't tell you what it was he was whistling but he and Chips seemed to join in cadence and whistled out a work tune to work together around the kitchen without colliding into one another and each time they delivered a plate to us at the table, they would raise a pretend top-hat and smile.

I think back to who I once was and I sometimes fear that as each day passes, it will be harder and harder to get back to being that innocent young girl I miss being. I fear soon it will be too late or impossible to undo many of the things I have done. I had a slight temper and streak of stubbornness about me as a teen; I was taught to be honorable and to not back down from someone by force. Lu raised me to be aware of my surroundings and to always have an escape plan; she feared that because I was a girl that I could be easily targeted to be kidnapped when we were out on rally rides. Chips, Pickles and Dexa all pushed to give me the skills to stand my ground against the same type of person Lu had concerns about so I had ample encouragement to be safe. Looking back I could have saved myself some punches to the face if I had learned a little better when to back down or even just to shut up, but that's not who I am. I have never had the ability to walk passed as someone was being bullied or pushed around. Something in my chest catches fire when someone is being picked on, I hated it when I was younger and that hatred only grew inside of me.

In the second high school I became friends with Carmen, she put our friendship to the test for her douche-bag boyfriend Scott but we still were friends after all of that business back at the park. Carmen had an amazing body, she filled out young and between her hips and her fuller chest, she looked way older than fifteen. With cheer leading there were plenty of times in the locker rooms that girls take notice of each other, it's human nature. There was once that a heavier set girl named Tiffany who was ridiculing a girl that was hardly half her weight named Dennia. Dennia was a small framed girl, by the early point of our junior year she still hardly had much in regards for hips or curves of any kind and you could tell it made her self-conscious. Dennia kept her books hugged tightly to her body as she walked the hallways and her eyes trained to the floor. Dexa often times found it hard to hold eye contact with many people for very long; even Lu or Chips or Pickle and he'd known them for better than a decade so I knew what a beaten person looked like.

Tiffany was relentless when berating Dennia; she was abrasive and pushed her weight around as often as she could. It was easy to read that Dennia hated herself which broke my heart because there was nothing she could do to change her body and she was pretty anyways so there shouldn't have been any reason for her to be insecure about anything. You only have one body and you need to be prideful about it, girls don't realize how much more incredible their bodies are than those of boys, we have evolved to create LIFE! And for those that believe in the whole god thing and Jesus stuff, it was a woman that brought a savior/god into the world. Tiffany did her best to impose her own form of authority on everyone, she bragged that she had all the answers and was the best at everything no matter how many people disliked her or proved her wrong over and over.

Tiffany was aggressive and "tifflee" about everything with everyone; after all "tiff" meant quarrel or argument, so being tifflee was one to start quarrels and arguments, looking back it all makes sense. Tiffany berated the smaller Dennia, she pulled at her clothes as Dennia changed and then heralded for everyone to look at the girl in her skimpy under clothes as she scurried to cover herself. Dennia was very light-skinned; she wore thick framed glasses and wore thick yarn ties in her hair to keep her dark hair back. Dennia cried several times over the torment that Tiffany doled out. I still feel ashamed that I didn't stick up for Dennia sooner but it took a few weeks before my boiling blood caused me to find the guts to do the right thing against the much heavier set bully.

I remember lying awake some of the nights after I heard Tiffany begrudgingly harp on the smaller girl; Tiffany was after all very non-petite for her height so it made it easier for her to bully. Dennia was quiet and meek but she was easy to toss for cheerleading. I wondered if maybe letting herself get tossed into the air was her way of complying or trying to fit in, I also wondered from time to time if maybe spinning through the air made her forget the crap that she put up with to stay on the squad with us girls. Dennia and I were about to be tossed and as I shot my legs straight, I had Marquina and Sherice as my base girls to catch me and Katrina as my backup catcher for safety, I looked to time my jump with Dennia whom had Carmen and Jackie as her base and Tiffany as the backup catcher, and I felt my stomach sink. I planted my foot and two spins into the basket toss, I tried to keep my bearings as I spun in the air and with each revolution, I tried to keep an eye on Dennia.

Little Dennia spun, her ankles crossed and her arms were tucked in tightly, she had a beautiful graceful spin. I tucked my thighs to my chest a bit for my catchers and kept my arms in so I didn't accidentally hit one of my girls and as I landed. I watched Tiffany push Carmen and Jackie to the sides to let Dennia slam to the ground. Carmen stumbled backwards into Marquina shaking my base a little and as Dennia whomped to the ground, her little body let out a loud shriek causing everyone to turn and look. Marquina and Sherice both held me around my back and waist as they let me down onto the ground as we finished our routine. I had enough, Tiffany played the victim and held her hands up while mumbling "Oh MY" and "OH dear what happened" but I'd had it. I had been a little warm from the jumping and twirling of practice but suddenly my veins ran hot with fury and I lunged towards Tiffany as she exclaimed that she merely bumped into Jackie by shear accident.

I didn't keep my hands open to slap box like I used to with Chips at the shop, I was ball fisted and swinging from the hip. I wanted to punch Tiffany on each freckle across her cheeks; I aimed to cave her face in. Her instigating bullshit and then reneging was tiresome and everyone was tired of it, I was just the first to call her on it and finally grow weary of her getting away with it. Our Cheer coach Kisha Theisson was in her later fifties and loved the brown-nosing that came from Tiffany so she enabled the vicious activity without any regards to the squad by looking the other way. Kisha conveniently didn't see what happened and then became frantic to help Dennia. I honed in my fists to beat the crap out of Tiffany for her bullshit and bullying. After I landed a few good hits to Tiffany she turned the tables and began to come back at me, her hands were wild and out of control.

Tiffany returned a few hits and we stood toe to toe and fought on the grass during cheer practice. Tiffany lurched towards me and as I tried to brace myself, her girth engulfed me and I found myself in a headlock. I grabbed a hold around her waist and pulled on her right arm that was wrapped around my neck. I couldn't get free so I exposed some of her right ribcage and then balled up my fist and hit as hard and as fast as I could, delivering blow after blow to her stretched ribs. My eyes wanted to burst out all of my anger in tears but I clenched my jaw and the rest of the muscles in my body to hold them back. I thought back to Pickle telling me not to give away my power over myself to anyone else and I held in my tears. Marquina and Jackie worked together to pull the two of us apart. I was visibly smaller in size but as she balled her eyes out from getting caught being a dick and then getting beat up for it, I was clearly the victor. Tiffany transferred off the squad not long after and told everyone that she quit because she couldn't handle the catty stuff of the squad, but most knew the truth that she was the biggest offender around.

I wondered if I was being tracked by my phone, perhaps there was a chip in it or maybe because I called Lu that there was a trace on the line and that was what lead the voice to find me so quickly, either way I was cut off and now back to being alone. The breeze was soothing and the gulls squawking like crazy as they swooped down from above and contended over small bits of food fighting each other. I didn't want to move from my bench even as hard as it was on my backside, I was content. I thought about Melanie, I thought about Dennia and Dexa and the many other people I had met in my life that were shy or reserved and because of that, were often picked on by assholes or pushed around. I felt bad that Dennia ended up with a broken collar bone after her fall but Tiffany ended up with a broken nose, which caused the raccoon mask double black eyes and four fractured ribs. I ended up suspended for beating up the coaches little girlfriend but it was worth taking a stand. I watched the white capped ocean waves and pondered what the next stage of my life might bring me; it is always easier to reflect near the water, ever so much more than when shoved away in a musty crotch smelling Mexican prison.

CH.4

I hauled myself up by my leathers and with near complete bodily defiance I turned to begin to stroll the boardwalk for a bit. I passed couples holding hands and vendors scooping out ice cream, there was a gaggle of people all scattered about and in the middle of all of it, was me, aimlessly wandering and doing my best to avoid confronting my adult life. I discarded my phone to a homeless person lying beside a park bench. I thought back to Chips once telling me that Vets have one of the highest rates of homelessness next to sexual abuse victims and it just made me feel sad, I wished there was more I could do for all of them. I felt the weight of my boots on my feet as each one clopped on the pavement as I strolled. I knew there were things I had to do, I knew there were risks I might have been taking by being out in the public but being in the sun and stretching my body in the ocean breeze was what I decided I needed to do for myself.

Pickle always assured me there was nothing wrong with putting yourself first once in a while and taking care of yourself when you needed to, it wasn't selfish. There were young couples in their bathing suits wrestling back and forth on the sand, men playfully tackling their girls and kids digging in the dirt and plenty of picture perfect happy families gathering for loving time at the beach, and none of them seemed to open their eyes to realize what happens in the world when you stop ignoring it, like sex slavery and endless bigotry, hate, blight, greed, deception and all the cruel evil things that stir in the minds of everyone around you that they hide behind a smile as they plot against you.

I used to hate; I used to hate with all of my being. I hated that my father was never around and that everything I did, I did without him. I often asked Lu if she was lonely without him or found her job of raising me to be more of a struggle on her own. Lu often skirted the question and even though they divorced before I was born, I was still born. I often told myself that my parents still loved each other; maybe the divorce was to protect Waylon County after he was caught and maybe it was some way of keeping the town from getting shut down. I missed my father Digger and my friends from the club, I could sure use a friend to talk to but I couldn't risk putting any of them in whatever spotlight I have brought on myself. I wanted to go back to being able to sit quietly at a booth and eat in peace, I wanted to be able to have a phone conversation and not be intruded by some strange voice that has eyes on everything I do, and I wanted to stop feeling like I was living on the run.

I made a large loop around the long boardwalk to try to clear my mind. I ran in school for pleasure and have missed it too some degree. I was still wearing my boots, leather pants and riding jacket with reinforcements in the forearms, including a bunch of money that was probably illegal and traced and what not, physically running wasn't anywhere on my agenda anytime soon but the walk seemed to help relax me a little. The sun grew blazen orange along the horizon and I was without some pressing need for anything specific, I was feeling insignificant again, dull and perhaps a little numb to everything that had happened since I woke up. I contemplated my long ass day and for the life of me I couldn't really find one point in my life that I can say; "that right there is where things went wrong" I just seemed to have one of those lives that was always in jeopardy.

The beautiful sky was just another sunset, the breeze was just a light wind and I couldn't figure out why I was feeling so icky. I was free after eight months in prison, I should still be kissing the ground all Count of Monte Cristo style and rolling in the sand, instead I was scanning everyone I could see on the beach for any sign of a gun hidden within a retail outlet suit or any bit of shady character that might be watching me for too long. I felt uneasy in the warm place of fun and enjoyment. I felt exposed and easily watched and vulnerable and it made my heart perk up a little as I finished my stroll. I felt the hyper-vigilance that Dexa spoke of when you have enemies that might be after you or find yourself in a place of possible attack; it makes your cheeks burn and then you get all emotional afterwards. The emotional letdown after your flight or fight responses is draining, you cry nearly uncontrollably and it depletes all of your energy, but I will say that the sleep you get afterwards is beautiful and when you awake it feels like being reborn again.

Down the street from my bike where I backed it in between a few other motorcycles and some trendy local mopeds I caught notice of a man staring me down from the driver's seat of his Expedition. The Expedition was shady black and blacked out like crazy with pitch black window tint, probably standard for Florida but I could hardly make out his silhouette with the exception that he was leaning half way out of the window staring me down. The lump in my throat grew, I didn't get a chance to look at either man that was chasing me from my shower back at the spa, the mean bastards ruined my rub down and that was enough to convince me that they were bad guys and that I was deep-fried if I got caught. I couldn't tell what kind of suit the man was wearing; it looked just like a dark blazer which further raised my suspicions about everything. Shay said both men that broke into my hotel room were wearing blazers and jeans. The man peering over his sunglasses was wearing a black or dark blazer; it was hard to tell against the black interior of the SUV. He had short thick black hair and was peeping like a total creeper.

I slowed my walk to my bike as I stared back at the SUV parked towards the end of the long narrow driveway. I tried to focus my hearing behind me to keep from being rushed or blindsided but also keep my attention on the SUV. I had my bandana around my hairline and my sunglasses on so most of my face was obscured just in case it happened to be some sort of surveillance or anything. The dude would not stop staring; the only thing he seemed to be missing was a camera for taking extra creep snapshots to wank-off to later, except there might have been on in the dark window behind his seat, but I couldn't see anything. Dexa used to tell me about people that sometimes followed people, he instilled extra caution in me to the point that I questioned myself about maybe sharing in his paranoia and then I began to second guess myself about being paranoid or just maybe noticing things. I took a deep breath and took four or five steps to my right to lean against the building post and debate if what I was taking in was correct. I tried to change my perspective before my heart rate got out of control and I panicked myself for no reason.

The brick column was warm against my side, the shadows beginning to fill the side corners began to grow and as I stared at the Tom Selleck looking man glaring down the parking alley towards me I tried to reassess what information I was noticing. The man was leaning on his forearm while staring down in my direction, he didn't seem to motion much and with a quick glance behind me, the only thing I noticed were sporadic people wandering around on the beach. I slowed my breathing, the whistling in my nose from the deep breathes dried my nose and it began to burn for a moment as my heart beat began to slow and come back under control.

I rolled my head and stretched out my neck a little and in doing so, I noticed a man wearing dark jeans and a black blazer over a button up shirt making a beeline for me from the beach side of the surf shop. The man walking towards me was younger than the man in the SUV, he had lighter hair but still wore dark sunglasses and walked with a motive, each foot kicking up sand as he trudged and swung his arms to keep his balance in the sand. My heart immediately began to race again; my gut hasn't led me astray by much so I wasn't ignoring it again. The memory of Shay telling me that two men had entered my room suddenly echoed in my ears and my fists began to clench as my fight or flight response kicked my adrenal glands pumped into overdrive, filling me with the adrenaline I needed in order to flee.

I nudged myself up from the light brick column; my body was already slightly at ease before I caught a glimpse of the man rushing towards me. I tried to keep from outright sprinting back to my bike but my jog grew faster and faster with each step and my fast walk turned into a full sprint for the last fifteen or so steps. I fumbled for my keys as I caught sight of the younger man beginning to jog towards me. I tried to keep myself calm enough to start my bike without fumbling. I turned the key over and pulled on the throttle to let the engine come to life. My chest was getting tight with anxiety as my suspicions were all confirmed instantly; I was being tailed. I felt my temples throb in my head as the roar of my exhaust burst to life.

With the pull of my wrist and leaning into the turns I was on my way to being the hell away from there. I stayed just out of reach of the younger man as he rounded the corner, as soon as I fired up my engine he stopped jogging and began to run all out to gain on me for the moment. I kept my head down and leaned left and right to avoid moving cars and swarms of people amassed in the parking lot as I snaked my way through back to the main street. The SUV man sat up as I sped towards him, I couldn't see behind his black sunglasses but his head following me assured me that I had his attention.

I wanted to keep an eye behind me to see how close behind the men were but I was trying to swerve in and out of cars passing by, all that I could was speed down the road and put some distance behind me on the highway. I headed back to the run down motel, my small nasty safe place to regroup and figure out what I was going to do, I figured it was quiet and ok. I turned down one street and up the next; I tried to think as quickly on my feet as possible to where I was going and tried to recognize streets and buildings as I also tried to ride chaotically to lose my newly acquired fans.

It was a little flattering really, but I just didn't have time in my life for new friends right now. As cars flashed by me I replayed the fast images of the man chasing me, he was in dark jeans and hiking boots, not the typical clothing for an agent, those uptight stiffs always wear suits because it represents who they are and their agency. The dress shirt and blazer told me that he wasn't some thug either, they wouldn't wear an off the rack suit either, I just couldn't figure out who the hell was after me, but I certainly didn't like it.

I took the long way around my shoddy hotel so I could park my bike against the back side wall that was covered with ivy, hoping to camouflage it enough to hide away. I stared back down the streets I rode up, other than light traffic it seemed relatively quiet, the alley behind the hotel was littered with dumpsters and other assorted trash but not obscuring my view of a pending marshal raid or something. If law enforcement was after me for the dead douche-bags I left behind in Louisiana then there wouldn't be a two man team chasing me, there would be all sorts of local and county sheriffs ready to whoop my ass. Miami-Dade county sheriffs are no joke, I've seen enough episodes of "Cops" to know that the mean business and don't play, so this couldn't have been legal things.

I couldn't put my finger on what the hell was going on, if they were government they would have notified the local authorities, if they were with the sex traffickers then I would not have out run a bullet, girls are worth a lot of money to the horny dogs over in the middle east that have to pay for ass because they get too old to keep raping for it. I couldn't wrap my mind around what they hell was going on. They found me in Florida after only a few hours, they weren't all that far behind me here in Miami Beach and I've only been here a few hours also, both times I was contacted by the phone voice chick, she's really starting to get under my skin, I'm canceling her from my Christmas card mailing list for sure. I tried to sneak around to my room, hoping that I could lay low and maybe catch some sleep for a bit once my heart stopped pounding in my ears.

My head spun trying to piece everything together; I kept my body close to the ivy as I walked up the back side of the hotel. I could see the empty courtyard, I expected to see the old Guido and one or two of his prostitutes lounging by the empty Jacuzzi again but it was dead silent. Before breaking around the corner near my room I tried to scan the other doors; the entrance across from the courtyard and around the corner, the parking lot across the way seemed quiet but that was a selling point when I first arrived anyways but I was extra aware and it kept my heart beating rapidly. I tried to flex my fists to keep my fingers from shaking but as my pulse surged through me, it was more important to keep my breathing under control than control shaking hands. As my chest wore heavy with worry my arms felt like weights hanging from my shoulders, I was growing more tired and I wanted a small itsy teeny nap.

I backed up against the ivy to hug the side wall as I neared the opening to the courtyard, the ivy cushioned the wall against my back and I squatted down slightly to lower my center of gravity. I dropped my arms and shook my forearms a little to get my sleeves feeling a little more comfortable as my muscles all tensed up from my feet to my head. I pigeon bobbed a few times to get fast scans further and further into the courtyard to get a handle on anything that might have been suspicious around me. Each view was of an empty clearing, it was reassuring and I slowly let my guard down before entering the small courtyard lounging area. I rounded the corner to ease my way to my room, I thought more about the two guys back at the beach; I was now certain that I had stalkers and I racked my brain trying to figure out where they came from and who they might have been. I turned the key with my left hand and the handle with my right and eased the door open. My room was still dark and crummy, just as I left it. The setting sun made my room seem even darker as I reached for the light switch on the lamp.

Click the light switch let out a snap and then it flickered to life. *Click* the door closed the rest of the way; I left it slightly opened to see well enough to make my way into the room and turn on the lamp. The slamming of the door caused my heart to jump with adrenaline, my breath was gone and I couldn't swallow with the lump in my throat. My body froze for half a moment, enough time to take in my surroundings and prepare to fight for my life, a situation I was gaining more experience in. I trained and fought plenty in my martial arts classes as well as brawls and scraps in various bars and other things but since I left prison, it was getting old and fast. I slowly turned to my left to see the old Guido sitting in a wooden chair in the corner near the door, and a shorter blonde girl standing at the door gripping a baseball bat like it was a dick. "Who are you" the old man with the white chest hair climbing out of the top of his low buttoned shirt asked. He

82

had his hair slicked back still but was wearing a khaki and black panama style shirt and he was using a butterfly knife to pick dirt out from under his nails.

"Don't kid yourself old man, you probably get a manicure twice a week to keep your hands from getting dirty" I snarked out referring to his bold but deflated attempts to intimidate me with a hooker and a bat, and his knife. "I happen to sleep alone, you both will have to find somewhere else to soak your dentures" I followed up. I wasn't sure what they planned to do in *my* room but I worked my feet side to side in my steps to get a good solid stance in preparation to charge the girl with the bat. The girl by the door wore a sleeveless leather vest, her blonde hair was in a bump on the top of her head, her eyes were coated with eyeliner and her tight skinny red pants looked pretty constricting. I eyed the girl at the door, her cleavage moved a little meaning she was flexing her chest muscles underneath, her leg muscles didn't move much as she also stood with a wide stance and tried to wring the pine tar out of her Louisville bat.

The old man was still half reclined in his chair as he stared at me waiting for a response, he seemed at ease that his girl by the door had everything covered but his kind of calm made me question if maybe he had a gun, you aren't entirely calm in a confrontation unless you have backup and a way to ensure that you'll come out on top, for me I had years of martial arts to whomp ass with. I turned a little to keep a shoulder towards the old guy, I narrowed as much as I could to make for a smaller target just in case he was packing at all, I was nervous at the situation and to have these two fools in my room made me pretty nervous. I can take a hit with a bat, if you rush in on someone you can take away some of the leverage they'd hit you with and in that case you just try to protect your head. The girl didn't have any sweat glistening on the top of her cleavage meaning they hadn't been in my non-air-conditioned room for very long, I wondered if they had been keeping an eye out for me or this was all circumstantial.

The girl by the door was probably in her young twenties, if she took a baby wipe to half her makeup she'd be pretty. In the shoddy lighting she looked to have light eyes and fair skin, even with the Florida sun. I had a bed behind me that stopped about right behind my knees, if she were to rush me I'd surely trip and I bet she had done this once before, except I know I am the baddest in a room, even with the geriatric pretending to be Puerto Rican with the knife. When things are not tougher than you then they are not a threat, if there is no threat there is no need worry, and with no worry, there is no fear, thus, I am not afraid, this is about to just be a quick little stand off and then they'll leave.

I ground my right foot into the floor; I could feel the carpet shift slightly under my heels as I glared at the girl with the bat. I stared down the girl between me and the door, her stance widened a little as she lowered her head and stared right back. I didn't like the prick glaring at me but I commended her for having the ovaries to square off back at me, but I was going to destroy her. I shrugged my shoulders up a bit to look defensive and then shot my face back at the old man. The man waited for me to talk and as soon as he said; "well" I charged to the woman at the door. I waited for the man to talk to distract the girl for a moment, I planned to swipe a forearm into her face and knock her back while jerking the bat from her hands and then caving in the side of the old man's head with it and then taking a nap once they were both tied up in the bathroom or something.

Chips used to tell me that taking a hit with a bat was easier if you were closer to the person swinging it, "the long end is the one with all of the leverage." I tucked my shoulder and raised my left forearm to take the initial hit from the bat in the reinforced part of my jacket. I watched as the girl closed her eyes while swinging, she wasn't a seasoned thug; she was just a scared girl following orders. I collided with all of my might into the girl, the hit to my flexed arm felt like a dull thud as she only hit me with the handle and not the full force of the swing, which would have probably shattered my arm. I raced at the girl with all of my weight and strength, I clobbered her between my body and the door, her body slammed into the door and she immediately fell limp after the clash. I held the girl pinned to the door until I got a good handle on the bat still gripped in her hands. My shoulder was sore from hitting the girl but the threat was neutralized. I propped my right leg back behind me to keep the girl wedged up against the door, her body did not fight back.

The old man rose to his feet as one of his working girls thudded against the door from my might. "Hey you bitch" he hollered out. I held the girl up on my left forearm under her neck and armpit with the left collar of her vest gripped in my hand, her weight was growing heavy. I worked my left knee up between her legs to rest some the limp body weight on my leg. I felt bad that I made the girl bash her head on the door because she looked pretty young and it was probably his instructions to do it. I held the bat up to ward off the old man from trying to charge at me as I tried to keep the girl propped up against the door. I ordered the old man to sit back down and prop his feet back up on the small table I figured that if his feet were up I'd have enough warning if he put them back down.

"Be gentle with Irena, she's a good earner" the old man began to plead once the tables had turned between my attacker and me. I had to bend down a bit to get a better handle under the girls armpits to half hip toss her onto the bed to keep her off the floor and from getting into my way again, I was cautious to watch him. The girl smelled of cheap perfume and her hair was without the shiny luster of a fresh washing, she was a worked girl and whatever this man had held over her, he used it. I squatted down to get a better grip on her when *Blam* I felt a hard hit to the back of my right side. I raised my arm to protect my face as I turned to barely catch a glimpse of some tall brunette with a nose ring begin to swing her bat back for another hit.

I felt my back begin to tinge as I tried to support Irena and keep us both from falling and ending up with an unconscious girl landing on me. With a handle on the girls leather vest I felt the girls' weight on my arm and I began to step backwards with her. My ankle began to roll and all I could do was heave back off my right planted foot and hurl the dead weight and myself towards the bed to soften our landing rather than the floor. My muscles strained, my legs fought buckling and I exploded from the ground to take an uneasy step to get the limp girl the span to the bed so we didn't collide together onto the floor.

I hoisted the blonde girl up enough to shield myself from the Brunette as she cocked back for another swing. Under the blonde hair I tried to keep an eye on the Brunette, her eyes were dark and staring at me as I carried her co-hooker girl with me as we fell. I struggled to use my momentum to my advantage to make it to the bed. My right leg buckled, I felt all of my weight bend my knee and my leg began to fold flat towards the floor. I heaved my arms upwards with the girl in my hands; my back and shoulder writhed in pain and then fell against the side of the bed. The blonde girl landed with her upper half of her body flopping onto the bed with a bounce as I collided into the side of the bed, not the top. My muscles burned along my back from getting hit as I crashed to the floor.

I folded onto the floor, the brunette that hit me while my back was turned stepped closer to me, she was wearing tall knee high black lace up boots that seemed much taller from my position on the floor. The stiletto heal on her boots must hair been eight inches long and even without them, the damn great ape towered over me with her bat cocked back. I followed the girls long lace up boots up her legs, at her knees her boots gave way to black fishnets and then to black tight hot pants. From the floor this girl looked nine feet tall, betcha the humidity from the clouds was a bear for her hair to deal with all the way up there.

The girl wore a fluffy black shirt to compliment her dark eyeliner, silver nose ring and brunette hair that I noticed had red streaks in it as it was all pulled up into a high pony tail on her head. I looked up at the girls' thin face under my eyebrows, I tried to keep my forearms ready to protect my head from a pissed off blow from the bat again as I tried to think of something to do. My back right side burned like hell as I leaned wedged against the wall looking for an escape. I was half wedged between the small coffee table and against the side of the bed; there was no where I could go in a hurry to get myself out of the position so I complied for a few minutes. I didn't like being in such a vulnerable position and I could feel that burning in my nose that usually precedes crying.

"I'm just passing through" I answered up. The tall brunette kept the bat pulled back, with the length of her arms the bat would have a long way to travel before it hit me but with the force put into it with the leverage, surely I'd be wrecked. Cheryl once came into the motorcycle shop that I was working at helping Chips to rebuild carbs and motors and such wearing tall heals. I was a little less than girly in my youth and she thought that Chips was alone. Cheryl walked like a dog on ice in the tall heals but she did it to surprise her husband.

Cheryl wore a sleek purplish blue corset for her husband for a surprise for him at work, she had no idea that I was there. I caught a glimpse of her and had no idea she could be so beautiful. Cheryl wore tall black heals with her corset get up. She wore a long coat over top but once in the shop she left it by the door behind her. I admired many different people for many different things, Cheryl was always a good friend to me and Lu and I admired her for that, now she gained my complete respect and admiration for confidently slipping into something so sexy and enticing for her man. I felt my jaw drop as Cheryl stepped around the corner looking drop dead gorgeous. Cheryl had her eyes on Chips on the other side of the room and didn't even see me in the corner; I was speechless from a far corner out of her view.

Cheryl slowly stepped across the room, I could tell by watching her ankles that she was a little unsure in the tall heels as she walked but she swayed her hips seductively anyways. Cheryl had her cute little butt all perked up in a skimpy pair of lacy panties, black garters on her nylons and she flicked her hair behind her as she neared Chips. Chips was often a smiley and goofy guy but I had never seen such a smile on his face as that time. I tried to inch backwards to the supply room, I didn't want to interrupt the couple, nor be present for what it looked like they were fixing to do, and they deserved their privacy for a bit. I watched as Cheryl bent over the table across from him and swayed back and forth, I watched her bend her feet side to side playing with her feet. I had to give Cheryl endless credit as he stood in a very revealing tiny outfit for her husband; it wasn't just her sexy body that I admired but her confidence too.

I hid away in the back supply room to stay out of the way and to not interrupt the couple. I was without my phone or any ability to escape so I did my best to block out, well, everything. I couldn't tell you who was snorting like a rabid gorilla-pig in heat but I didn't want to know for sure but they sounded like they had their fair share of married fun, and good for them. I laid out my work shirt to insulate me from the cold ass floor and I tried to take a nap. My nap mostly failed as it wasn't quiet or conducive for rest but I tried to lay still and stare into the backs of my eyelids. I don't know how long I was in the supply room because when you work with oil and grease and all that, you don't wear anything you wouldn't risk getting ruined like a watch.

I was alerted to a knocking on the door: "Yo Dollar" Chips was seeking my whereabouts. I rose up and cautiously answered Chips, "You all good man?" I heeded to the nuances of his voice, he was slightly out of breath. I cracked the door open, praying he was still dressed, or redressed, or whatever. Chips was blushing slightly and still smiling largely while averting his eyes from mine while apologizing. I was nervous to open the door, Chips was my friend and I'd see more of him naked at the bar than I would have ever preferred but this situation was plenty different. In the distance over his shoulder I could see Cheryl fixing some of her clothes and tying things back together with some jiggling bounces and shuffles to get bows and ties to where they needed to be, I was so embarrassed.

I pulled the door the rest of the way open to reveal Cheryl in her coat leaning back against the table, also staring at the ground while still playing with her heels on the ground in shame. I was hesitant to step out from the supply room; it was pretty awkward to be honest. "We are so very sorry" Chips began to plead for my forgiveness; of course I had the upper hand to bust his ass in every way possible. Immature comments like; "that was quick, oh Quick Draw huh? Didn't picture you as a four-stroke fan" and dozens of other ways to bust my friends ass came to mind and with each one I struggled not to blurt them out. I stopped for a moment, I looked at the sincerity that Cheryl truly loved him so much that she stepped out of her comfort zone and out of the house out of love for Chips, and rather than make some comment to make Cheryl any more embarrassed, I waited for Chips to open his hand as he slid it off the door frame and I high-fived him.

Cheryl shook her head lightly and apologized over and over as I walked closer to her. Chips explained that he forgot all about me when he saw his wife walking towards him and to hell with the rest. I nodded that I understood and I really meant it. As Chips began to apologize again I put my hand up to hush him, neither half of the loving couple had any reason to apologize and the topic was silenced. I asked Chips to head to the office for a few minutes to get us both a soda; I figured I'd be less embarrassed asking her questions with him there, because we were just pals in the shop. As soon as Chips was out of earshot I reached up to hug and reassure Cheryl, she was still shaking and worried that she had reason to be embarrassed. I hugged Cheryl and confidently boasted "Damn girl, damn *hot* girl" and even though her cheeks grew even more red, her mouth cracked a smile. I coaxed Cheryl to unfold her arms and open up her long coat so I could get a bit of a better look.

I wasn't ogling Cheryl out of some lust filled teen same-sex curiosity but rather I admired the work she did to keep herself in shape, plus getting all sexy'd up like a lady was fairly new to me. I asked Cheryl plenty of questions; how uncomfortable some of the stuff was and how she knew how to get all dolled up. I was often referred to as "Dale" in the shop because of "Chip and Dale" the cartoon, it was the reference to Chips being like my daddy uncle and the camaraderie we shared when slap boxing and such. I adored Cheryl and Chips as a couple; they were an aunt and uncle that I would choose for anyone and they were adorable in their love. I was a little nervous and Cheryl detected it, she realized I didn't have the girliest of upbringings but she wriggled her hips in a bit of a dance to make me laugh and to lighten up the mood. Most of the walls of the shop were slathered in pinup girls on bikes and whatever else, I never once felt objectified or insecure; I admired each of the bodies and regardless of state of dress. I was confident in myself but I was also a tomboy in my youth so my teen years were filled with learning and experimenting to be more feminine, even if my body didn't get the memo till a bit later on.

Cheryl showed me the snaps and how she got into most of her slinky gear, the rest was pretty self-explanatory and even though she was mostly embarrassed because she didn't make sure the shop was empty, she was still holding her shoulders back and her head up high with confidence, which was what really made her sexy. Cheryl was still had pretty sweaty cleavage and as I admired her fit body and her get up, Chips showed up out of nowhere. "Man I have a sexy wife huh?" he disrupted the silence; I felt my muscles tense up for a moment but knew it was just a small startle, I wasn't doing anything wrong. Chips grabbed the waist of Cheryl and pulled her to twist her body a bit as he also admired. I tried to avert my eyes a little and keep from looking too longingly. Cheryl flung her arms up for a moment and caught my attention; I thought she was going to fall. "You know why heels are so dangerous Dale?" Chips asked. "She's about three feet up off the floor on those stilts" I replied thinking I was being funny. Chips spun Cheryl around and raised one foot; he showed me that even though his wife was a tiny little critter, all of her body weight was concentrated onto the point of the heel, especially dangerous on ice, or sand, and also for larger girls I was informed, it was very intriguing.

I flashed back to the physics lesson from Cheryl and Chips; ironically I was being faced down by a girl wearing skimpy sexy clothes and very high heels when it came back to me. I had no other play than to kick as hard as I could at the girls' ankle and heel with the reinforced toe of my boot. I kicked my foot as hard as I could and connected with the soul of her boot, I watched as her ankle buckle sideways and the long heel of her boot cracked and bent underneath her, causing her to collapse like a building in an earthquake. The tall girl came tumbling down as her ankles wobbled and gave way; I tucked up my legs to keep from being landed on. I tried to shield myself just in case she tried to swing the bat on her way down. The girl let out a slight groan as I connected with her boot. I though back to the many times I wore high heels especially when I was strutting around shiny chrome bikes in tiny swimsuits for money a few years back, the heels are meant to support weight from the top to the bottom, not designed to take a sideways hit; I found my way out: crippling her big ole hooker heels then hurrying to my feet.

I scurried to my feet before the old man could take his turn to rush me next. My right shoulder now hurt worse than my busted left ass cheek and I was intensely angry about getting jumped and hit with a damn ball bat, especially in *my own* room. I snatched both bats from the floor and paced for a moment. The amazon girl was stumbling as she tried to stand up from the floor but failing because her ankles kept buckling without the heel on her boot to help support the high arches of the boots. I pointed the end of the bat to my attacker and told her to just sit on the damn bed and keep an eye on her friend or risk joining her. The old man dropped his feet from the table as I dropped his tall brunette while she stood above me but he didn't rise to his feet faster than I did. The tall girl coddled her unconscious friend by petting her hair and holding her to keep her close. My right arm hurt like hell, my riding jacket softened the blow but a hard hit was still a hard hit no matter how you take it, and getting hit by the long limbed lady, well it hurt a whole lot.

"What the hell are you crazy bastards doing in my room, I just wanted a night of sleep" I fought back my cracking voice as I howled my demands. My knees wanted to give out under me from my sore lower back and sharp pains running down both legs but I fought off gravity and remained standing, even if it was unevenly. I hobbled a little towards the door to lean back against it to ease the pain on my shoulder and keep my back to an exit to keep from getting rushed again. The old man crossed his arms and continued to chew on his cheeks with anger as he stared right through me. I offered up that I was simply riding through and needed a cheap place to stay and it was all as simple as that. The old man just gnawed at his own teeth and hardly flinched, I figured I wasn't getting anywhere with him.

I looked over at the two girls sitting on the bed; the blonde was still passed out and the brunette still running her fingers through her friends' hair. "Start talking sister" I ordered as I waved the bat in my right hand towards her. I was in a piss poor mood and growing increasingly inpatient. I didn't want to waste my time in the room talking to myself while they just took up space. "What the hell?" I demanded as I lunged with control at the slender girl causing her to jump to defend herself and friend by cowering and covering over the other girl. I knew immediately that the slender girl cared enough for the other girl to protect her, it's those subtle clues that Dexa told me to look out for with people, it helps to read what they are really made of.

"He make us come to get you, he in control" the slender girl began to speak with a choppy accent. I watched as her dark red painted lips parted and wriggled while she spoke, I couldn't identify her accent but with her pale skin and sharp cheekbones, I'd guess she was Eastern European of sorts. "Tallia, you hush now" the old man barked. The brunette Tallia shuttered and withdrew from him. I was already hurting and the pain made me impatient but I watched for her bodily cues in response to him. The girl was willing to smash me up with a ball bat for the hairy old fool and that pissed me off to no end, I slammed the bat in my right hand against the end table to force my point that I was done dangling like string in the wind, waiting for something to grab onto.

I wanted to know what the hell was going on. I had the upper hand because I had the exit and both bats so I wasn't going to go without answers. "Shut your old mouth wrinkles" I shouted to the old man while waving the bat once again. I refused to let the old man control the girls anymore. I turned back to Tallia and knuckled for more about what the hell they were doing in my room, not that I was all that surprised with that child-molester looking guy *Carl* that sat at the front desk running the place. My neck throbbed and my right shoulder blade felt hung up on a thick swollen bruise as I tried to roll my right shoulder back to straighten up my posture. Trying to lean against the door only pushed on the giant softball size clump of muscle and bruise that was feeling hot and tender near my shoulder blade.

"He say to come get you, he like the pretty girls" Tallia began her choppy narrated story to tell me all about how Davor (the old guy) would move girls around and when he had them unable to flee by taking their papers, he would throw parties which was when several girls would be given many drugs and then the men gathered them in a big pile of bodies, more men would arrive and rape them. The girls would all be awake but unable to move. Tallia remembered each man as they undressed and then took turns climbing onto them over and over, laughing and joking.

Each girl was kept in a room in a run-down building somewhere; big men would come and let other men into their areas to have intercourse with them, sometimes up to fifty a day for the newer girls. Each girl was wiped down with a wet wipe by a guard man between each stranger so they smelled nice and was clean. The guards would be rough with them and put their wipes and fingers inside of them, sometimes the cloth would be dry and it would cause pain that felt like tearing or would cause bleeding sometimes. Most of the men in the big building had accents, some you could understand while others you could not, but each man would slap or hit you if you fought back. Tallia pulled aside the unbuttoned top of her blouse and under her red lacy bra strap she showed scarred bite marks on her chest.

Tallia wept a little as she recalled how the week long party resulted in a beaten and battered body for days, an abuse that left each girl completely aware of Davor's brutality and his ability to control them. The old man with the sleeked back hair and gray chest hair was white knuckle gripped on a knife and was trying to inch from around the far side of his table, each move he made was not stealthy nor silent so I was full well aware of what he was attempting to do and I anticipated his attack. Tallia continued to talk about flying to some warm island then then being loaded onto a boat with several other girls in a tight space before arriving in America. Tallia closed her shirt up and wiped away her tears. Tallia lifted up the vest of the blonde girl and showed me more small scars on her stomach. "One man paid very much to use his knife on her, he made cuts and then put things into the cuts" Tallia explained. I squinted out of uncertainty at the slender brunette and then she wriggled upright finger and in the air while nodding, then she put her finger down by her crotch and wriggled it like a penis. I cocked my head to entice the lady to explain what she was trying to tell me; I couldn't believe the imagery that was forming in my mind.

"Man cut into her belly while she was held down, then man put his penis into her cut and continued to hold her down until he was done." Irena could not fight and she could feel the blade enter her just below her navel and after, she had to watch as he wriggled his fingers into her abdomen to make room under her skin before he used it to have sex with. My mouth was dry from hanging open as Tallia explained the crudeness of these scumbags. I was appalled that Davor in the corner could take money and let a man have sex with a knife wound in another human being. I felt a little lightheaded, my vision was shaky as I filled with rage and my knuckles burned as I held onto both of the bats I acquired. I stared are Davor sitting in the corner while he just stared hard back at me, I felt like I was staring into a vast emptiness that could have possibly once contained a form of a conscience. I figured he was picturing stabbing me and then raping the wound. My head spun with everything I had heard, processing it was difficult, but much easier than containing the anger that ran rampant in my chest.

Davor took in girls from all over, any girls he got from around the area he sent out on a boat and girls from other countries he brought in, girls that didn't know the language and have no way of getting away. I wrung my hands on the handles of the bat; I wanted to swing it as hard as I could against the skull of the old man in the corner. Drugging girls for fun and having "parties" to rape them into submission as they lay paralyzed from drugs but fully aware of what was happening to them bewildered and infuriated me, I was sickened and saddened, but mostly pissed the hell off.

The tips of my ears began to get hot with my raging blood pressure and I began to see spots in the corner of my right eye as my heartbeat throbbed. Tallia wept and bowed her head as her mascara began to streak down her face, not something she would risk for just some sympathy. "So who is this guy?" I asked Tallia. "His name is Davor Varkonavish, he grow up around here and learned from his uncles that much money can be made from women." Davor had family in Europe and they traded smuggled women like playing cards. Davor learned from his uncles how to smuggle women for money and how rape and brutal abuses kept them afraid, imprisoned with fear.

Ch. 5

"Serbian first name, Croatian last name" I muttered to myself as I tried to sift through the things I was just told. I was hesitant to take a big bite of the story and swallow it, it could have just been bullshit by some girl that was all hopped up on drugs and trying to avoid jail. I turned my head towards Davor and told him it was his turn to speak up, he leaned back and passed a cocky smirk, he didn't seem all that convinced I was willing to press him for answers. I raised the tip of the bat towards his throat, he swallowed hard enough to make the bat move in my hands but he still didn't look convinced of my seriousness about the situation. "She's telling the truth" I asked with slight encouragement from my new bat, he just perched his lips even tighter together. I kept one bat to his throat and the other gripped tightly in my other hand, it could have all been a rouse but I wasn't in a very trusting mood.

"Another girl, Servina, she try to escape one time, Davor tie her to pole naked, he bite off her nipple and then spit it into her mouth as she cry, he hold knife to her neck and he make her swallow it" Tallia cried out as I had my eyes locked on the man still trying to kill me with his stare. I raised my second bat to tap the first, sending a hard thud into his neck. Davor still clenched his knife in his hand, I hadn't forgotten he held it tightly but I didn't let on I was on to his antics just yet. "Put the knife on the table big guy" I instructed. Davor was of course resilient so I pushed back with my bat against his neck. Davor slowly raised his hand, the knife blade quivered as it neared the table. Images of him biting off a girls' nipple and spitting it into her mouth flashed through my mind, the thought of the sight sickened me and gave me a small shiver. This guy made his living with pain and torture; I didn't understand what drives these sorts of people.

I waited until Davor began to reach his knife across the table, it inched little by little and as fast as I could, I slammed the bat from my right arm down onto his clamped hand. Davor lunged forward to curl around his busted hand; his stern face began to turn red as he bent over his lap. Davor spat and grunted as he held onto his busted hand trying to ease his pain. It's often the ones that love to dole out the pain and inflict it on others that can't handle any themselves, the dicks just sicken me. Davor kicked his feet on the ground and unleashed slew of curse words and slang terms meant to degrade me; well all women really. I understand that the easiest thing to use against someone is what you can see, call a black person the "N" word, call a white person a honkey or cracker (yes they're racist terms you idiots), and of course call a girl any name from the long list of derogatory terms that men have come up with to inferiorate women, but honestly, you can't be more inventive?

I reached forward and pulled the old man by the collar of his shirt to jerk him onto the floor. Tallia squeaked at my sudden outburst of anger and the noise of the bat clashing onto the table. I knelt down onto Davor as he lay curled on the floor. I left a bat in my right hand and ready to defend myself against Tallia if she decided to try and attack me as I knelt and searched Davor for any more weapons. Davor mumbled and sniffled as he fought to keep from crying out while clutching his busted hand. I heard plenty of the small bones in his hands crunch between the bat and the table and was pretty sure, he won't be using it anytime soon.

"Sorry about your love life there padre" I offered my half-assed condolences. "You're just a man, there's plenty of you to slap around, isn't there?" I asked as I used my free hand to slap him harshly in the face after searching him for weapons and coming up empty. I kept my knee on the ribcage of Davor and looked back to make sure that Tallia and Irena were both still on the bed where they belonged. I didn't know what to do, both girls did not belong here and both were horrendously tortured and tormented so sending them back to wherever they came from was just as mean as letting them stay under his care I suppose.

"Uncles" it clicked in my head that Tallia mentioned that Davor was raised by his uncles to be sadistic and controlling towards women. "Got any nephews around here you smelly old prostate?" I asked Davor before standing back up. I realized that the old man surely wasn't working alone and at his age, his uncles have probably passed on but he would have to have close men to rape women with. I'd guess it might be a bonding thing to steal and torture women together, you'd have to have very trustable guys in order to ship girls with them around the seas together. I stood back up, shoving my bat into Davor's neck to push myself up wlth. "What else do you know skinny girl?" I pointed my bat at Tallia hoping that she knew more. I was dreaded with having to hurry because I had two dudes now tailing me and I didn't want to hang around and find out what it was they wanted from me, but I just couldn't leave this guy and his nephew/lovers to keep shipping girls around the world.

I was torn, I leaned back against the wall and alternated between looking at the old man curled up near the corner and the two girls so far from home (wherever that was) over on the bed. I held one bat with my left hand and leaned on it like a crutch, I released the other bat setting it up against the wall and used my free hand to rub my shoulder and try to ease some of the swelling tension in my neck for a second as my head began to throb. I was always raised to have honor, to do the right thing and to serve others and my country and here I was, hanging my ass out on the line for strangers again, and stumbling into even more human trafficking of all things. I couldn't believe it's only been a day and here I am, embroiled in more underground shady human selling bullshit.

I don't get how these things keep happening to me and I was lost over it. "Look out girl" Tallia spoke out as Davor was trying to reach for my leg to grab me. I wasn't sure what he was trying to accomplish because he was unarmed, one handed and damn near sixty, but good for him for trying. I raised up my bat and hammered it down into the side of his temple, pretty hard, his legs kicked out and he let out a meaty exhausted grunt. Davor rolled back and forth as he held his head from the pain. "You done yet? You need to think back to everything you ever let anyone do to a girl, that's the kind of night you're in for buddy" I leaned down and warned the old man. I let my warm moist breath fall on the long scraggly hairs that corkscrewed up from his ear hole as I warned him that he was utterly screwed and I wasn't going to be nice in any way. For immature fun I let some spit build up behind my lips and once I parted them, it stringed down into the small tuft of his graying ear hair, causing him to spin his head a little in protest.

I was never raised to be an animal, never encouraged to be mean or vindictive in retribution, but I was also incapable of just idly letting horrible things happen to people. In my sophomore year I lived with Otis and Trish, they were both members of the Lucifer Squadron in the earlier years that moved out to Arizona from Waylon to retire. I spent my junior year living with Pickle and I already told you how that ended up. So Lu asked if they would consider being my host parents for the school year.

Otis was a bald man with a gray goatee, Trish had dirty blonde hair she kept spiked up and together they were a funny couple to live with. I enjoyed my stay with them and looked at them both like grandparents; they were the closest thing I had anyways.

Otis was slightly hard of hearing, his service during Nam put a dent in his hearing and when he would shout "Huh" Trish would change what she said each time. One time that had me laughing heartily was, " You want ham"(referring to dinner) turned into "bears like jam" and that quickly turned to "you really married a man" of course when she followed up with "I have boy genitals" his response quickly became "ham sounds great." The two of them were more adorable than I could handle for long, they still held hands together when they walked, he would hold the door for her and even tucked her in then walked the house to double check the door locks and lights so she didn't have to walk through the house in the dark and risk tripping over anything.

I was living with Otis and Trish when I snuck out with Carmen and her douche-knocker boyfriend Scott tried to get me as naked as she was. One night Otis took Trish and me out to a movie, I wanted to see that Bourne movie but Otis had opted for National Treasure, it lacked Matt Damon but the Riley guy was a cutie, and Sean Bean lived through it. The movie got out on the later side, not a big deal but as we rounded the corner of the theater in the overhead lights, we noticed the side wall covered in grasshoppers or locusts, apparently there was a run of them and they swarmed to the sun heated wall for the night to stay warm. Trish was grossed out by the swarms of bugs and swatting at as many as she could to keep them out of her hair but they were falling on us by the hundreds. I was fighting to keep them from falling down the front of my shirt and the whole time, it grew harder and harder to hear over the buzzing sounds.

Otis suggested that Trish and I wait back in the doors while he went and retrieved the car to save his lovely wife the wallowing in all the bugs, I didn't mind getting them out of my clothes and hair as well. Trish and I took a few minutes to reach into clothes and slowly pull the twitching brown bugs from *places*, I had a few under my shirt and trying to trap them to remove them squished some, and that made me shiver with grossness. After stopping a few bugs from getting to second base I realized that Otis hadn't pulled the car around yet so I grew suspicious. I told Trish to wait and I headed back out through the gauntlet of swarming bugs as they jumped off the wall and flew back over and over again. A few steps from the doors I noticed two men standing close to Otis in the shadows of the parking lot. I stutter stepped for a moment, I was scared that something was wrong and that small moment of panic stopped me in my tracks.

I watched Otis' body language, he was standing erect and rigid, I didn't recognize the two men but they pretty rather close to Otis and he didn't seem to be reacting well to them. I tried to walk softly in my Keds, the softer souls helped to keep my footsteps quiet-ish as I crept towards the faded red Cadillac. I tried to narrow my vision on either man to make sure they didn't have a gun on Otis. I was pretty frightened and wasn't sure if I had a game plan or idea of what I could do but I had to stand up for my bike club brother, and friend.

"What would Bourne do" I asked myself as I made my way unnoticed closer to the car, I tried to keep quiet and low as I moved closer. I ducked behind one car parked next to our car, I thought about trying to look like a fellow motorist just walking to my car but my mind was racing and I was coming up empty headed. I made it to the back of the car, I tried to listen and as I inched closer I realized that the two men were holding a knife and threatening to stab Otis if he didn't fork over his keys. I wondered how Otis held them at bay for the last few minutes but the old guy was still a badass.

"OOOGA BOOGA" I popped up from behind the two men to startle them. With my hands raised a little and a semi squat stance, I paused and asked myself: "where the hell did that come from?" I was embarrassed that Otis even heard that. What kind of stealth combatant would pop up with such a stupid phrase to spook someone? I was an idiot. Both men were sure enough startled and as soon as they turned to face me, Otis managed to leap onto both men and tackle them to the ground. Otis pounded up and down for a moment to smash the men against the hard pavement until they stopped fighting. I kept my fists clenched and in ready stance to defend myself as I had in jujitsu and boxing but luckily, Otis had everything under control. Otis bossed out beating up the two would-be carjackers and in a hurry. We dragged them to the middle of the parking lot and then we loaded up to get Trish after tossing their knives into the trunk and then hopping into the car. I had no problems fighting and of course the entire night I shook my head and mumbled: "oooga booga," wondered why in the hell that popped into my head, I was such a dork.

Otis told Trish he dropped his keys and had a hard time reaching down under the car due to bad knees and being slightly rotund until I helped. Trish was certain that because of his slight smirk he was full of crap but she trusted him and let the issue go. He didn't want her to worry. Once we all got home Otis nudged my shoulder and suggested I hit the ice cream, he helped Trish to bed and he made his late rounds to double check that everything was tight and tidy. Otis pulled up a bar stool and joined me at the counter as I heaped on the caramel sauce, "you did damn good kid, thanks." I dropped my head and replayed my stupid *oooga booga*. I explained that my head went blank and my mouth took over. Otis admitted that when he saw the knife he flashed back to being twenty and at war and was ready to grab both men by the throats and jerk their wind pipes out and make quick work of them, then his follow up notion was of his adoring wife and what might happen to her if he messed up. Otis realized he wasn't twenty but almost sixty and reality hit him harder than the two thugs could have.

Otis talked for a while about the sadness of growing old, remembering how you once were; young, virile, in great shape and at the top of your life, and then comparing it to how things are now; "hard to button your pants, hard to hear your sweet wife's voice and each day is one closer to finally taking that dirt nap." I remembered sitting and thinking about everything that Otis said to me. I enjoyed being young and able bodied and still had the rest of my life ahead of me. I dreaded the day when I'd realize I had longer behind be than ahead of me, I didn't sleep all that easily that night after everything.

I told myself as I laid in bed that night thinking about Otis thinking back to his youth and comparing his arthritic knees to his mud kicking, ass stomping days in the jungle. I didn't want to trudge through days being ashamed of myself or prone to my self-worth being based on anyone else's opinion of me except my own. I knew that when it was time to look back, that I wanted to see pride and I wanted to always have the image of myself standing tall. I also knew that I would spend some time when I was at my physical peak, getting plenty of pictures of myself in bikinis and proud of myself, that was one of the things that lead me to model for a while. I can always say that I indeed did model and it was tasteful.

I was in control of my body, I am my mind and when I first began to get tattoos I spent a long time designing and mapping out what I wanted and where, it was my body to decorate, not to trash. I felt certain that I was strong enough for anything; it bothered me when people doubted me so I made sure I worked out not to show off but rather to show myself what I was capable of. I needed to know that my limits were far beyond what I thought they were and I wanted to validate what I thought of myself. I know what I am capable of and that overruled what anyone else ever thought of me. People that hardly know me are often quick to judge and if we were over in some shit filled litter box desert, those opinions could quickly get me lashed or beheaded. I was bullet proof against the slander of jealous bitches; it was easy to judge me without getting to know me based on my small frame, once long bleached hair, willingness to smile or even my willingness to keep an open mind to many things. Being heckled or judged for made up illusions or faults was something I was victim of a lot. It becomes flattering when girls that don't know you talk trash, it's a sign of jealousy which meant I was rocking hard enough to make complete strangers jealous, which also meant that I caught enough attention for something I was doing that other's lacked the courage to.

Tallia continued to stroke the blonde hair of Irena as she still lay silently on the bed. I had Davor lying on the ground by my feet and two random men chasing me. I wanted to go back south and finish the massage that was interrupted and be done with this day. I gently swung my bat and let it connect with the top of Davor's head on the ground as I encouraged him to stay put. I eased over to the bed and asked Tallia to move to the far side so I could check to make sure I didn't severely injure Irena. The girl laid with her lower legs hanging off the bed and her arms down by her sides, I was nervous to get close and risk getting caught in some ambush but I wasn't about to move to the other side of the bed and give up protecting my escape. I raised Irena's legs onto the bed and grabbed the pillow from beside her to prop her legs up with; it's always good for the heart so why wouldn't it help the brain also? I pried open the girl's eyes and her pupils were slow to constrict, if they were blown or remained open then I surely would have been deep fried but it just seemed that the girl was unconscious still, and luckily.

I gently slapped my fingertips against her cheek to rouse her slightly before stepping back and letting Tallia get back to caring for her friend. Tallia took up sitting next to Irena again and resumed stroking her hair. Tallia's body language changed when she noticed that I was truly concerned for her friend and not a threat. I had to leave but was afraid that the man curled up on the floor holding his head would live and return to his sick ways. Urgency slowly replaced adrenaline, my need to preserve myself and flee was filling me but the voices of all of the honorable vets that raised me were resonating in my mind to do the right thing and help the girls out somehow. Irena slowly moaned and began to stir a little which took more of Tallia's attention. Tallia broke her eye contact with me and looked to smile at her friend lying beside her.

"What can I do" I finally asked Tallia. I was at a loss, I had crushed the shit out of Davor's hand, his whimper as he curled around his beaten paw assured me he was much less of a threat, the blade of the knife had a forty-five degree bend to the side in it and it lay on the ground by the far wall. I still didn't quite understand what his intent was breaking into my room; I am a thin girl sure and maybe he thought he could just take me and sell me off. I'm definitely not some agent looking chick, especially with the way I dress or manner in which I carry myself. Did he just think I was a fed, or some girl he could put in his stable?

I expected to find a gun on the old guy cowering on the floor at my feet, the fact that he only brought a knife and two obedient hookers tells me that he was small time, if he were part of some large ring or intricate set up then he would have been much better connected and had back up that wasn't some of his workers. The girl on the bed continued to stir, Tallia kept her hand on the girls cheek and leaned in to whisper her name, my heart went out to the two girls but I had two blazer clad dudes out after me so staying idle for too much longer was not in my best interest. Tallia's voice cracked as she tried to speak, the tears in her eyes began to well up and her mascara began to trickle a little at the outer corners of her eyes; " he has brother that help to run girls and nephew to drive the boat, they are very mean to girls. The brother runs a liquor store and the nephew drives a boat between South Beach and somewhere in the Bahamas where they change boats and then go on to Free Port before flying to Europe." I couldn't believe I was caught up in such turmoil and tried to figure out what I could do as Tallia continued to talk while stroking Irena's hair. I was obligated to meet up with the random voice lady and figure out what she had on my father and then return to Waylon and live my life. I have too much of a headache for the mess I am finding myself knee deep in, and I'm tired of the shadow chasing mess of it all.

Irena rubbed her hands over her own bare stomach, covering over her scar and then she lurched for a moment, her gasp for breath was full of terror as Tallia was doing her best to comfort and assure the poor girl that everything was alright. Irena flung her arms above her and grasped for handfuls of the bed to struggle backwards for a moment before full consciousness finally returned to her. Irena kicked her feet and attempted to put more distance between myself and her after she recognized me. I raised my hand out to try and make some attempt at peace with the girl that squared off with me and then ended up on her ass. Honestly I was impressed that Irena was bold enough to stand her ground, there aren't many girls out there that are willing to throw down with someone to stand up for what they believe in. Irena didn't sound very coherent for a moment as she tried to make sense of why I had both bats and their pimp lying on the ground at my feet. Tallia continued to shush her friend and just tell her that everything was ok and to not worry.

I had two ladies that had been stolen from some other country and an old coot with a penchant for being a dirty old bastard and total sleaze bag and all I could do was ask myself what the hell was going on. I had one butt cheek purpled with bruise, now a knotted shoulder and the beginnings of a tension headache and all with my morning smoothie causing some bloating, I just want a bourbon and water and a hammock to fall asleep in. Davor rolled back and forth and something in my gut knew that he was up to something so I made sure I stayed behind him and each time he tried to roll back a little, I kicked his upper shoulder to keep him on his side, one of the better positions for him to keep me from getting suckered.

Irena clenched her jaw; her gaze at me was one that made my skin shiver with her hatred for me. "Yes I knocked you on your ass, and you're still on your ass, deal with it" I told her. Dexa used to tell me that the only way I could feel small when someone else was staring me down was if I let them seem bigger than me. Dexa dealt with hoards of garbed citizens during the Gulf war, he learned to grow eyes on the back of his head and become skilled at deciphering all sorts of small nuances to determine if someone was a threat or just being a dick. I am not ever in a hurry to get punched (it sucks) but I'm also not one to roll onto my back and submit either. Dexa always encouraged me to stand my ground, he knew the marital arts I had studied, he and Chips had also shown me plenty of moves they learned from their training and time in the military. Chips and I had hundreds of hours of slap boxing behind us which definitely keeps the hands fast and agile so I wasn't the least concerned with Irena staring me down, not while we're on even ground this time.

Tallia whispered to Irena and after a few inaudible wisps, Irena let her thinly penciled eyebrows part from her scrunched forehead before her whole body set back with some ease. Tallia told me that Davor's brother Mucxim used to help run girls but now he helps to train them to be slaves and working girls. Mucxim's son Szeda smuggles the girls on a boat, he runs a phony tour guide boat and brings girls to Mucxim to lock them away to train them. Mucxim is much younger than Davor but they all work together and move dozens of girls a year. Szeda also disposes of some girls into the water of the ocean or cuts them up to chum for chartered fishing tours when girls don't behave or try to run. Tallia continued to tell me about as much of Davor's business as she could, she was much younger when she was picked up and then flown to a few different countries before her longest run in Miami. Tallia balled her hands into fists and then shook her fingers out as she tried to fight off the shakes and aches from withdrawing from whatever Davor kept his girls hooked on.

Irena began to speak up;" I was fourteen when two large men grabbed me and my sister. They grabbed me around my waist and pulled me into cargo van. It was dark but I heard my sister gasp and squeal as her body thudded onto the floor. My sister and I were walking home from a picture show; it was the first one I ever got to see. My parents did not have much moneys so they saved for enough for my birthday to go with my sister. My mom wanted to go to the picture show with us girls but had to work more at the laundry house to pay for me and my sister to go. One big man smelled very badly with very much cologne, he knelt down on me and tied my hands behind my back; my sister Kelsa was also bound. I cried and cried; Kelsa tried not to cry but wept as she told me over and over to stay brave. In our town sometimes people were taken and then brought back after a ransom was paid. I was wearing my nice brown coat and I thought it made me look fancy. I laid on the floor of the van and cried because I looked fancy in my coat and thought the men must have thought our parents could pay the money to get us back, but they didn't have any money.

The van drove for a while and Kelsa and I had hoods put over our heads. I caught a glimpse of one of the men; he had a large belly and a short beard. Kelsa was three years older than me, she worked part time after her schooling to help our parents with the bills and she also helped to look after me too. Kelsa always had good marks in school to show me that it could be done, she was much prettier than me and even though all the boys liked her, she never got to go out for herself because she worked too much. Me and Kelsa were moved a few times before we were finally allowed to see from under our hoods, we were tied to posts in a big room, there were twelve other girls around my age, most of them had tape or ties around their mouths.

I was very frightened and kept my eyes on Kelsa to hope that there was hope coming. I cried out for my mother to come and rescue Kelsa and me, and each time a man would slap me in the face. Kelsa just kept telling me to behave and listen to them and not to get hurt. At the end of the first day being tied up the men took turns taking us one at a time to a bucket to use for a bathroom, it was very gross and I did not want to use the bucket in the corner for a bathroom. I cried and shook my head as a big man pulled down my clothes to force me onto the bucket, Kelsa shouted and tried to kick her feet to get the man to leave me alone. One man held a large gun walked over to my sister and began slapping her over and over. I used the bucket and shouted for the man to leave Kelsa alone but he did not stop hitting her. The man shouted at Kelsa in a foreign language, he was all tan and had dark hair and was wearing a brown leather jacket with black pants. The man smiled and laughed as each slap sent my sisters' head whipping side to side. I shouted and screamed so much that I could not hear anything else as the tears ran down my face making my shirt wet.

Kelsa was slapped a few times and then the man punched her and her head slammed back into the pillar she was tied to, her body went limp after she hit her head very hard. I felt my heart stop, I wanted to vomit, I wanted to yell and run but I just froze there staring at my lifeless sister. The man guarding me put a cloth around my mouth to make me quiet before he shoved me to the ground. The man that hit Kelsa kicked her while she was on the floor, her body shook but she did not move. I was frozen with fear, I could not move, only look over to my sister on the ground. The tan man took out a large knife and began cutting Kelsa's clothes off, making sure to yell and shout to all the other girls to watch. The man with the gun behind me shouted also, "watch what can happen, you see?" he leaned in to speak to me. The man with the knife cut all of Kelsa's clothes off and then he grabbed all of her hair in one hand and dragged her around on the floor after cutting her ropes. Kelsa was dragged by each girl that was tied to a post or pole and the man kicked their feet to make sure that each girl looked at her limp body being dragged by her hair.

The man in the leather jacket raised Kelsa up and then dropped her to the floor. He kicked her arms and legs out as she laid face down on the cement floor. I couldn't catch my breath to shout, the cloth in my mouth tasted like dirt and old metal. The man in the leather jacket stood in the middle of all the girls tied up and began to remove his pants, letting them fall to the floor. I had only seen small boys naked at the beach and this man just looked like one of them, but with black hair all over his legs. The man continued to shout as he knelt down and then laid on top of Kelsa, he grunted and shouted and spit when he spoke and he climbed onto her. The man with the gun shouted when the man on top of Kelsa shouted; "this will be you if you do not behave, you belong to us now and if we tell you to please a man, you will please a man, you are only girls, property which we own, and if you do not behave, you will just die." Some of the girls cried, others tried to shy their eyes away, I could only lay on the hard floor and pray for my poor sister.

The man with the leather jacket humped at Kelsa for a few minutes, his face grew red and the veins in his neck and face bulged out as he arched his back and shook his head while howling. The man stood back up and pulled his pants back up, he stared down to Kelsa and continued to spit on her and shout curses at her. Kelsa was barely alive, she began to move a little, I was sure that the man had killed her, but she moved a little. Kelsa tried to move her legs together, wriggling her waist side to side a little while her long curly brown hair was a messy pile matted with blood on the floor. The man bent down quickly and used his hands to pull Kelsa's hair into a handful behind her again, he stepped on the handful of hair to pin her head to the floor and then returned back to waving his knife at all of the bound girls around him that made up his audience.

The man with the gun called him *Tarak* and translated many of the things he shouted. Tarak barked that if anyone does not behave that we don't have to be alive or awake to please a man and that there were men lined up to kill us if we did not want to behave and that they would still use out dead bodies for pleasure. Tarak bent down with his knife and with a sawing motion with his arm, he cut between his foot and the back of Kelsa's head. Kelsa began to weep softly after the beating to her delicate body. Kelsa tried to curl up into a ball on the floor to shield her body, she began to weep and cry as Tarak sawed and ripped through her thick bundle of hair. Tarak ripped his blade through her hair and then stood tall with her ponytail in his hand, his trophy for having conquered the much smaller and younger girl. Tarak waved the wad of hair at each girl until they looked at him and made eye contact so they knew he was talking to them. The man with the gun kicked me to get me moving, it hurt my side.

I desperately wanted to crawl to my sister, she was so strong for me and I could not help her. I slowly tried to crawl to her and as soon as I thought I could make it past the pillar I was tied to and get close enough to kneel down by her, I made a sprint for it. Tarak quickly turned to face me to protect himself and his victim from the rush, I was a small girl but he still jumped at the notion of someone coming at him. Tarak laughed and smiled a big toothy grin with his eyes wide open right in my face when I got close for a moment. Tarak held his knife out close to my neck and then waved it to get me to back up from him and her. The man with the gun dragged me backwards to the pillar and retied my hands behind the post. The man with the gun was very rough with me and I thought he was going to break my arm but I could not look away from Kelsa, I worried for her. Kelsa tried to cover her head with her hands, she had red marks on her back and as she tried to curl her legs up to her chest, I could see her run her fingers through her now short hair.

Looking around I saw that there were some girls not crying, but just one or two. Tarak continued to shout and spit into the air, he was like a madman. Kelsa tried to push herself up from the ground, there was blood underneath her from her face as well as from between her legs, her body shivered with the cold. I tried to shout for my sister but only mumbles came out from behind the cloth in my mouth. Tarak turned to kick Kelsa back down to the ground, he shoved his foot down onto her top shoulder to pin her to the ground. Kelsa tried to fight him off with her free hand but he kicked into her face and sent her head backwards to the hard floor again. My blood was hot with anger, I was so scared and mad and hurt but I was still tied up and could not move. The man with the gun knelt down beside me, he grabbed my throat and leaned in to talk to me; "you better watch this, everything he did to your sister, I will do to you, I will not wait until you are very bad, I will find you in your sleep and that is how I will wake you up, watch and see."

Tarak leaned down and with his big hand; he grabbed the right breast of Kelsa and pulled her up from the floor a little by it, turning her upward as she raised upwards. Kelsa was slightly lifted from the floor as Tarak pulled tightly on her skin; he leaned down with his other hand and began to cut her breast from her body, his wild hyena like laugh was the only sound in the building. I couldn't move, the blood poured down her white skin and began to make a puddle on the floor beneath her. Tarak pulled the chunk of flesh from her body and discarded it at one of the two girls that would not cry. Kelsa's arms shook as she fell backwards to the floor her feet twitched and Tarak licked the blood from his hand and he turned to circle the room.

I could not believe what I was seeing, this grown adult man raped my sister and then, to make other girls cry, he cut her breast off of her while she was still alive. My hands were numb, my mouth was dry and my shirt was wet from crying. My sister lay naked on the hard cement floor with blood leaking from between her legs and running from a large hold in her chest. Tarak bent down to roll Kelsa over, he lifted her up by her neck, he seemed strong with rage and as he pulled her from the ground, her body dripped blood from all over. I stared as I watched blood pour down Kelsa's pale white body; blood ran down her legs and began to drip from her toes onto the floor. Tarak hoisted Kelsa into the air and held her there with one hand; she just floated there with her arms dangling down beside her. I stared at my sister, her head was facing the ceiling so I could not see if she was alive or crying or moving at all. I slowly lowered my eyes, most of her body was covered with blood and then I saw his knife.

The man holding my neck licked some tears from the side of my face and as his warm breath moistened my cheek, he spoke: "I want to do this to you" as Tarak moved his knife from above Kelsa's knees, smearing her blood on her legs and then up between her legs up to her crotch. The blade moved along the bleeding skin, the knife moved forward and then backward with the blade cutting into Kelsa. Tarak made a sawing motion two or three times and then as her legs spread a little from the knife prying into her, the point began to move upwards and into her just like he had just done. Kelsa let out a loud shriek as the large knife sliced into her womanhood, letting even more blood to gush from her and fall to the floor. With one movement like a monster Tarak shoved the entire knife into Kelsa, hardly the handle he gripped onto could be seen under all of the blood. Kelsa wriggled and kicked her feet as the knife sliced into her belly then and deeper into her. I tried to close my eyes but the man holding my neck choked and shook me to watch any time I tried to turn my eyes away.

My sister must have been in agony, her poor body mutilated, disgraced, and taken by the filthy man, and I couldn't help her. Every muscle in my body tried to clench, I wanted to break free and save my dear sister but I was not strong enough. Tarak lifted Kelsa a little higher and with both hands, he slammed her small body onto the floor like he dropped a heavy weight. Tarak stood over Kelsa, his right hand still clenching the knife he ripped from inside her as he threw Kelsa to the ground. The ground was covered in blood; some of the other girls were splattered with my sister's blood as she fell into the puddle and splashed it. Tarak was also covered in her deep red blood. I watched as Kelsa looked at me for her last moment of life after she hit the ground, her brown eyes slowly closed away behind her eyelids as she let out her final breath of life. And just like that Kelsa was forever gone from me. Tarak licked the blood from his knife and his hand and then made each girl also lick some of the blood from his shoes, reminding us that we all belonged to him like dogs.

Szeda let go of my neck and within days, he was loading me onto a boat to sail to another country to begin working for him to please men. I thought Szeda forgot about me and the promise he made to rape me but after a few days on a medium sized boat locked away in a small hole with six other girls, he made good on his promise. Szeda pulled me from the small holding space on his boat where he smuggled girls, he bound my hands to the rail of the boat and began to remove my clothes. Szeda had his way with me, he was a mad man and I was still just a child. The pain made me pass out, when I awoke I was covered in blood and lying on the floor of a small building looking up at Davor shouting directions of what my new life was going to be like. It's been several years since I have seen my parents, even if I was able to, I do not know if I could return to them and tell them of Kelsa. I do not know if I could even face what has happened to me. I do not even know if I can still speak my language anymore either. I died when Kelsa did, I do not exist anymore, I am just the shadow of a whore now."

I felt sick to my stomach, my cute dainty salad with bright orange tangerine pieces and dark green kale was trying to charge up my esophagus with a warming feeling. I felt the hot sweats warm me over and my mouth began water. I fought back the spots in my eyes but not very successfully. I felt woozy and my blood pressure began to drop. I tightened as many muscles as I could to force blood back up into my head and to keep from passing out I leaned back against the wall behind me. As my teeth began to go numb and tingle in my mouth, Davor rolled to try to get up and get even footing with me. I felt my face grow pale, I suddenly had no strength in my body and everything started to slow in motion. My knees struggled to remain straight but they slowly began to ease me towards the floor. I imagined Davor cracking me with a bat and then using my body for a cum-dumpster for who knows how long, maybe he'd even invite that pedophile Carl to come on over and use my carcass as a spank rag.

My vision blurred slowly and I watched Davor rise up, his height rose over mine as I continued to slump. I held a baseball bat in my left hand but failed to do anything but grip it as I slid down the wall. Davor growled as he stood tall, his face squinted and all of his wrinkles packed together around his eyes and mouth. The speckles of white in his hair blurred in my vision and right before my face, he raised up his bleeding and disfigured hand. Davor began to cock back his good left hand, all I could do was stare blankly at him and wait for the hit, I was too woozy to even flinch or brace as I continued to fall to the ground, the corners of my vision grew white and blurry. As I neared the floor I felt some of my blood pressure return, I couldn't fight gravity or change my direction, I could just fall slower. Davor was beginning to deliver his left handed punch and his shaking jowls around his grit teeth showed that he was putting as much of his force into his punch as he could muster.

Whomp a vision of the other wooden bat collided with the side of Davor's head, averting his punch enough to avoid hitting me in the face and sending him to the corner chairs. As my double vision aligned my eyes made contact with Tallia, her long lengthy body stood stern, her legs apart to brace herself and her arm quickly cocked back to deliver a second hit. Davor toppled to the corner table and chair, my blood pressure began to return and I clenched tightly onto the bat I was half propped up on, trying to find the burst of strength to keep from getting my skull cracked. Tallia stood in a very baseball player stance, I was dreading having to take another hit with a bat and my back was still hot and raised under my jacket from her first hit but I have the inner strength of a pissed off bear and the willingness to fight to the death if necessary. I pulled my right foot back to set it against the wall behind me for a push off and drew in a deep breath. Tallia's pupils were pinpoints as she stared at me, there was ferocity in her, her years of lying with men under the order of Davor had built up and the chance to snap his controlling chain had finally happened and she was now taking her life back.

Tallia dropped her elbows and let the bat rest on her shoulders, much to my relief. I stopped struggling to stand back up and let my butt drop the last few inches to the ground, a moment with my head between my knees helped to push my dinner back down my throat and eased the throbbing of my temples. Tallia shouldered the bat and turned back to Irena to help her to sit up. I pressed my thumbs against top of the bridge of my nose to ease some sinus pressure before fighting to return to my feet. I looked at Tallia and nodded with thanks for saving me from getting slapped around, looking at the blank stares of Irena I could tell that the girl was long gone; she meant it when she said that she died years ago with her sister and there was nothing left in her. I felt helpless except that I was also being hunted and it was pretty pertinent that I haul ass out of town quickly.

I convinced Tallia to take Irena and go; they knew where Davor was based out of and what he had stashed away that they could pillage in order to give themselves a moderate attempt at a living if they tried. Irena unbuttoned her black leather vest and smiled at me as she let her bare chest lead her out the door and across the courtyard. I followed Irena out the door while Tallia remained behind to clean up the room I gathered, she assured she was not far behind and that I should hug the sides of the courtyard while Irena distracted Carl.

Once I saw that Irena had Carl's attention and convinced him to unlock the door to his bullet proof office I rushed to barge in through the door. Most men are dumb enough that when they see a pair of honkers they become pretty oblivious to anything around them. Irena volunteered to distract Carl since it was often her job to earn their rooms from him, she knew what he liked. Tallia hung back in the room with Davor in the room, I wanted to quickly draw attention to the scummy motel and since I was a wanted woman, a simple phone call to Lu would flag the source of the call and then my fan club would be on their way quickly, hopefully with some authorities.

I trudged up behind Irena as she stood at the doorway waiting for Carl to open up, I tried to run on the outside of my boots like Chips taught me in order to remain as quiet as possible but running with an extremely bruised ass and now a knot under my shoulder blade just made me short of breath and put a hobble in my scurry. Irena stood behind the closed door so I crouched a little as I navigated lawn chairs. The sun was ducking behind some of the taller buildings and the shadows were once again becoming my friend. I watched as the door cracked open, the light began to beam out and as I neared Irena, she bowed her head to begin to button her vest. I "pssst" at Irena to step to her side and as Carl pulled the door open, I jumped over Irena as she began to squat down and kicked as hard as I could at the door Carl just unlocked. My boots collided with the door, Carl's girth on the other side of the door forced the door back at me but with my momentum, Carl stumbled backwards and I fell almost on top of Irena.

Carl began to blubber and groan; he wasn't even wearing pants, just piss stained briefs that had as many holes in them as his shirt did. Carl had pasty white thighs and the hair on his legs seemed matted and globbed together, I don't want to guess what he got on himself that caused that. Carl tried to fumble up from the ground after I knocked him back, his mumbling was jumbled and incoherent, he almost sounded drunk because he had a slight cry to his blubbering gibberish. I rolled off of Irena, her response was: "look, enough already have you not done enough?" which caused me to let out an exhausted huff in response.

My back ached from tailbone to the back of my ears but there was no time to be bothered with the ashes, there was work to be done. Irena pulled herself from the ground right behind me and gave me enough of a push to regain some momentum as we plowed through some of the clutter in the office. Carl tried to crawl away and I almost thought about grabbing him by the waist and pulling him back but the sight of his clothes was putrid, almost as nasty and skanky as that TV family with all the slutty daughters, just gross.

I kicked my steel toe into the thick mushy ass of Carl, he jerked forward and nearly face planted into the side wall as his mass collapsed to the floor. The room was littered with tug mags and trash, every other pile was of used tissues and the bulge of gagging balled up in my throat. I stopped for a moment to look at Irena to get reassurance that we were in the right place, she shrugged and smirked while raising her hands, sure enough this was the way it was. I found a small phone on the main desk, there was no telling what half of the stains and globs of stuff on the phone was but I was sure that there was enough DNA in the office to train two dozen forensic science students. I found a box of tissues on the desk; I didn't even want to touch the box so I knocked it down with my foot and stepped on the box to rip it open. I used one tissue to dial the phone and I decided to call Lu.

"Car Thirteen" Lu answered. "Ma, I'm under a scope and no time, ben dirty, love you later" I did my best to code that I was going to send her something. Ben meant Ben franklin as in money and dirty was in reference that it needed to be laundered. When Digger used to move some easily acquired goods he would run up to the casino's in Vegas. In Vegas Digger and some of the club guys would take turns cashing in their money for chips and then trade hands and then cash the chips in for clean untraceable money, it was a bit of work but cleaner and easier to launder a few grand at a time and some casino's would even give cashier's checks, which then were mailed to contractors or construction crews for work in Waylon, and all for much less than most laundering fees of anywhere else. I had two big bundles of cash in my forearms still and knew that it was a dangerous amount to be carrying, even if no one knew I had it. I planned to bundle up the cash and mail it to Waylon so it would be waiting for me when I returned; I also wanted to warn Lu that I was under a microscope and being watched.

I left the phone off the hook to make sure that my new secret admirer had long enough to trace the call. Irena stood over Carl, her blank stare was locked on him and there was no telling what she was thinking. With what Irena and Tallia were made to do to earn Davor money, there was no limit to what they may have been capable of, just like all other girls, they just needed to realize that we are the stronger sex and that they were no longer slaves to a man and his ill lusts. Carl was still cowering on the ground; his hands were raised to protect his face which was red from his blubbering. "Do you know what he liked" Irena asked me. I hesitated because I wasn't sure I really wanted to know, by just looking at him I had a suspicion he liked to watch himself take a dump in the reflection of the water in the toilet and probably got off over it, and that made my dinner begin to climb up my esophagus again. I shut my eyes for a moment and shook my head, hoping, even praying Irena wouldn't complete her sentence.

"Carl liked to rub me with mayonnaise with his hands while we were both naked. After being covered in mayonnaise he would wrap my whole body up in plastic wrap until I could hardly breathe. Once I was covered in plastic wrap and unable to move, he would then take a large piece of plastic wrap and hold it to my face until my vision went cloudy and I was close to passing out. Carl liked to choke his girls until they passed out a few times and after several times of passing out, he would then rip a small hole in the plastic behind me and roll me over and then have his way with me." Carl was very degrading, he would make use of a girl two or three times a week depending on how many girls were staying, he and Davor worked out the details that both got what they needed. I felt my face sink after Irena finished telling me the lighter end of the scale of things Carl liked to do, I had enough ugliness for one day and there were still hours of light left.

I suggested that Irena get moving to avoid when the cops showed up but she shrugged off my suggestion by waving her hand towards me. I stepped past Irena on my way out the door and something caught my eye, she was rolling a nudie magazine she picked up from the floor. "What are you doing?" I was inclined to ask. "He never got enough girls, now he'll get his fill, I promise" Irena said with a demonic undertone in her voice. I didn't hesitate to leave, I had a mission to get back to my bike and be gone. I nearly stumbled in my rush to get out of the office but my fear of touching something kept me upright. As I hobbled quickly on my sore leg around the lawn chairs and back towards my bike, Tallia stepped out of the room: "You can find Mucxim in South Beach near Seal Head Harbor, he runs a liquor store for boaters and offers fishing and sailing tours with his son Szeda's boat, they need to be stopped." I stuttered as I tried to explain that I was needed up north, I couldn't head back south again to deal with the two shit-birds. I tried to insist that she deal with that mess, she had Davor as leverage and they'd probably put up some money for his life or something if she demanded it.

As I panted from my hurried rush I noticed that there was more than a light on in my room, I stopped breathing out of my mouth and inhaled deeply through my nose; SMOKE. Tallia reached forward to grasp and shake my hand, I tried to explain that I couldn't go after Mucxim but she spoke over me before she made a beeline towards the office. Tallia hurried to pull Irena away after she turned a skin mag into a suppository in Carl and get away. I let out a deep huff and returned to hurrying back to my bike. I don't know if the truck that turned into the front parking lot was that of my admirers but I sure as hell didn't wait to find out, I was in a bind and really had to get away. I couldn't believe what the hell I was tangled up in, still, or again, or I don't friggin know. I started my bike and worked my way passed the dumpsters along the back alley and towards a much more open road where I could better see if anyone was coming at me.

I have no idea if Irena popsicled Carl and frankly I don't care, he earned it. I don't know what exactly Tallia did to Davor but it was her prerogative and I hope that both girls stick together. Girls need to stand by one another because the world is full of assholes, they don't need to berate other girls to make themselves feel better. I made my way to Collins Ave When I was stunned for a moment, my head was telling me to hike my ass north for a bit to steer clear of the heat and to make my way to Philadelphia like I was supposed to but there was also a sinking feeling in my gut thinking about Kelsa, Servina, and Tallia and Irena and who knows how many other girls that were cycled through the hell of becoming forced sex slaves. My stomach was wishy washy after picturing Kelsa and what that animal Tarak did to her.

As often as I am conflicted about public places, they often are advantageous in regards to quick escapes and easy coverage to blend in. I used to be a long haired blonde and I would have fit in very well in the Florida area but now I had a short bob and back to my brunette hair, if I were donning a skimpy bathing suit I wouldn't stand out as much but I'm in my riding gear, not very low key in the cabana boy filled beach area. I decided to pull to the side and try to relax with a smoothie at the straw topped little outlet where the boys were wearing white polo shirts. A guy with dark hair had deep Mario Lopez dimples and a strong chin served for as a pleasant distraction from my stress for a small bit. I needed something yellow with mango to lighten my mood, I needed some time with the sun on my skin to reset and defrag my mind, maybe a few minutes with a smoothie would be enough.

I ordered something with pineapple and sauntered over to a brick wall that lined the parking lot, I took caution to look around before removing my jacket and shirt to sit in my bathing suit top for maximum sun exposure, plus I look super cute in my small top and riding pants and boots, pretty badass if I do say so myself. I tried to blend in in just a bikini top as I sat, I let my shoulders slump to duck down a little and I tried to keep my head from whipping side to side as I kept a look out while sipping. The pineapple and mango was creamy and helped to soothe my parched throat as I let my heart rate slow and tried to let some of the knot in both my butt-cheek and shoulder throb with soreness. I watched as many other beach bodies roamed around the cabana and through the parking lot, it was easy to let my guard down a little because a weapon would be easy to spot on someone in a bathing suit and that was just about all that was around me.

I felt myself sizing up everyone around me, I often think back to all that Dexa taught me about watching not just people but their body language. Dexa explained to me about how many war weary soldiers deal with enough emotional trauma that they eventually just look right through people, snipers are the worst about it. When you watch someone through a scope long enough you don't see people as human anymore but rather just an entity, a target, just sort of like a movie character on a screen that if they die so be it, you lose the emotion necessary for life. I felt the coarseness from prison harden me and most of the young college kids wandering around me were all happy and oblivious to real life. I on the other hand would bareknuckle scrap to the death with anybody in this parking lot and not think twice if it meant me walking up out of here. In high school I thought about how cute most girls were and how much energy we all put into ourselves just to feel confident with looks, the gym, the makeup, the fitting of our clothes, now I am covered with tattoos, scars, and bruises and I've never felt sexier in my own skin.

Dexa spent plenty of time in a bottle to cope with his depression and post war trauma; he struggled with compartmentalizing what he had been through and his buddies dying mere feet from him. Dexa slowly learned to differentiate what he had been through and what he was experiencing, he was still extremely claustrophobic and that was mostly mostly lead him out to Waylon, to avoid having to ride in a car during the snowy northern winters and being able to see for miles in any direction would be the best way he could function normally and begin to feel like a human again. Dexa struggled with finally leaving the war behind, he had a hard struggle and even after having grown up around him and having heard everything he had dealt with, I still felt bad for him and millions of other soldiers that return with emotional scars that get shirked when it comes to the government failing to help them when they need it.

The sun felt warm on my skin, the breeze wasn't enough to keep me from perspiring but sitting in just my top was comfortable enough for me to begin to relax a little. I let the icy bits of tropical fruit slide down my throat, I couldn't hear any sirens in the distance so I assumed I was far enough from the hotel or perhaps the fire Tallia set didn't consume the meth lab of a motel I left behind. I was torn finding myself at a cross road again. Last time I missed my meeting time because I tried to skim through Atlanta but in my defense I was still at the bar on the day I was supposed to be, the phone lady bailed so it wasn't entirely my fault but at least dinner was good.

I was a two day ride from Philly but only half an hour from Seal Head beach but if I head south I'll be sure to miss my dead line. I want to cut Szeda's nuts off and feed them to him for Kelsa and whomever else in his life he mistreated and then wait for him to choke to death on them. I can live with myself for the rest of my life if I miss another meeting, I'm not entirely sure why I feel so obligated to seek this lady out anyways but I guess I owe it to Digger. On the other hand I'd never sleep again if I knew there was something I could have done to stop something so wrong, something such as sex abuse or the wrongful imprisonment of a child, those are the people I would gamble my life for. Whenever Chips was in a tight spot he'd always say: "if my aunt could pee standing up, she'd be my uncle." I never fully understood it but it seemed to apply right now.

I needed to get to get my battered butt up the coast, a ride I almost looked forward to, all scenic and tranquil, might ease my soul for a bit. The deeper calling was to do the right thing and head down to Seal Head harbor and unravel some twisted human trafficking. I knew what I had to do, I knew what I wanted to do, and I knew that sitting on the light brick wall much longer would further make my left butt cheek hurt as well as put me at risk for getting caught by the secret admirers that were following me. The weather was nice and the view was splendid but my inner demons pulled at me. I worried that blowing off Philly was going to leave me up shit creek for the scumbags that died on my way to Florida, which were only partially my fault I remind you. If the one bad guy hadn't been trying to rob the gas station nor pointed a gun at sweet Melanie then he wouldn't have been body dropped when he considered pointing his gun at me, it was his fault that he hit his head, and his fault he bled out like a dick, that's what he gets for aiming a gun at me.

The pineapple soothed my desire to hurl as I sat on the wall with my riding jacket across my lap and my t-shirt shoved into my back pocket, it was comfortable and helped me to keep a low profile. "Oh my gawd, what happened to you" a high pitched random voice suddenly spoke up from behind me. I hopped to my feet and turned wildly to find the source of the voice. I turned to face a young teenage girl walking with a girlfriend of hers. Both girls were strutting in their bathing suits and flip flops, the blonde had a drawstring bag hanging down her back while the cuter redhead had some clothes rolled up under her right arm while her left hand held a pink smoothie. The blonde held her eyes open widely staring at me while the redhead let her straw hang from her mouth waiting for my answer. "I love your tattoos" the giggly blonde blurted out as she looked at my left sleeve and other tattoos as I was preparing to ask what the redhead was talking about. I raised my eyebrows in confusion as I looked at the redhead and all of her freckles that adorned her shoulders around the strings of her pink bikini.

"What do you mean" I finally swallowed enough to ask. The redhead waved her free hand back and forth while telling me that my back was covered in bruise, she didn't even bother to take the straw from her mouth as she spoke she just pushed it to one side. I tried to look back over my left shoulder but had no luck before raising my left arm and seeing the back of my hip continuing to purple over and make its' way up my side, I assume from the fall from the hotel window. "You gather some scratches when you don't watch life from the outside" I mustered some lazy philosophical aversion to answering with the truth. The blonde swung her bag from behind her and began to rummage through it. I continued to glance around me to watch as people came and went from the small smoothie stand, I was nervous about having my back to so many people but my bike was next to me and I was all but ready to leave once my smoothie was finished.

The brunette pulled out a bottle of Motrin and offered me a few of the mild pain killers inside, I was unsure to trust the girl but as I opened the bottle, the pills were uniform and familiar to those I had taken before, assuring me that they hadn't been switched for anything shady. I decided to only take one pain killer, enough to reduce some of my swelling but not enough to do anything crucial to me if they were anything other than in fact pain meds. I thanked the young girl for her help and for being concerned for me and then I tucked the swinging part of my t-shirt into my other pocket and slid into my jacket. "Hey chicky, where's the nearest mail store from here" I asked before the two girls moseyed off. The redhead cracked a smile and pointed to follow Collins Ave south a bit and I should see it, I thanked the young girl for her help and complimented her on her adorable belly ring before brushing my hair out of my face to put my sunglasses on and climb onto my bike.

I kept my smoothie clutched in my left hand as I rolled out of the parking lot, I let the wind blow in my half unzipped jacket and kept the sun on my right as I headed south on Collins Ave to find a mail shop to make my jacket a little lighter before I made sense of things around me. I stopped at a pharmacy to pick up measly supplies including another throw away phone and some pain relieving cream for my back and now shoulder. I was still tight and sore from sleeping on the hard slab in prison just a few days ago as well as the ground plenty of times since.

I needed another massage I thought to myself as I slid my jacket off in the corner of the parking lot and removed the two bundles of cash I had stuffed away. My sleeves were wet from sweat and the money was beginning to smell a little but that wasn't my problem. I broke the bundles up and folded what I could into three small padded envelopes, hoping that the mail x-rays wouldn't detect the wad of cash folded over itself rather than sending a banded wad of hundreds. I put an even three grand in each envelope and pried the marker from a package to send them to three different addresses.

In the mail store I sent one envelope to the garage, one to the bar and the other to *Dale* at the gas station, each letter was secretive enough that only Lu would know what was what and then take care of things for me. I had about a grand left rolled in my pocket to take care of what I needed and then I was on my way south again. I knew I was headed to Seal Head harbor to find a sleaze bag named Mucxim and then figure out how to kidnap his son Szeda and then feed him to the sharks. I wasn't sure how far from the harbor Freeport was but I had a feeling I was going to end up crossing international waters and that was stressful enough that I was starting to get a migraine. The thought of ending up in another third world prison fending off rape and other flirtatious advances made me a little woozy, I didn't have the nerve to get back to playing the assault game again anytime soon, even though I haven't lost yet.

I finished my smoothie on my ride through some of the streets and then dropped the cup into the bed of a truck; I thought about the cell phone I did the same discard trick with back in Arizona. I thought about calling Lu in order to alert her about the two men that seemed to have a crush on me and send them to follow a big rig, maybe find a gravel hauler or some construction truck hauling gear somewhere far from me in order to keep them tracking the phone and keep them busy. It was eating away at me who the hell had the ovaries to call me in the rotten crotch of a prison in bung-hole el Mexico, and then to have me sprung. I couldn't figure who had the kind of connections it would have taken to make the last few days all happen and it left me reeling trying to make sense of it all.

Seal Head harbor was a little more than half an hour ride down the ocean highway and it didn't give me enough time to figure out what I was doing with myself, again. I wondered how Melanie was; I sort of missed her holding on around my waist and her chin on my shoulder while riding, it was comforting. I missed Melanie for her cheery companionship and I could certainly use a hearty muscle rub on that knot that keeps bulging under my shoulder blade from Tallia. The sky ahead of me was blue turning orange, the long orange stands silvered along the tops of the waves in the far distance to my left as the sun continued to sink over to the west. I found Seal Head harbor on the southern end, I wondered what genius named it such since seals were a northwestern territory type of animal, where it's cold, not tropical, but I didn't have the energy to entertain such nonsensical things. I could smell the change in the air as I neared the large marina, the ocean wafted over hundreds of yards of beach front and traffic before filling my lungs on the ride but near the point it took on the salty nut-sack sort of pungent smell.

I realized one of the problems I faced was that being a marina, there were dozens of liquor and supply stores as well as shops that retrofitted boats or sold boating supplies for everyone. I was trying to find a douche-bag in a dumpster full of douche-bags at this point. I pulled my bike into a small lot for trucks and longer term cars for anyone that had a slip or a docked boat. I backed my bike in behind some larger pickups to obscure it from view from the road or the entrance and then decided to walk the docs to see if I could pick up any signs of the turd burglar I was out to find. I passed all sorts of people, happy old couples that wore matching velour jumpsuits, cocky middle-aged guys wearing boating shoes with white khaki shorts and long sleeve dress shirts and one old timer just playing with his rod in the water wearing a Vietnam cap over his gray hair fluffed out on the sides. The old timer looked up from his perch on the doc, his hat proudly displayed the unit he served with for our country and all I could say to him was the admirable sentiment: "welcome home" as I nodded and passed by.

I wandered into some of the small boat stores with an excuse in each one, a pack of gum, a bottle of water, a stringer of

Zots and so on until after my fourth store where I found a man with a bit of an accent and the same trashy chest hair fluffed up from beneath a half unbuttoned silk shirt. The store was a white building with a larger boat storage building behind it. I was immediately on alert when I saw the older man behind the counter, my hands trembled and my boots suddenly felt like they were sticking to the floor with each step. I pulled each step from the floor and wandered up and down each sparsely stocked aisle trying to find something that would be good enough for a purchase.

I found a boot knife with the fishing and tackle gear and figured it was a bit too on the nose of a purchase, but it had a cute black sheath and it matched my boots. On my way to the counter I snagged a pack of sour straws from the shelf and then stared at the old man behind the counter. The old man had more gray on the sides of his temples but just like Davor, he had a gold chain hanging around his neck and it was tangled in his white chest hair. I caught myself glaring at the old man, I felt the heavy stare in my own eyes and I was nearly at the counter before I realized I was even doing it so I broke and let out a smile.

"Can I help you young lady" the man at the counter asked. I didn't have to strain to listen for an accent; his was thicker than Davors' so I wondered how close of brothers they were. As I set my knife and candy on the counter the man did his best to pass along small talk by asking what such a young girl needed such a knife for. I suddenly felt like I was back in elementary school and was being questioned about making a big girl decision over something trivial, I didn't like it. I wanted to unleash hell and drag the old man from his side of the counter but at the last moment, good sense reared its' stupid presence in my mind. "The knife is a gift for my friends' brother; he dropped his so I wanted him to have a new one before we set out to go fishing tonight." The old man nodded his head and parted his lips for a smile as he rung me up, I could hardly contain my breathing and felt short of breath but I also needed to be sure of who I was dealing with.

"We don't get to go out very far because his boat isn't that big but it's still a chance to do some fun fishing, sometimes we even get a good catch but not often in the more shallow waters." I tried to bait the old man into proffering up his son and the charter fishing they used as a cover, I needed something concrete but was quickly growing inpatient. I eyed the large corkboard behind the counter and tried to notice something I could use in any of the pictures of fishermen and boats but nothing stood out, just the usual tackle store owner taking pride in the success of his customers and friends in the forms of pictures tacked up on the cork board. My heart slowed a little in my ears, I felt the tension in my fingertips let up and my hands didn't even shake as I reached forward to grab my knife and candy from the counter. *Wham* the old man slammed his hand on the counter and reached forward to grasp my hand as I gripped the knife, my body jolted because the prick scared the crap out of me. The old man pulled my hand towards him and he leaned his face in to mine; "You be safe out there, doesn't take much for an accident to happen you hear?" he let out an ominous warning with an eerie undertone as he spoke.

My skin exploded with goose pimples and even the hair on my forearms stood up on end. I pulled my hand back quickly out of sheer reaction to being grabbed and in the slight flash of a moment I was ready to strike the old man out of trained and ingrained habit after years of reflexive martial arts training, but I stopped myself in time to not randomly assault the clerk. I was back to square one and headed out to keep looking for my guy. I was determined to find Szeda and maybe even find my way to Tarak and castrate him with a rusty coat hanger, back alley abortion style. I stepped out into the waning late afternoon sun and felt discouraged. I missed my first meeting with the lady from the phone because I took the higher road and honored my father and the servicemen and women by having the courage to do what was right and go and jack up old Putty Nuts and hopefully put a foot in the ass of the people smuggling he had going on.

I wondered if Melanie got the other girls back to their parents on the cruise ship and what she was up to. I thought about how easy it seemed to just make some girls disappear from a big ass cruise ship and how fast they were about to be shipped out of the country to some goat raping country in the desert, all of it made my head spin a little. I supposed if someone is motivated then they will find a way but I also couldn't understand how someone could be so pathetic and deplorable that they would ever have to force someone to have sex with them, wouldn't you rather have someone that wanted it with you? I could never like anyone that didn't want me back, I couldn't imagine living with someone that you had to force into anything, like having wives you had to keep cloaked to force them to stay with you, it's slavery and it's abhorrent.

I decided not to head back to the docks but rather to duck away to the side of the bait shop to lean up against the side of the dumpster tucked along the back fence and enjoy my sour straws in peace. It was getting dark and even though I felt exhausted, I was still pumped with enough adrenaline that falling asleep would be a struggle so sitting and feeling the warmth of the sun slip away would bring peace to my mind. There was no breeze I noticed as I slumped down to sit next to the dumpster. I was completely out of view from the docks and parking lot and the only thing I had to face was the large building on the other side of the chain link fence.

I had spent many nights sleeping on the ground next to my motorcycle, most times when the Lucifer Squadron would make a cross country ride for a charity run or go to support our VETS we would often find a pavilion to park under and lay out a bedroll on the ground and call it a night. Sometimes as many as forty or fifty of us would lay out in a field near the highway off ramps on our bedrolls if the weather permitted until we met with larger groups closer to our destination of where we were going. I have no problems sitting leaned up against a dumpster and a fence, I was protected on two sides for safety and I was a pretty good distance from anything that would be a threat or unnerving like people milling around. I was a light enough sleeper that if someone walked across the small alley way then I would most likely hear them and wake up with enough warning to defend myself if necessary.

I missed pack riding. I loved taking the long drawn out roads of the southwest like Arizona, New Mexico, or northern Texas, I loved seeing the road stretch on into the sun and chasing it for hours. I missed riding for a long time but after having spent eight months locked away in my cell with a few random voices to break up the monotony of being alone, Melanie was welcomed company. I liked riding with Melanie, she was a cute girl and seeing her back at the bar was a pleasant surprise. Melanie had a gorgeous smile and an impressive body, when I throttled the bike she held on tightly around my waist and even though my hair probably whipped in her face she still kept her chin on my shoulder. Occasionally Melanie wrapped her legs around me when I leaned back to relax, it was only a short time we rode together but it was an immense comfort having her with me. Melanie was a good travel companion and was extremely funny, especially when she ran off to chase down that naked buff dude only to find out he was happily married.

The pavement was warm beneath me; leaning against the fence wasn't the most comfortable but no biggie because I was trying to enjoy the serenity I had with the splashing of waves just a bit away and the engine noises far enough away to barely make them out. I enjoyed my sour straws and sipped more of my water as I tried to regroup and think about my next step. It was nice and quiet and I was comfortably blocked from the small wind gusts that made the tall patches of grass bend in the middle to bow. The small wind wisps tickled a bit at the back of my neck and of course that tingle feeling of Mother Nature calling made me have to move from my comfortable sitting position, much to my dislike.

I stepped to the downhill portion around the dumpster to pee and as I returned back to the tucked away corner I planned to sleep in, I saw a short stocky man creeping towards the boathouse. The parking lot near the boathouse was cracked and had tufts of grass sprouting up but on the other side I watched the grass tips sway and slightly obscuring the silhouette of a man. The short stocky man looked as shady as someone could, looking back over his shoulder with each step and everything. I kept my profile down and slunk back into the shadow of the dumpster to just perch on my heels and watch. Each bite I ripped from my sour straw I chewed with anger, I didn't know the man I was watching but I immediately despised him, he was a stocky man with a big head and with each short step he took, I grew more and more mad at him. I tore at my straws, ripping and tearing away chunks like a hyena feasting on a zebra in the wild, and I felt just as wild and angry.

The pudgy man let himself into the boathouse and I knew I had to follow him in. Once the man was out of my sight I stood up and stretched for a moment to look around and ensure that there was no one else around in the area. I braced my left elbow on top of the dumpster and then pulled myself up enough to toss my legs over the top of the fence in order to be up and over as fast as possible, and silently. I dropped down to a squat next to the dumpster again to look around, the shadows grew larger and the sun was no longer insight in the distance, the unknown lurked around the corners, but so did I.

Ch.7

I crept along the pavement to the door of the boathouse where I saw the short stocky man enter, there were no windows to peer into and if I went in blind I might end up deep fried in trouble by anyone waiting for me inside. I listened to the thin corrugated walls for anything but it was dead silent inside. I snuck to the opening on the waterside where boats drove in and were docked or lifted inside, my heart beat like the double kicker drums of a heavy metal drummer. The pavement stopped abruptly to a wood plank that dropped down to the water, I laid flat on my stomach to peer down to the water and try to look for a ledge to stand on to edge around into the boathouse. I slide my body down the side of the dock and into the building, there was no ledge but I braced my feet against the wave break of a wall and inching my hands over one another, I slid under the steel wall. The inside of the boathouse looked just like a garage from what I could see in the shimmers of sparse light, just enough to give some contrast against the dark.

There were a few boats floating in the water and a few on the far side on a rack. I looked around for any sign of the short man but everything was silent and still except for the small waves cracking and splashing against the cement siding along the water beneath my boots. I pulled myself up to sit on the side of the wall just inside the garage. The back half was intensely dark and even with the large opening to the boathouse, hardly any light shone on the walls. As the surface of the water rippled and squirmed there were scant sparks of light that seemed to dance along the shallow tides moving the water up and down in the boathouse. I felt let down for a moment that the place seemed empty but I was certain the short Danny DeVito shaped man was inside somewhere.

I rolled to my knees slowly to begin to stand up when I heard a *ping* and a *snap*. I stayed crouched on my hands and knees, my entire body froze. My heart beat in my ears and my lungs burned from my racing heart but I tried to clear away the cloud of fear in my mind and focus on what the pin and snap sounded like. The snap didn't sound like a gun cocking, nor was it all that close to my head so I may have just heard something strange from the boats shifting on the water behind me instead of someone getting ready to shoot me. The shadows of the boats rose up and back down on the waves, the eerie sights made every beat of my heart echo in my brain.

My hands clenched as I stood up, I slowly inched my steps forward, gently setting each one down to the ground to be as silent as possible. I couldn't make out any sign of a person standing in the dark so I remained the most dangerous thing in the warehouse that I could run into, unless I hit that water and there was a freaking shark down there, then I'd probably be done in, well I might be able to mess up a shark I suppose, but anyways. I took a few light steps towards the direction I thought the door was, I squinted to try to make the most of any light I could find but the lack of anything just made me feel absolutely blind in the pitch blackness.

One night in high school after cheerleading practice Carmen and two other girls and I decided to go to the mall. Denise was a shorter girl with long dirty blonde hair and a dangly belly button ring she showed off with every belly shirt wearing chance she got. Denise was funny about most things but easily distracted when there was a chance to get a boys attention, which her belly shirts did fairly quickly. Denise liked the bubble gum pop music, the uppity stuff that you don't need all that much talent to produce because there weren't any real instruments played. I love metal and the heavier rock, the stuff you can blare in a gym and sweat away your pounds and stresses of your day. I loved wrapping my hands and spending half an hour with a speed bag before going to kick boxing with a heavy bag, the late nineties early two-thousand rock like Trapt and so on that just filled you with rage with power chords and grueling songs and kept you pumped. I liked some country and also classic music when it was time to relax but my body often craved the harder stuff.

Denise and I never agreed on music, I felt it was because I wasn't thirteen, she felt it was because she didn't have testicles. Denise and Cailey had their inside jokes as they were closer as friends. I often hung out with Carmen because she lived closer but I often had to deal with whatever dickbag she was dating but that was often how it is when you're in high school. So Denise and Cailey caught the eyes of some boys and decided to part from us to chat them up while Carmen and I went to get some more spankies for practice. Calley agreed to remain put until Carmen and I returned but sure enough she wasn't going to let Denise out of her sight either when she followed some jock named Zack outside to make out in the dark corner of the building. When Carmen and I finally found our friends in the dark Cailey was being manhandled and trying to fend off one boy that was pulling at her clothes rather aggressively. Denise was tangled up in her shirt and the "nice boy" she started talking with had her shirt pulled up like a hockey player ready to fight and he was using it to trap her arms.

The two boys took our friends to a shadowy corner by a loading dock. It took Carmen and I a few rushed moments of panic before Carmen noticed them and shouted for me to help. I was wearing my shorts from cheer practice and a light shirt and I had my hair still tied up, not really a great fighting get up. I wasn't dressed as cute for the mall as I had preferred but there was only so much you can do in the locker room after practice right? I told Carmen to call the cops and to get security so I could break up the boys. I darted to one of the boys, it was hard to tell who he had pinned underneath him but when I finally got close enough I saw that Cailey, who was often a much more reserved and self-respecting girl, was struggling to keep her shirt down and keep the much taller boy out of her pants. I squared up, clenched my fists and side kicked as hard as I could into the stretched ribs of the boy. I hugged the shadows enough that the laser of light that beamed over the top of the loading dock platform hit the boy in the eyes and gave me enough of an advantage to deliver a second kick followed by as many rabbit punches as possible to the already tendered ribcage.

Cailey couldn't catch her breath from being frantic and crying and just closed herself off as I dropped the first boy to his knees and kneed him in the side of the head as hard as I could. My kneecap felt like it shattered when I drove it into the other boys head. My adrenaline rushed but I felt myself smile, I liked sparring in the gyms and this was much more fun than just trading punches. Cailey continued to cry and back away towards the wall as she wrapped her arms around her torso. Cailey was such a cute girl and seeing her crying broke my heart. The boy grunted each time I kicked him and I found myself hitting harder and harder trying to get him to heave and grunt louder than the hit before.

I had kick-boxed and sparred and when you hit a pad a few thousand times you get really sweet abs but you also expect to hit a bit of padding. When you actually use the strength you've built up to knee someone in the side of the head with all your might you are willing to swear on everything in existence that you shattered your opponents' skull, and your own knee. I felt my eyes burn and my nose start to run after the first hit to my knee made it feel broken and trying to put pressure on it to hobble over made the tears pour from my eyes. I fought to stand up and face off with the second boy that had most of Denis's clothes off of her, I did my best to grit my teeth but I still started crying from the pain. I kept my jaw clenched but my tears streamed down my cheeks, the pain shot like lightning from my ankle to my hip, it hurt so bad that it nearly took my breath away. I imagined back to sparring and even though there were pads, there was always the occasion where you clip your thumb or smack a bare elbow and immediately begin praying for death so the pain would stop, I did my best to keep my focus.

I tucked a little and upper cut the boy holding Denis's shirt with his left hand and working her undies down with her jeans with his right hand. The boy was so focused on nuzzling her chest and working her body over with his hands that he had no notion I was on his side and readying to pounce. I hook jabbed as fast as I could; I felt my fists stop on more muscle than the last boy had. I didn't hit the ribs as hard as I had hoped so I kept hitting. The boy pulled his hand from inside Denise's pants and right back to back hand me, I was mid-strike and focused on what I was doing before I saw his hand coming, and by then it was too late to avoid. It was dark enough that seeing all that clearly in the commotion made for a bit of a challenge to fight evenly.

My right cheekbone felt like it was going to explode and my eye was going to pop out but I kept my fists braced. The boy let Denise go in order to face off with me, he seemed enticed at the idea of a fight, anything to keep his blood pressure up I guess. I kept the light behind me for my advantage and ducked and weaved a few of his jabs. I ducked my shoulders down a little and as he reached his long arm to deliver another blow to me I got inside of his reach and exploded upward as hard as I could with a fist under his chin. I felt his teeth clamber together with my punch and to be honest; I tried to collapse his throat when I hit him.

"Shipping off to Boston" blared in my ears as I lit a shit-storm on fire with my rage. I ducked and jabbed as I attacked the boy delivering punch after punch. As the boy gained a slight bit of footing and stopped backing up I twisted my hips and swung as hard as I could to deliver kick after kick to his knee over and over until it no longer supported him and he fell to the pavement. The first boy was groaning and calling me all the wonderful names a strong girl gets used to hearing; bitch, slut, "c-unit" (but the real word) and so on as I kept my fists balled tightly and heaved my breath in and out after my warm-up workout (the first boy). I was the one standing, both boys were nursing wounds and even though I was injured, I still stood, it was an amazing feeling.

I hurried to help Denise up from the ground, she was struggling to cry and untangle herself from her shirt at the same time, she looked more to be rolling around on the ground than making any real progress but still. I knelt down as best as I could to start reassuring Denise and to help pull her to her feet to help her to get her clothes back on. Cailey was frightened and panicked a few feet away; she just let her tears fall down her face in disbelief of what had happened. I could only move so quickly with me leg hurting and now my hands were sore and I was slightly winded.

I learned long before high school that I never wanted to freeze in fear. I never wanted someone to have enough power over me to take away my sense of identity or my own personal strength. The desire I had to be strong in my own skin was enough to push me through my martial arts and kick-boxing in order to stand my ground and protect myself no matter the opponent. Cailey was much less disheveled physically but having been raised in a conservative household, she never imagined such a thing could happen and it really bothered her for a long while during the school year. Cailey had the mentality that bad things happen to people that make poor decisions, she had a fairly privileged and ignorant view but she learned quickly.

When the cops arrived right behind a heavy set mall security guard that just fumbled his words, both boys remained on the ground. The girls and I had to stand around to help the cops fill out a report about what all had happened. The junior officer that arrived wasn't much older than the boys that were charged with sexual assault, he had short black hair and bony cheek bones. The junior officer began listening to Denise talk about just being willing to make out but not wanting to do it in the public of the mall so she agreed to step out with the boys in order to sit on the brick wall until Carmen and I caught back up with them. Denise spoke about starting to make out until the boy began aggressively coaxing her towards the loading dock and really getting handsy. "You shouldn't have provoked him, look at how you're dressed" the junior officer spoke out his opinion while taking notes. Denise began crying even harder, the pig had the balls to suggest that anything that happened against her wishes was somehow her fault.

I felt my hands clench again and I couldn't contain myself, I pivoted and dropped to one knee as fast as I could and power punched the prick right in his giblets. The senior officer turned from talking with Cailey and braced his hand on his gun to find out what had happened. I stood up and raised my hands as the junior cop wobbled on his feet trying to gasp for his breath. Denise began to panic loudly as the snot bubbles began to form from her crying so hard. The junior officer cradled around his waist and groaned in agony, he should have, I dropped that foreskin with a hard straight punch to the scrote and let him think about how wrong his ideology was. The senior officer threated to pepper spray us if we didn't back up. Admittedly it was worth the extra hour of having to explain everything over and over until finally we were granted the right to leave but the junior officer probably wasn't smart enough to learn his lesson and is probably still a wad of hognuts.

I eased closer to the door of the boathouse, my eyes slowly adjusted to the dark and my heart rate continued to calm down enough to be able to hear better in the silence. I continued to listen for anything more than the sounds of the large boats rising and falling along with the level of the water, it was hard to distinguish but I felt there was something strange happening on the larger boat with the tall cabin. I stepped easily towards the boat, each step made me nervous to step on glass or something that would give away my presence and ruin my advantage in the dark. I reached up for the ladder and leaned over the buoys below me to push off of to pull myself up the railing on the boat. I saw some lighting along the bottom of the door of the cabin; I decided to put my new knife to use and grabbed it with a reverse hold to better protect myself if I needed to.

Chips not only taught me slap boxing but we would also wield Bondo left over's that were shaped much like daggers. Chips liked the Steven Segal "Under Seige" style knife holding and made a point to further my martial arts learning's and actually practice knife fighting with me. "In case you're ever in Puerto Rico or Brooklyn" he would always joke. When I started riding heavy bikes I always heard the tales of bikers that carried chains and hammers and pipes and so on, most never carried legally descriptive weapons like guns or knives to avoid harassment but a simple tool like a hammer was deadly enough as a weapon to carry and if you got stopped you might only lose a few bucks if it gets taken away. If a car cuts you off in traffic you aren't morally bound to be nice and you can remove a side mirror because the dick doesn't use it, that's when a hammer comes in handy.

I began keeping my wallet on a chain like most others for two reasons, one: you won't accidentally let your wallet fall out of your pockets and not know about it until two states later, and two: a wallet chain is decent back up if you need to defend yourself. I began wearing soccer shin guards inserted into the forearms of my sleeves when I started riding. The built in elbow padding of a riding jacket helps in a wreck if you have the wherewithal to jam them to the ground and slide on them, despite that you'll most likely still end up with a broken elbow or shoulders, it is still better than road rash to the bone. Wearing shin guards to protect your forearms gives you much stronger than leather protection especially if some crazy chick decides that she is going to cut you because her boyfriend checked out your ass.

My extra safety in forearm protection also comes in handy to guard against a direct hit from a hammer or pipe and when you spend ample time in biker bars growing up, you learn the small things you can do to save your ass in some scuffles. One night I was in a bar with Lu, I was only fifteen so I was riding on the back and we met up with some distant club members in Northern Cali for an Honor Ride, it was one that Digger always wanted us to participate in as a club. So I was enjoying a Pepsi and watching some guys play pool when a tall dude with a shoddy Mohawk started chatting me up. "Rip" introduced himself and offered to buy me a drink. I had no interest in drinking anything but my pop and I wasn't giving someone the chance to lace my drink so I politely passed. Rip was over six foot tall, he had a douchy chinstrap beard and was ultra-scrubby but he was one of those guys that would be sort of good looking if he cleaned up and dressed better.

I declined Rips offer for a drink and returned to watching the pool game continue. Rip missed the point that I had no interest in him and a moment later, some heavy set *chica* came raging towards me. I had my back against a tall wooden support beam and was sitting on a flimsy bar chair (hoping it wouldn't buckle under me) when I was caught off guard. I had no idea the lady was charging me, I kept to my word to Lu to not drink and risk putting any bar at risk if I was ever in one so I always stuck to a soda and nachos. The *chica* was adamant that I was enticing her man Rip despite my utter lack of interest and that my "little white ass" needed to be taught a lesson. The bigger gal swung a few good jabs and I remained on the defense as to what all I had done. I did my best to just block her hooks and caught most of them in the forearms rather than the face as I tried to navigate each jab. The brainless guys circled around us and with each failed jab while the girl grew angrier at me.

I tried to explain that Rip had hit on me but I turned him down, she then growled that no one turns him down and how fine he was and so on. As the men in the crowd began to ignorantly chant for us to fight I continued to block her hits and dodge when she tried to run and grab at me. Rip stood at the outside of the ring and continued to drink his beer and watch as everything unfolded. I had no idea why the lady felt the need to attack, her ability to reason was long gone but I kept trying to talk to her rather than have to punch her in the face. "I'm fifteen" I finally found the right moment of silence to holler out my age, putting a fast stop to the lady and her jealous rage. The lady dropped all of her facial expressions and looked befuddled. I nodded and kept my defensive hands up to prove that I had no interest whatsoever in the dick-wad beside her. Rip quickly tried to make his way through the crowd of cheers still encouraging us to fight. The lady turned from me to him and picked up with him where she left off with me.

It turned out that she was his baby mama and she didn't want to have to share the child support she was getting because it paid for her bike and he was too chicken shit to man up and get a snippy snip to prevent having any more kids that he didn't want anyways. Lu was proud of me for not destroying a lady twice my age, and twice my size. I never understood the deep seeded desire in most women for drama, I used my energy to stay cage cut (meaning fit for a fighting cage) and I loved it. Rip was some low rent schlub, he might as well have been a fluffer for porn for all I was concerned, I was at the bar with friends and other members of the club for a VET rally, I wasn't there to meet dudes, and besides, I was fifteen.

My biggest desires and crushes were of idols or fit girls like Julie Kedzie and Morgan Tran, chicks who are more bouty (meaning ready and able to brawl in a bout) than ninety-nine percent of guys in the world, and endlessly sexy while doing it. It took a majority of my sophomore year of training and hard work but I was able to achieve one-hundred hanging sit-ups from a heavy bag and fifty handstand push-ups along with a five mile run every other day, it was a hard uphill climb but once I began running and seeing my muscle tone under my skin, I loved the feeling of my stamina and energy to face each day. I fell in love with myself when I took long looks in the bathroom mirror and watched my body slowly change. I transformed from a little teen girl into a strong tone woman that slowly sculpted her body. I built my self-confidence in myself, I earned ever rep and every pound of raw iron on the weight bars in the gym and nobody could deny me or take it away. I ran every mile, I worked for every drop of sweat and I earned the right to shed every tear every time I pushed my body passed the desire to give up. In races, marathons and even on emotionally bad days, it was all me and it was all my doing.

I inched closer to the cabin door of the boat gently rocking below my feet. My palm was sweaty gripping the knife but I kept my left hand open and prepared for anything that might come at me from the other side of the door. I fixated my eyes on the handle and reached forward to pull it open and begin whatever I was getting myself into, all because I am too stubborn to just let stuff go. The long handle in my left hand barely had any resistance as I slowly turned it. I kept holding my breath to hear if there were any sudden movements or noises that might alert whoever was inside. My pounding heart made it hard to keep holding my breath and I struggled to let it out of my nose slowly while still listening.

Click the metal springs on the latch opened and on inhale, I pulled the door back and prepared to rush in. I gained my momentum and headed into the cabin left shoulder first to begin brawling if necessary to find out what was going on. The short pudgy man was lying face down without any pants on, his acne pitted pale ass jiggled as he shunned in surprise and jerked his head over his right shoulder to see what the commotion was about. The sight was sickening, his huge round ass with dark hair running up the crack squished together as his muscles flexed deep below the surface, his back arched as he turned his head over his shoulder to look back at me for having surprised in on him.

I jammed the brakes to stop myself from landing on top of the stranger; his torso was dressed in a striped dress shirt with sweat stained white undershirt underneath it. The man was as bald as a baby's nut-sack and his eyes squinted behind his thin framed glasses, his open mouth and wide eyes said plenty in regards to his surprise. The man's jelly ass squeezed together with surprise, his pants and drawers piled on the floor of the cabin of the large boat. In a moment of surprise I was stunned to find half naked pudgy guy, he wasn't the shop keeper nor did he look European in any way. "What do you want, who are you" his high pitched voice nearly squealed out. I gasped with surprise and immediately began to apologize until I saw the rest of the bed. A body began to wiggle from under the man and it stopped me mid-sentence, the portly man was laying on top of a girl, not an adult female lady kind of girl but a small Asian girl, who looked ten or eleven.

The cabin of the boat had a long wooden tool bench on the right, some once rust orange looking carpet riddled with stains making a small path from the door up towards the front. There was a shelf overhead that had a handful of radios all wadded together, boxes and crates of rags and junk scattered about, and a bed. The bed on the left didn't look all that big but there it was, covered in dirty sheets and a fat pudgy little bastard wriggling and heaving into a small scared little girl that was trying to look at me from under the flailing open flap of his dress shirt.

I felt my mouth fall open, my heart sank into my stomach and I couldn't get a foothold enough to take a breath in in that moment. My blood turned ice cold and then back to boiling hot, I felt my forehead burst forth with sweat and every raging song I've ever heard played at the same time in my head. Every kick to a heavy bag or punch with a trainer was for this moment, there was a beast in me that roared to life after a lifetime of slumber and years of pissed off aggression were just below the cute look on my face hiding the rage. I reached over and dragged the tub of shit from on top of the girl by a handful of his sweaty oxford button up shirt.

The man's body jiggled with waves of fat as he thudded to the floor. I began stomping and kicking the man and when the opening between his arms presented I took the shots to his softer ribs that didn't have as much blubber on top. I wanted to bend down to punch him also but the space was cramped and my muscles were still very stiff. White hot rage consumed me, everything happened in an instant before I realized he was covered in blood and my body felt like it was on fire.

The poor little girl wriggled and cried under her duct tape gag, her small body was laid out on the bed, her hands taped together above her head. The man cried out and whimpered, pleading for me to stop as his tears mixed with blood on the floor below him as bloody spit seeped from his mouth as he begged for forgiveness. "I'm a teacher, please stop, I have a family" he recited over and over. I stood in disbelief as I tried to cover the poor little girl with a measly blanket from the bed. The man kept his tiny little erection even after I kicked the crap out of him, literally from what I could smell. "You are a sick bastard" I broke my aggressive stride and actually tried to talk, briefly. I was appalled, confused, just mortified and I felt my right eye begin to twitch trying to understand everything that I had just come across. I began asking questions about what was going on but each time he tried to sit up I pointed my knife at him to keep him on the floor and away from the poor little girl.

The man's name was Terry Jargani or something, he was a middle school teacher and a few years back he met a man that ran a bait shop: Max. Terry and Max spoke bait and tackle a few times and the conversation volleyed between eyeing some of the hot little girls walking out on the docks to the notions of actually doing something about it. Max sent Terry out on a few fishing tours with his son Seth a few times as friendly favors and then soon enough, Terry was paying a thousand dollars to spend a few hours with young girls once or twice a year when his wife and kids thought he was out on a chartered fishing trip. Terry begged that he had two kids in the school band and his loving wife had no idea and that this was the youngest girl he'd ever been with. I grew short tempered real quick with all the pathetic crying and pleading of a fat desperate loser with what I'd say was a toddler's sized little pecker tucked under his fat belly.

I insisted Terry pull his pants up because I was tired of seeing his doink when he kept trying to roll over. Once Terry was up I ordered him to lean onto his rotund stomach on the bed and then began to bind his wrists together behind his back with some of the tape I found on a bench. Just as I was wrapping layer after layer around the fat hairy wrists of Terry I heard a voice; "You almost done? Your time is up my friend" I heard someone shout. With the stretching tape noises I didn't hear anyone enter the boathouse, I quickly dropped down to a squat to keep from being seen or caught in the boat windows. My pulse burst back to panic mode and I was once again short of breath as my breathing raced like crazy in my chest.

I kicked Terry to the floor between the bed and the bench, the tight space was sure enough to keep him wedged for a while reassuring me that he was not a threat anymore. I watched as Terry wriggled his crown of gray hair around the sides of his head back and forth but ultimately unable to even move himself in the slightest. Terry was crammed into the tight space and even trying to wriggle he was pinned; he looked sort of like an elephant seal with his large double chin hanging from his face.

I stepped up next to the bench and waited for the new voice to come to me, he had to pull the door outward so I waited to reach and grab whoever was on the other side and jerk them into the cabin. I motioned to shush to the small girl still lying on the bed, I couldn't speak to her but I tried my best to be reassuring as I waited for my next a-hole to come at me. The door slowly opened and as soon as I saw the darkness from the door cracking open, I kicked the door back to move it to charge through. I was nervous to race out because there might have been more than one other person but I was already charging forward before that realization hit me, and then I just felt stupid for rushing to get myself killed, or raped by these freaks.

There was a younger man in my way as I toppled through the cabin door; I was actually expecting the older shop owner man. I saw flashes of skin and outstretched arms as I hurled my body out of the open door and towards the person opening it. I landed on the man and scrambled to hold my knife to his throat. I neutralized Terry and did not have to worry about him behind me, now I was at arm's length from a complete stranger and holding him hostage on a strange boat in a dark boathouse. As my chest heaved warm air in my nose and out my mouth, I could only ask myself how I get myself into these situations, maybe it was because I am a girl raised on *Fight Club* and *Bloodsport* and around bikers and VETS, but whatever the reason, I was more and more convinced that maybe I don't make all the best decisions for myself.

I moved the younger man into the cabin and gave him the same tape treatment that Terry got, minus the gag for the initial questioning. The man told me his name was Seth and he just chartered fishing tours. Seth told me the he didn't know what Terry was up to and he had no idea how the poor little girl got into his boat, all the "not me" blah blah blah. Seth conveniently didn't have any ID on him nor much else in ways of weapons. I questioned Seth for several minutes and of course I got ample resistance from the prick. Seth was wearing black canvas pants and had a long black coat on, I had a funny suspicion he liked to play pirate out on the big water. I stood in the doorway of the cabin and watched over towards the door so I didn't end up with more surprise company coming up behind me. I needed time to think. I turned on my throw away phone and dialed the bar after taping Seth's mouth shut.

I asked to speak with Lu and knew that I was now on a timer before my admirers arrived and ruined things for me and my new friends. "I've got two tickets, I'm Lonely Island and I'm Paul Walker and Jessica Alba, Police Academy 5, I'll tell you everything when I can, sharky jock nod" I filled a brief minute conversation with as much code as I could come up with hoping that Lu would decipher it all. "Two tickets" referred to Eddy Money and that I was going to be near Paradise, meaning Nassau which is also known as Paradise Island. Lonely Island referred to their hit song "I'm on a boat" and the mention of Paul Walker and Jessica Alba was hopefully a hint that I was going into the blue. Police Academy 5 was titled "Assignment Miami" to give her an idea where I was leaving from. I lingered on turning my phone off. Sharky is a type of hearing aid to remind her that our conversation was most likely bugged and jock nod meant that I loved her, something that Digger and I did on our way out of the prison visitation booths as our little secret "love you" to one another.

I ended my phone call with Lu and I waited in the silence of the dark. If my random lady voice that first called me was government, then she'd have had that call traced and be calling me back shortly, if not then I was on my own and would just have to call the cops. The cops would have much less power to comprehend the magnitude of the situation I was embroiled in but they would have to do. I untied the little girl as I waited for the phone to ring, the poor girl barely spoke except to mutter "no" and shook her head as she cowered. I tried my best to comfort the girl by wrapping her in a blanket and petting her hair, she was reluctant to uncross her arms or even look up at me from the bed she sat on.

I waited for minutes for a call that wasn't coming and the minutes ticked away, each one slowly toyed and teased my anxiety. I pulled the tape from the portly man's mouth and warned him that he had two options, rat on his buddy to the cops and admit to everything, or I tied a brick to his winky and drop him in the ocean two miles off the coast, I didn't have the room or patience for passengers, especially pudgy whiny shit-bags that had a thing for very young girls. I searched around for anything string like as well as something I could use for weights to tie to his stubbiness. Terry tried to struggle and each time he got all ambitious to try to escape and make a bit of a rustle he would quickly run out of breath and just lay his head and pant.

R-R-R-RING my phone broke the still of the darkness. I had the overwhelming suspicion that the voice was government something but there still wasn't much for confirmation but I decided to put all of my chips in and make her show her hand. "You there" I answered the ringing phone. Yes Miss Griffin, now why aren't you" the lady voice queried in response. I told the lady to listen and that if she truly needed me in Philly then she needed to pony up and put up some more faith. "I have no idea what you could want from me but because of you, I keep getting my ass thrown in hotter and hotter water and I'm sick of it" I expressed with raw emotion before explaining my latest discovery. I descried most of the events that I continued to fumble into all the way up to the boathouse, I left out my intent to leave the country by way of boat but I told her that I needed the bait shop owner picked up and that I had a hog tied pedophile for a gift for her if she did.

"You need to bring your ass up here or stay and ride up with my two friends that are almost there, that's enough running around" she demanded. I apologized for flaking on our plans again but still insisted everything that has happened to me in the last ninety-six hours was all her fault; I also added up that she can't argue that I already broke up one human trafficking ring and international customs fraud stuff in Atlanta so I earned some leeway. "You don't understand the severity of the situation" she insisted. I recognized that I was toe to toe with a stubborn lady, I was a little impressed that she didn't back down but this wasn't time for a pissing contest. I was growing short tempered that she was failing to understand my dilemma and I suspected she was stalling until her blazer clad lackeys closed in on me. I interrupted to suggest that she hit record on our conversation because I was going to give her a gold star for catching up with me by ways of a confession from Terry.

I climbed over Terry and heaved to yank him from the floor of the boat to prop him onto his knees, his girth was wedged between the seat and the bench, he was hard to lift up, especially with as sweaty as he was. Terry was still a blubbering mess and crying about his family and his love for being a teacher; I was tired of hearing his pandering so I slapped him. I hauled Terry out of the cabin and dropped his whale like carcass to the deck of the boat, he was covered in snot and sweat and his skin was sticky and gross. I put the phone on speakerphone and told Terry to start from the beginning. Terry whined and blubbered through his entire life story before finally landing the plane and admitting to paying to sleep with little girls from his ole fishing buddy Seth.

Once I got Terry to finally spill his guts I headed back into the cabin to smile and wink at Seth. I searched the cabin for a pen and to ensure it worked, I dragged in on the cheek of his face in circles until the ink ran from the blue pen, he squirmed and wriggled like wimp the whole time. I asked the voice on the phone what the hell I should call her; I was tired of chasing a random phone voice; "Carol" was a good enough name to identify her by. Carol sternly demanded that I stop running and to get in the car with her agents and let them take me to Philadelphia so everything can get worked out in order to clean up everything and put the last ninety-six hours behind us. I was actually tired of running, I was tired of riding and I was tired of getting beaten up. My ass still hurt from falling from the canopy of the hotel, my shoulder hurt from taking a hit from a bat from Tallia, my neck was still sore from falling asleep in the back of the cab heading away from Atlanta airport two days ago and above all, the bitch interrupted my rejuvenating massage.

I pulled my sleeve up and wrote down the phone number on my bare skin in a space that lacked dark tattoo ink that Carol called out; I needed a direct number so I could get in contact with her. Carol made me promise three times that I would stop dicking around and get my butt in gear and head to Philly, which I totally intended to do, one of these days. I heard plenty of commotion outside of the boathouse and I knew it was time to get the little girl off the bed and on to the solid ground. I ripped Terry's shirt open while trying to pick his chunky ass up to hustle him off the boat. I didn't give Terry much help in ways of climbing down from the boat, I power kicked him in the back and let gravity do us both the work. Terry let out a howl as he thudded onto the pavement, in my mind I could just picture man titties flopping in the wind and then shock waves rippling through the rest of him as he bounced on the cement. I untied the boat from the two posts and then headed into the cabin. I yanked a screwdriver from off the small bench and headed to the front of the cabin.

Once I jammed the screwdriver into the ignition I cranked the engine over and made myself familiar with the cockpit to begin to drive the ship out towards open water. I tried my best to wriggle the large ship out of the boathouse gently and quietly. I felt a few jars and jams as the boat bumped slightly against buoys and the other ships floating in the water nearby but I did good. Seth hummed and moaned in displeasure as I tried to ease backwards to get turned around. I flicked most of the switches I could reach in hopes of finding lights rather than fumbling in the dark trying to back out of the boathouse. Seth struggled to free himself so much that he rolled onto the ground from the bench seat, his long coat wrapped around his legs. In the panic Seth was almost able to kick my legs out from under me when I was focused on not wrecking the boat or getting caught, sneaky bastard. I was more focused on getting clear of the boathouse and from the two agents on their way to make me their guest and escort me to Philadelphia (against my will I suspected) and I was nearly hitting several of the boats in the small dock area before I got out into more open space in the very late afternoon hue on the water.

I debated on keeping the lights on once I found the right switch, the waterways were growing dark and as I backed away from the boathouse I saw the door burst open. My two hotel buddies finally showed up to scoop up the little kidnapped Asian girl and the portly Terry and his potato shaped body. "Carol" had all the evidence she needed to prosecute most of the people I left in my wake. I felt like a typhoon after the few days I had, and now I was skipping the country to do what I had to to stop such grisly atrocities like what happened to Kelsa. I watched as the two men stormed into the boathouse hoping to find me inside but instead

161

finding the fat bodied skeeze and the poor girl he paid to rape and have his way with. I was hardly out of the harbor when of course my phone rang, "Carol" I shouted as I motored a little more on the throttle.

Carol began to berate me for being an idiot and that I had no idea what I was getting myself into by not getting myself to Philly and quickly. "Big Whoop" was all I had in me to respond. I was doing what was right and doing what would make me proud of myself in ninety years if I lived so long, to hell with what someone else wanted me to do for them. I decided to start talking to Carol like she was a crush and to no longer feel that sense of dread when she spoke, like I owed her something. "Do I stay to the right or left of the green lights on boats, do you know? I can't remember" I asked Carol. I realized that my perception of Carol was all wrong; I felt that I owed her for springing me out of prison except that I had a suspicion that I was sprung for her benefit, not mine. I took my own ass off the figurative clothesline and took back over control of myself. Carol grew angry and hung up on me which I found her timing pretty well convenient as I was trying to figure out what I was doing with the ship and didn't want to crash or anything.

Piloting the boat was a little nerve racking at first but I found it relaxing, even with Seth murmuring like a cat in heat on the floor behind me. I maneuvered through some of the water ways and no wake zones to the wider shipping lanes and deeper cut-ways for ships. I popped all my lights on and cut east to the ocean. I wasn't entirely sure where I was headed but the first thing I wanted to do was get clear of men trying to grab me. I picked up my phone and called the number that Carol gave me, I smiled as I called to further have fun with my new found friend. "What are you wearing" I opened as soon as she answered, her reply of "A GUN" wasn't nearly as playful as I had hoped. "Is that all? That's pretty daring and sultry on our third date" I responded. If Carol wasn't going to find any of our conversation funny, then I was. I tried to remain jubilant even though I was freaking out over trying not to crash a borrowed boat in an area I had no familiarity with, I tried to just swallow hard to keep control of my emotions and keep my head straight.

"What could you possibly want with me" I asked, following up with the fact that I might not have much reception for long. Carol replayed the same story about being my father's case worker and that she needed to meet with me pronto. I doubted every word she said for a multitude of reasons, beginning with the secrecy. Carol wouldn't budge on sharing why I was so important or who the hell she really was. I unloaded many of the observations I made regarding what I knew, such as obviously working for the government based on the wire taps, and that our initial meeting was conveniently across from a military base. I applauded her for the ballsy pull to get me thrown out of a Mexican prison, and Mexico for that matter, and having tracked nearly every move I made over the last few days. I rambled even further down the list of my suspicions, I figured if I showed my hand then perhaps she wouldn't feel such a need to hide things and I'd finally get some answers, ugh she was a vault.

I continued to goad Carol about who she was, what branch she was working for and how was I supposed to trust her to not set me up to go to prison for the rest of my life for the terror spree she sent me on while I was en route to meet up with her. I was the victim for most of those situations, I just so happen to be a crappy victim, and Fred wouldn't have died if he had just remained still and not suffocated himself by blacking out after struggling so much, yes I zip tied him to the headrest in the van but I'm still saying it wasn't all my fault.

I felt my stomach sink, my throat became hard to swallow and my hands felt clammy as I realized that I really made a mess of things and I was really looking at major trouble. I held my head up high and decided that if I was going to end up in prison for the rest of my life it will be because I choose to help other people get their lives back. Maybe they'll move me to a prison back in Colorado and save Lu some driving, she could make a family day once a month and visit me and Pops if we have the same visitation day. I wondered if the money I mailed to Lu would cover postcards and postage for my whole sentence, and maybe enough commissaries to get the cheese and crackers they sell.

I didn't go very far out into the water; I pulled back on the throttle and chose to hang to the outer edges of the large marina for the night. I couldn't decide what I was going to do, it was dark and I had no flipping clue where I was going or what I was doing, I just knew that I didn't want to go to prison and I certainly didn't want to get tagged crossing into international waters with Seth hogtied on the floor. I pushed the throttle forward and made a wide turn back towards the docks where I just came from, it was safer to tie off in a random slip rather than drift half the night and I certainly wasn't going back to the boathouse. There was a metal ammo box on the floor by my feet, it was full of pieces of a socket set but it was perfect to drop my phone into to kill the GPS tracking capabilities of Carol while it was encased in metal. I slowly motored back to an empty docking slip and did my best to tie off in the dark. The boat came to an abrupt halt as it hit one of the wooden pylons harder than I was supposed to.

I tore the cabin apart looking for a safe enough compartment to shove Seth into, one that even when he licked himself free of his mouth tape and chewed through his wrist bindings, that he was still not going to be a threat to me while I try to take a small nap. I thought back to Tallia and Irena telling me about smuggling holds in the boat, I didn't know if I was on the same boat and I didn't feel like questioning Seth so late at night but I figured I'd look. Beneath the bed was a small long crate, I wasn't sure how comfortable Seth would be but it looked like it would be a good enough fit. As lifted up the mattress and slid the crate over, a small latch caught my eye. I stepped over the side of the bed and into the space beneath and revealed a larger hidden hold beneath. The compartment was big enough for three or four larger adults and it had scraps of clothing strewn along the bottom from what I could see in the dim cabin light. It looked like it was reinforced for people to lie in and be locked away for the duration of an ocean trip, it was perfect.

I re-tied Seth's wrists and over his shirt sleeves so his sweating skin wouldn't loosen the adhesive of the tape over night. I flipped Seth over the side rail and braced my body to kick him into the hole for the night so I could get some moderate sleep finally. As I was pulling the mattress down a thick zip-tie caught my eye on the bench, it was more than perfect to reinforce his wrists, the timing of finding it after all I had already dealt with sucked but it was worth the extra effort to dig Seth back out and better secure his wrists, his eyes were rife with pissed off and clenched with hatred each time he saw me, I alternated between smiling at him and blowing him air kisses to further enrage him and support my dominance. Seth was a squirmer and he certainly tried to lash out at me for shoving him into his own slave hole where he forced girls to stay. Seth was a handful and wrangling him proved to be challenging as he was larger and stronger than I was.

The mattress was lumpy and Seth knocked and bumped in the cargo compartment under the bed for half the night before he finally gave up. I tossed and turned for a bit but I slept. My left ass cheek was insanely stiff and my shoulder knotted up overnight but I was up with the rising sun, just staring at the ceiling in the boat and watching for shadows lurking outside the cabin windows. I cautiously poked my head out of the cabin to make sure that I was still mostly alone and free to head back out to the ocean and find out what the hell I was truly caught up in. The water traffic was low and the waves were relaxing as the motor hummed beneath me. I found the compass on the instrument panel and found some wrinkled maps. I had no nautical idea what I was doing but I did get to drive a boat on Lake Denali with some girlfriends in high school so I at least knew how to steer and make it go faster. I tossed and turned plenty overnight, I awoke with dreams of being back in that prison and it was unsettling but I wasn't running and I wasn't sleeping on the ground.

My eyes still felt puffy as I eased the large ship back out through the cutway and towards the deeper ocean. By navigating by best guess and crappy maps I headed towards the open water and I had plenty of room to work, it was looking to be a fine day out on the water. If the steering wheel had those old pirate knobbies I thought about bouncing and whistling like the old Mickey Mouse steam boat cartoon, it was pretty fun to drive the boat I must say. I made it a fair distance from the harbor and found myself distanced enough from any other passing boats to finally get to work interrogating my newest scumbag buddy.

Seth looked like hell when I pried him from the same cargo hold he used to smuggle girls. Seth's face was sweaty, his pants soaked with piss and the rest of him stank like a soiled gypsy. I found myself looking around into the distance with paranoia; I kept waiting for a boat to come speeding towards me at any moment. Seth must not have learned after his night in a box because he still struggled against my pushing him out onto the back deck of the ship, you'd think he would have learned to just go along because I don't tolerate the fussy fighting of his very well. Seth tried to jerk his head back and head-butt me as we neared the door, he almost caught me had I not pushed him a bit further forward when I was taking my swaggering steps on the rocking boat. Seth and his attempt to bust my face open with a headbutt only pissed me off, it was too early for it but he was trying my patience.

It was stupid early and with my muscles aching and my stomach rumbling I had a very short fuse. I knew Seth was disgruntled when he started giving me crazy death eyes as soon as I opened his box. "Did you spend all night thinking about all the girls you locked in that box" I prodded him to get his memory going, he just hung his head down and moved towards the back of the boat with my convincing shoves. Seth took a hard thump onto the desk, I half expected him to slide a little but he tumbled onto his left side, he had this look in his eyes that if he prayed to something that existed I might have actually caught fire.

The air was still a tad chilly out on the water but I didn't bother to put my jacket back on, I wanted more of the sun rays on my skin. My tattoos always darkened up and looked much sexier with some sun and some lotion on them anyways. Seth reeked of urine and half of his long jacket was soaked in it, I probably could have let him out overnight but he was a piece of garbage so I had no reason to care. I tripped Seth by kicking his raised root out from underneath him to let him fall with his still bound hands to the deck, an a-hole trick I was accustomed to because of my prison guards.

Seth continued to mumble and grumble but the gag in his mouth made hearing the darn fool near impossible. Seth was beat red around his eyes and the corners of his mouth were chapped and looking pretty sore. I was disappointed in the man for his lack of survival skills that he couldn't even free himself from his tape and zip-tie bindings, I didn't chain him nor cement him together but he was still as tied up as I left him when I shoved him into his box. I just shook my head as I gazed down on my new friend. I took a seat on the hard wood bench and kicked my feet up to rest them on his chest to establish my dominance, I wanted to make sure he knew well and good that he was the subordinate, not this girly girl with a cute bob haircut and adorable flowy shirt looking all chic on the back of my new boat.

I opened my arms to rest them on the rails I leaned against and began to speak to him while taking in some sun; "alright Seth, I know about you and your daddy and the damn awful things your sick family does for fun. I met two lovely girls' named Tallia and Irena, and in fact, one of them happened to accidentally kill an old nut-sack named Davor, your uncle right?" Seth tried to struggle for a moment but ceased and dropped his head as soon as I mentioned his uncle. I decided to remove Seth's gag and let him begin to speak for himself, besides, you can't get answers from someone that can't talk.

I leaned in to remove the tape from around his mouth and Seth tried to lunge forward to head-butt me again. I slapped

Seth in the face for misbehaving; I should have rolled a newspaper to whack him on the nose with for being such a bad dog. Seth made several attempts to accumulate enough saliva to spit in my direction but he was easily blocked with the soul of my boot, the prick was being totally uncooperative. I explained that I knew about a holding building for exchanges over in the Bahamas and assured him that I might even let him live to see it if he offered up as much as he knew, but the fool kept his mouth shut. I will say that Seth held out pretty well, I bit my tongue and even walked back into the cabin a few times to keep from losing my temper, but the jackoff held out.

It took me half an hour before I finally lost my temper, his hostile personality and excessive name calling was so rude and I had had it. I decided to finally make some headway rather than sit afloat out on the water getting berated. The back deck of the boat was nearly ten foot from the back of the cabin to the back rail of the boat. There was so much crap strewn about, floaty buoy things, fishing gear, lengths of rope, wrappers and trash, so much crap and here I had Seth lying on the aged wood deck like a caught tuna. I had the boat turned towards the sun, so East, I wanted to go to the Bahamas to find out what all I was looking for and then an idea struck me.

"When I was younger Pickle told me that the way they castrated hogs was with a tiny rubber band, like the ones the used on your braces except thicker. Farmers stretched the teeny tiny rubber back with a massive pair of pliers and sneak up behind the hogs and slid the stretched band up around their massive hog nuts. The rubber band would snap shut and tighten down on the skin and over the course of a day or two, they would turn black and fall off, the rubber band sealing the skin shut and healing over." I spun more of the story than I had actually been told but I made it pretty juicy and I slathered it on thick. I kept my face in an upward emotion, trying to focus on the warmth of the sun on my face rather than the story I was telling, it would be more threatening if I told it calmly and as if it was just any other story.

Seth turned his crazy eyes to those of slight concern when I let up my clenched eyebrows with my idea. Seth's look was much more like the thousand yard stare that soldiers have and I could tell he was either trying to look right through me or merely saw me as some girl that was only good for selling for sex. I rummaged through some of the piles of trash that accumulated in the corner or the deck looking for what I needed, while Seth let his mind spin. When I was younger Pickle took Lu and me camping over at Lake Nighthorse. I wasn't sure why and I'm still not but it was a fun week of campfires and fishing. After a day of fishing I began to feel bad because Pickle spent more time untangling my fishing line than actually fishing but he seemed to have fun with us either way. Fishing line tangles worse than long hair, that windy twisty line coils up on itself and is an absolute hell to undo and there was always plenty of it that had been cut and discarded anywhere you could fish, the same went for on a boat.

I pulled a mass of tangled line and wrappers from the floor of the boat, I was too ill tempered so early in the day to spend the time pulling and getting caught up so it looked like my idea of getting Seth to talk wasn't going to work until I realized I was on a fishing boat, sure the chartering was probably more of a cover than anything else but there were still plenty of tools and crap for actual fishing, including a spool of line in a box in the cabin. "Hey your daddy Mucxim is probably waking up from his first night of many in jail, you won't be so lucky there sport" I shouted to Seth to keep up my end of our conversation. I grabbed my knife and the spool of fishing line and sat back down with Seth, he mumbled and grumbled and called me names and continued to not cooperate while I got to work, and continued to smile. I could slap Seth all day long and threaten him with every prostate swelling notion of torture but I didn't think he would roll over on his father and late uncle; family ties are usually pretty tight like that.

I tied one of the blue and white floaty buoys to a piece of rope and then tied the rope to the end of some fishing line, Seth watched with worry and uncertainty as I whistled through my joker smile while I worked ,still with steamboat Mickey on my mind for some reason. "You get one chance buddy, what is your real name" I had to make sure I had the right dick-bag I was out for and not some other sick customer of the bait shop owner that was out to have his next turn with the small girl I found under the fat-bodied Terry the school teacher pedophile. "Seth, my name is Seth" the man on the ground shouted at me. "Are you sure" I asked with a big grin on my face as I began to unbutton his pants. Seth wriggled and squirmed and panicked demanding to know what I was doing. I was disgusted working down the zipper on piss stained pants, sadly it wasn't my first time with urine soaked pants though.

Seth wore black canvas pants, they were partially worn through in places with random threads coming undone from the woven pattern around the cuffs; his boxers were crimson red with dark scarlet swirl patters, very "ladies' man." I pulled his shirt up and out of the way so I could tug and work his pants down below his knees. For being a man with a boat he had some awfully pale legs. When I was younger I would lie out hidden behind privacy fencing without anything on because my tan-lines from my cheer uniform would look terrible so I had to even things up.

I had no concern for his little limp pecker in the whole world as long as he wasn't trying to force the earthworm looking thingy at me, but to emasculate him I snickered and sneered. I was grossed out having to grab Seth by his mcnuggets because they were matted in piss soaked hair and that was just gross but it had to be done. I wrapped my fishing line around his pecans two times and tied a nice cute little bow. Seth kicked his legs so wildly that I had to stand on his pants to pin his legs down in order to do my work. I rinsed my hands off in the water behind the boat and turned to face the man wriggling on the wooden deck. The ocean below the boat grew dark blue, a good sign that the bottom was pretty far down below. I waited for the boat to sink and the water towards the back to raise up while holding on as tight as I possibly could; honestly I was slightly concerned to fall over the rail.

"Alright douche-monkey, you are about to really find yourself in a hog-nut castrating kind of a way, tell me everything" I warned Seth what I was up too and even though his legs kicked and his head wobbled, his hands remained tightly tied behind him so he wasn't going anywhere. Seth argued with me for minutes about what I was doing, his bare white skin reflected the sun like a mirror and it was almost blinding. I discussed possibly leaving him exposed in the sun while I sailed around in his boat, his skin pealing back from the sun exposure. I could threaten him with my knIfe, maybe even circumcise him like he so desperately needed, I mean GROSS dude. Seth continued to argue and spit at me, he was a disgusting pig. His language grew more vulgar as I tried to cheerfully whistle while I worked. I felt sociopathic that I didn't feel bad for what I was doing, he was a scum bag and he deserved what he was getting. I left it up to Seth and his attitude to decide how much more of my friendship he was going to get.

I warned Seth that he was down to his last chance before he was certain to regret calling me the "c" word or *c-unit* as I call it. Seth kicked and spit with fury, I wouldn't let him get up from the floor and kept myself on the defense as he kicked and tried to sweep his feet to knock me down. I was furious inside but I refused to let Seth have any power over me, including the power to really piss me off. I wanted Tarak to pay and Seth, err Szeda wasn't going to get in my way. I smiled and shrugged at Seth as he growled and kicked, I flashed a sarcastic smile and pouted out my lips that he didn't want to be my friend. I picked up the blue and white floaty buoy attached to the thirty feet of rope that was tied around his balls like a dog leash and tossed it happily into the water over my shoulder.

Seth stopped fighting for a moment, as the buoy splashed his eyes grew real big, realization was beginning to set in for what I had in store for him, I bet each and every name he thought about me, or called me, was running through his mind at lightning speed. I continued to whistle as I headed back into the cabin to start the motor. "You might want to tell me where I'm going, cause if I have to find out for myself it'll be at a much faster speed in order to end up where I want" I shouted to Seth. "What do you want you crazy bitch, what are you doing" Seth begged and pleaded, panic filled the frantic mans voice.

"First what is your real name" I hollered behind me. "Szeda, ok it is Szeda, my father is Mucxim, and he owns the bait shop and I have this fishing boat" he began to open up to me. I was touched that we were finally bonding, if only he would have had such strong feelings for me before I had to handle is nasty ass gonads, but I suppose that's how men are, they need the physical contact before they will emotionally let themselves open up. "Where am I going to in order to find what I am looking for" was my next command. I only moved a little in the water but as I kept watch out behind me the slack on the nut line was growing taut.

Szeda was trying to trap the tightening fishing line with his feet against the bench to keep it from tugging on his little hairy chesters, his feet were still tangled in his pissed pants but

174

his ugly shoes sure kicked frantically, if he were standing I'd swear he was dancing an Irish jig. Szeda turned his yelling to hollering, his hollering to shouting and then shouting to shrieking as the thin fishing lined continued to pull from the tension of dragging the buoy bobbing in the water. I was hardly idling but the pressure was enough to begin to pull the fine line into his skin, causing a yelping and shrieking, like someone kicked a dog. The water out front of the boat grew dark blue compared to the lighter greenish water behind me, I knew it was getting deeper out and the air temperate began to confirm it. I slapped the throttle lever back to kill the motor and let the boat just bob with the waves again. I turned to head back out and damn near tripped over the ammo can filled with sockets and wrenches. Jamming my foot flared up my pissed off and I instantly angry again.

I was sick and tired of being sick and tired. I wanted a good night's sleep, I wanted another salad and I sure as hell wanted to be far away from a ringing cell phone and the dread of not knowing who the hell was on the other end. Nearly killing myself tripping sparked a fuse in me, I was furious. The rising and falling of the boat hadn't bothered me all night but now it was messing with my coordination and also my equilibrium. Szeda remained on the deck, he was still struggled to ease the slack on the fine fishing line that was looped around his marbles and his body was tensing up. I wanted to run at him and just kick him soccer style in the back of the head and be done with this silliness but I needed his cooperation.

"Tarak, you piss stain, I want him now" I commanded angrily as I stumbled my way back out the cabin door. Nearly breaking my neck in the fall made me mad to the core, I could have ripped bites of lead off with my teeth and spit bullets I was so mad. I stepped onto Szeda's chest to force him to stop wriggling; I watched his balls begin to drip blood as they pulled tight with the string down between his legs. Szeda began to mutter everything he possibly could through gritted teeth while forcing his eyes closed to deal with the pain. When the back of the boat dipped down some of the waves the small blue and white floaty buoy could be spotted in the distance, the string had ample tension and when the boat rose up so did the tension.

"You can find him at a yellow water front building with a dark blue roof in Roar Channel cove by Freeport; his building is where we exchange girls. He lives there and moves girls from all around the world." Szeda shared that he had a GPS unit tucked away under the helm (the boat steering wheel apparently) and the setting was "number 4" to find Tarak; number five was to return back to the bait shop. I pulled out my knife and snapped the tight line but didn't bother to untie the knot from around his beanbag. I left Szeda in a comatose state of elation, grateful his nuts were still dangling from his body and I headed back into the cabin.

The handheld GPS took a moment to figure out; I didn't bother to care about Szeda, with as still as he laid on the floor, I figured he passed out. The trip looked to be an hour or three maybe, nothing I couldn't handle, the ocean was pretty and the sun was rising. I heed and hawed but finally opened the damn ammo can that almost killed me and turned on the throw away phone I shoved inside. I wasn't sure why but I decided to call Carol and chat, it was a pretty morning. If I called Lu or any of my friends she would listen in and Dexa didn't need the stress and none of them had anything to do with my predicament so I fought to continue to keep them out of my drama. I leaned back against the side wall so I could steer and navigate without having to turn my back on Szeda, I wasn't threatened by him but I certainly didn't want any of his nut blood on me if I had to beat his ass again, yucky. I wanted to keep an eye on him and still steer in the direction the small GPS told me to go.

"Don't tell me you're on a boat" was how Carol answered the phone; she sounded vaguely tired this time. I could only respond with deep sarcasm due to my already inflamed annoyance for the outside world; "be nice to me or I won't bring you some candy." I bit at my lip as I spoke; the tone in her voice sounded like it was full of disappointment. I owed this lady nothing since her springing me from prison wasn't a favor to me, and frankly I don't like feeling like a pawn but I still wanted to know a lot of things, especially what she wanted me for. I had already tried to bluff up my hand once and with the notion that I am headed out of US coastal water I was out of many other options other than to start telling some truths.

"So you owe me some information Carol, start by telling me who you are and what you want with me" I didn't bother to beat around the bush any longer. My happy bouncing whistling mood disappeared when I almost died tripping over the stupid metal box. I was tired of the secrecy, the mystery and the manipulation and was seconds from being done with Carol all together. "I will tell you all in time but it needs to be face to face and private, there's a lot at stake including your home town of Waylon, your best interests have aligned with mine and you gotta trust me" Carol spun more of tale and continued to sound like a desperate car salesmen, which is a major turn off. I felt my blood pressure rise up when she spoke about putting Waylon in jeopardy; that was my father's legacy she was threatening.

I wasn't getting stirred up by her chum any longer; I was tired of taking her bait: "Say something before I hit international water and may not return, you also might want to hurry before I lose service Carol." Carol stuttered and stammered, I took her hesitation as her frantically searching for another angle to bullshit me with and it only made me more angry; "I don't even know why I called you, you have dragged me all over the damn country and can't even be straight with me, I don't know you nor care to, how about you lose my number and know that if I ever find you in Waylon, that it won't be my cute smile you'll be getting." I was about to hit the end button when Carol stopped me, "Alright, I was a little involved with Waylon before you were born, I get it and I support it but it's getting hairy and I can't get directly involved, but for the same reason you chat with Lu in strange patterns, we have to do the same, except in person."

Carol had me conflicted and confused, was I being baited to end up in federal custody for who knows what because they were too lazy to follow up on busting the first sex trafficking ring? Were they just going to peg me with the murders even though I acted in self-defense? The phone began to crackle as I throttled up the motor, "You get yourself back here safely....please" were the last words I could hear from Carol through the phone as I sped up and down waves. Szeda continued to moan and groan and roll around on the floor, I could have gone and helped him get his pants up but his white as paper thighs needed some tanning, plus he needed to dry from wetting himself. It was kinda fun driving the big boat, up waves and down waves, much different than Otis' small fishing dingy or the slightly larger fast boat I got to drive when my girlfriends and I went with one girl's dad to a big lake for a weekend of tubing and relaxing in high school.

The GPS took me past the western tip of an island, the little dots on the screen lead the way and I followed without any real clue where the hell I was going. My fist remained clenched on the wheel and my jaw clenched with angst as I rode up larger and larger waves and back down the other side. I thought back to the pirate movies I enjoyed and imagined myself captaining a much larger vessel, when I found myself disappointed that I wasn't I'd randomly shout to Szeda that his vessel wasn't big enough. I mentioned small things to remind him of his place, things like telling him he was a scum bag and just another limp dick trying to be tough through force. I slowed down as I came within eyesight of a beach in the distance. I've seen plenty of movies where the coast guard patrols and then people get busted and I didn't know my way around so I was nervous about getting pinned for something, anything, that I was doing. I slowed my engine down and decided to go and drag Szeda back in the cabin; I could always drop him into the people hold under the crate under the bed in a hurry much easier if he was close at hand.

Seth moaned and groaned as I dragged him by his shoulders, the bastard was much heavier and bending to drag him was certainly felt in my poor bruised butt cheek and sore lower back. I could feel the moss forming on my teeth from not having been able to brush them in the morning, my hunger pains had gone away but I could tell I was slightly lethargic from the hunger and my mind kept thinking about another tropical salad with lime flavored grilled chicken slices and a smoothie. My stomach garbled a little from emptiness and it sucked. I imagined that somewhere on that beach, some sexy half-dressed tropical man was selling jerk chicken and rice. *GHRRRBBLLL" my stomach rumbled again. My mind wandered to some of the potential street cart vendors; oh I wanted beans and rice or chicken and peppers with a hint of mango or pineapple, just something tropical and fruity to reenergize with.

I loved hitting the gym hard, I loved pushing myself farther than I thought I could and finding that elation that comes from surprising yourself. My last two years of high school I continued to work out and train with my kick-boxing. I would hit the weights and then also work on my forms and sparring. I toned up like crazy and after my gym time I would go to a small diner around the corner with some of the football players from the gym. I often impressed the guys by eating eight scrambled eggs with a cup of salsa on top for a post workout meal, the guys would all watch in amazement that little me ate so much and stayed cute (except for being all post workout sweaty which was a little gross). I often ate a cute salad for dinner but I would gorge to fuel my muscles after my work outs.

I always enjoyed a yummy smoothie before school (it was worth the stop at the Bear Claw coffee hut) I always got mine mixed with green tea of course. Lu explained to me that when I got my first bike that I would have to be able to stand it up if I laid down and I'd definitely have to keep it upright. I enjoyed physics as much as the next person but a ninety-eight pound girl was no match for a five hundred plus pound bike so I began to leg press. There were many days when I would squat and leg press until I was vomiting up water. The warm rush that climbs your esophagus and causes you to break out in sweat sucks but you know that you earned it by moving several times your body weight in cold steel. There were many times I had to call for a ride and then get help to walk out of the gym, the amount of lactic acid that builds up in your throbbing legs makes them quiver and shake, the funny freshly birthed giraffe like walk is proof to the world that you put up one hell of a fight.

I loved doing hanging sit-ups with my legs wrapped around the heavy bag, all the boys would come and watch me rep them out and even though my abs burned and I often times just released my ankles to fall to the floor I never let them see me wince. Some of the boys I worked out with like Marc and Tyler, who were running backs, would sometimes try to keep up with my workouts in the gym but offer up high-fives out of respect when they failed out. Marc and Tyler were both manly guys but also had the confidence to wedge themselves into sports bras for football practice, it drove the coach nuts that they'd do it but they would shove the bra cups with ice packs and keep themselves cool in the blistering heat, and they would sure flaunt it too. Tyler would pucker up his lips for a pouty face every time the coach looked over at him and even though the coach would get mad and make them all run, he'd keep doing it because that was who he was.

Tyler was a mixed kid, his skin was a smooth brown and his eyes were amber, sort of like a light beer color and they were beautiful. Marc was a white guy with a long jaw and Tyler's best friend. Tyler caught a bit of shit as a kid for being mixed in a pretty predominately white school which is bullshit because he was always a positive and easy going guy. Marc grew up close to Tyler so of course the two guys naturally bonded and stood tall as friends all the way through graduation. Marc got in more fights over people being dicks to Tyler than Tyler did, Tyler knew not to let anybody be a threat and handled it all with an easy cool that came with true confidence. Marc wasn't so easy about most things, he was quick to brawl if anyone dissed his pal and he was admirable for the chivalry, his dad often high-fived him for being so stand up when he had to come and pick him up for being suspended for fighting.

As the school years progressed the classes became more integrated and Tyler found much less hassle in being who he was. Marc followed Tyler into football and as workout partners; they exploded with their natural abilities. Tyler, Marc and I would all moan and limp our way to a diner after the gym, it was only a one block walk but after a harsh leg day, it might as well have been up Everest. Marc and Tyler would load up massive amounts of weight on a bar and lunge it back and forth across a parking lot.

On occasion they would have me saddle up on their shoulders and then they would compete to see who could squat me more, which often ended in a tie to save someone's ego. Marc, Tyler, me and a girl named Becky all went as a group to the junior prom, there was no weird sexual tension but just a group of friends, to keep it classy we hit Taco-Bell for our dinner and had a soft taco showdown for dinner.

Tyler went on to serve our country in the Air-force after graduation and Marc was killed in action in Afghanistan serving for the Marines saving a young boy from getting caught in a crossfire, Tyler and I were both at his memorial. Marc was always the guy willing to take and throw a punch if it meant getting his point across. Tyler never took much shit or grief over the petty feelings of someone that was dead wrong anyways but Marc was deeply irritated by the ignorance of people and their willingness to infect others with it. Tyler was Marc's brother and the two of them were my friends and I was fortunate to be theirs. Tyler stood stoically and tall at the funeral, he was always strong and even when the day after leg day came and no one could muster the strength to lift themselves up from the toilet, Tyler always put on a brave face and flashed his big toothy smile to get through the day.

Seeing the tears fall from Tyler's amber eyes, wetting his cheeks and falling down to the ground was impossible to see, he kept his strong stance and thousand yard stare but I knew what was going on behind his beautiful eyes. Tyler was an amazing man and I loved him as my brother, he and Marc both. The darker brown skin under the tear trails glinted in the light as Tyler stood firm, he fought to keep his emotions held back to honor his uniform, and his brother, but the pain of losing his lifelong best friend swelled up in his throat, and as all men do, he couldn't fight it any more when TAPS began to play.

The twenty-one gun salute and full military burial is the highest honor anyone can receive, Tyler and I had always known that Marc was going to get one; we just always thought it wouldn't be until we were old and gray. Tyler only had half of a day of leave for Marc's funeral, he was robbed of his chance to weep and mourn for his friend. Tyler and I walked together and quickly discussed his arrival home as well as quickly tried to catch up as best we could. Tyler used to see me in gym pants and a sports bra back in school so when he caught glimpse of me in a black lace dress; the wide smile on his face when he turned the corner walking with Marc's parents was precious. Tyler's eyes let up and his lips broke in a smile that parted for his big white teeth.

Tyler is a gorgeous man and when he chooses, he will be a beautiful father and husband and I look forward to the day I get to be an aunt to his children. Tyler lit up from his somber military stare when he caught sight of me in my long sleeve black lace dress. I wore my black heels with my dress and hid my sleeve tattoos out of respect, which he complimented with some sarcastic needling as well. Tyler took the lead Pall-bearer handle and with sharp military snapped salutes, his friend was promised to the same ground he shed his blood for. I did my best to put flowers on Marc's grave every year for his birthday and there were many occasions I would take a beer and go and just sit and talk to him like I used to. Many good men risk their lives for our country every day, and sad to say, there are too many assholes that don't respect them and it pisses me off.

I thought about Tyler as I honed in on some of the dark skinned Bahamian guys strolling around on the far away beach, thinking of him and how easy-going he is always makes me feel a little bit better when I feel like I'm under a lot of weight, sort of like when we were working out. The waves on the crossing were fairly large and a little intimidating but come hell or high-water, I was going to find Tarak. I followed the GPS on the boat and tried to match the inlets and outlets along the coast with the dotted map on the small device. Roar Chanel was unmarked but I had the GPS to lead the way and I followed along. I sat on the side rail to steer and to get the best view from behind the steering wheel while not turning my back on Seth. I had a sinking feeling in my belly about everything, I was out of the country and illegally from my understanding, plus the unfamiliar territory always heightens my adrenaline and my awareness while tugging at my nerves.

I felt my forehead begin perspire as I slowly turned the boat into the cove, there were several boats moored to large wooden posts floating in the brownish water. Bits of white trash easily caught my eyes as I scanned the water looking for anything that might clue me in to where I was supposed to go. Szeda continued to moan and groan with his hands bound behind him on the floor. I found myself staring at him with curiosity, for being a big bad tough guy that beat women and treated them like meat, he was a major sissy. I found it strange that for a small inlet, there weren't all that many people in sight and it made me nervous. I let the boat idle as I found a small end of a dock to tie off too, there were tires tied to the sides of sun faded planks to keep from beating up the sides of the ships that docked there.

I poked and prodded Szeda with the tip of my knife for more information about Tarak as I eyed the quiet building fronts; I gently traced parts of *him* with my knife blade. Szeda tried his best to remain all heroic to his cause but a light filet motion with my blade against his already tattered boy parts he become my little chatty friend. Szeda was pretty fond of the same sack of skin that probably got him into the very same predicament he was in and I made sure to express my willingness to part him from his favorite little toy if he wasn't willing to cooperate. Szeda clammed up when I asked him questions on where to find his boyfriend but a small tap to his little ratty looking nuts and he became more gossipy than the Gilmore girls. I found it so strange that I find myself crying over stories of injured or abused children on the news but I found myself numb and remorseless holding a knife to the whoppers of a man that doled out torture and punishments, maybe there's a little psychopath in me. Szeda twitched and flinched each time I slapped his face with the flat side of my knife, I watched his shoulders to make sure he wasn't making much progress in freeing himself but I had a suspicion it was finally on his agenda, especially now that we were near his buddy Tarak.

When Szeda heard me turn of the motor from his semi curled up state on the floor he began to toss and turn again, he must have figured we were or close enough to maybe draw some attention to get rescued. "You retched bitch" Szeda began to call out over and over, his balls were half purplish and still bloody and he kept referring to his genitals and to me in a slurred spitting kind of rant something about what he was going to do to me. I was too hungry and too tired to waste the energy focusing on what all he was being slanderous about, I didn't really care anyways. Szeda gave me half of an idea, I pulled the socket filled ammo can out from under the bit of shelf near my feet, it must have weighed forty pounds so I lifted it up to about chest level. The height scared me a little so I closed my eyes and turned my head. "Chang, clang clank" the ammo can crashed to the ground after it bounced off the side of Szeda's head after I opened my hands to drop the ammo can onto him. Szeda was out cold and I only had a few minutes so I began to hurry. I used my knife to work the zip-tie off then to cut through Szeda's tape bindings and work his jacket off from his arms. The jacket was still damp from his piss from the earlier morning but it would have to do. I pried Szeda from his jacket and re-tied his arms before he woke up.

I thought about how lost Tallia looked as she watched over her friend on her lap, the story she told me about some guy making a slit in Irena's stomach to insert himself to make love to it while she was conscious and aware was beyond disgusting, the thought of it crept into my mind once or twice when I shut my eyes and it sent full chills of repulsion riving through me. I felt the some tenderness in my backside go away as I gritted down my teeth as I squatted down to undo his ties and then stand back up. I thought about Kelsa getting raped by Tarak and then getting raped again, to death, by a knife. The atrocities of people make me want to be sick, I want to ball up and cry and wish that it all went away, the problem was that too many people turn an ignorant eye to the things that happen all the time and no one has the tough enough ovaries to do anything about it, but I do.

People often say that dicks are tough; they might be for a short period of time but be real, turn the air conditioner on and see how long that lasts. A uterus must stretch, accommodate and take a beating from the inside for months during pregnancy, there isn't a man tough enough to endure what most women have to and I'm pretty sure that the "tough as balls" propaganda was all started as an over compensation so I don't buy it. Men have no idea what women go through but have the nerves to put us down every chance they get. I wish more women had the sense to stand together for each other and not get sucked into the competition among one another, that's the same competition that will often destroy us with petty jealousy or drama and it all needs to stop.

I fought back my eyes welling up and throat pulsating with the urge to gag as I slid into Szeda's long coat, with my riding jacket on underneath I was already sweating and hot but I wanted to cover over my petite frame and seem a bit more bulked up as I moved around the boat and then to the dock. I sauntered with a wider stance as I walked out of the cabin, Szeda was still and concussed on the floor with a small bit of head blood matting his hair together before trickling to the floor under his head. The cabin was filthy and each time I glanced at the bed along the left wall, all I could picture was the short Terry guy with the Danny DeVito body wriggling and grunting underneath that poor small Asian girl I found him with. I probably should have thought longer and more clearly about what I was getting myself into but at this point I was already sledding towards hell, I might as well just go with the momentum and see where it leads me.

I found some ropes along the side of the boat and tied them tightly onto the wood posts that jutted out of the water. The inlet cove broke up many of the waves that would have traveled in from the deeper water with more energy in the form of big waves that would normally toss around the smaller ships tied to the docks so luckily the boat didn't rock as badly as I stumbled a little back and forth. I shoved the bed mattress back against the wall and pried open the small space underneath and grunted to heave Szeda up and back in, when his half naked ass rubbed along my arm I felt my empty stomach try to empty itself with a squeeze but there was nothing there except a stinging burp in my throat and nothing I could do. I untied my new knife from my boot and tucked it into my left jacket sleeve for closer access. If you have to raise your hands being held hostage it's handy to have a knife in your forearm sleeve to get rather than your pantleg.

My armpits leaked sweat down my sides; I felt the fabric of my t-shirt stick to my skin as I headed out of the cabin to make my way up the cracked wooded dock and towards the ramshackle looking buildings along the water line. I knew I was looking for the yellow building with a blue roof and in fact a majority of the yellow was chipping off, the building looked rather rundown and shiesty looking but it was close enough to what Szeda described to lead me to it. The boards creaked beneath my steps as my boots thunked with each step, I tried to step lighter but I wanted to keep up a look that I belonged there. I felt eyes on me as I walked and it was unnerving but I did my best to keep my head down and move quickly.

I held my breathe on my opposite steps, inhale on my right step, hold it, then let it out on my right step again as my boots thumped down the iffy looking dock. The trees in the background were bushy and green with foliage growing in between the battered looking buildings giving everything a weathered and almost abandoned appeal; very "Texas Chainsaw massacre" meets "The grapes of Wrath." I tried to keep my head down and tucked into the tall collar of the jacket and eyeball all around before heading on my way onto the solid land and towards the chipped yellow buildings a few docks down where I was informed where Tarak would be. Everything around me was wrong, the quiet fronts, the water barely moving, it felt like the calm before the storm and even with all of these red flags making a strong argument that I should turn around and go back; I pressed on.

Once I laid eyes on the building I was interested in I slid into the side shrubs two buildings before, one of the long leafed plants smelled a little like lemony furniture cleaner and the course leaves whipped me in the face which pissed me off some. Some of the small shops or shacks had signs hanging above the doors but there wasn't any foot traffic. The beach I passed along the way was beginning to come to life with bodies breaking out their coolers and lawn chairs, but not here, the only life around me was the breeze coming in from the ocean and abrasively rocking the leaves around me. The breeze from the water broke just a little of the humidity but almost none of the heat, sweat poured down my sides as I ducked and hid. As I stood in the bushes I could hear the buzzing of some of the small bugs and I fought the urge to frantically swat them as they buzzed at my ears or landed on the bare skin of my neck and face. I tried to keep looking back to keep a watchful eye on the ship I commandeered from Szeda to make sure nobody was sneaking aboard and going to steal my stolen ride.

My dad Lil Digger always used to tell me that "if you always face the wolf it can't sneak up on you." I often thought about his little parable, I would recite it before going into a kick-boxing match, especially if the girl or guy was much larger than I was and I would feel that urge in my stomach from nerves to hurl or that moment of fear numb my legs. My thighs quivered and my palms were sweaty as I tried to fight my runaway heart beat in my chest. I didn't want to walk into some trap and began to doubt myself and what I was doing; what if Tarak saw the familiar ship and was already on guard or sighting me into a rifle or something, then what? I wish it were more like the movies where I could radio in some distress call and then Jason Statham shows up; whoops everyone's ass, and we disappear into the sunset on a massive yacht to sip Champaign all naked and sexy; "damn it Jason where are you?" I thought to myself. My anxiety grew as did the tension in my head, the knots in the back of my neck felt like they could snap my vertebrae. As I snuck along my mind raced wildly around my last few days; I missed my massage ladies and Shay, oh and the smoothie as my stomach grumbled loudly again.

"To hell with Carol, I'm getting a massage and a large pizza for myself when I get done with this, maybe I can find a smoothie or food vendors here and mug them for my fill of food and have a cocktail while on my first crappy vacation in the Bahamas. Perhaps I won't even bother leaving, Lu can wire me some money and maybe I can start a small shop, maybe I can just click my heels together and wake up at home and all of this be over, too many maybes. I calmed my breathing as I remained squatted down watching the area; the windows on the shops were dusty and hard to see into, making everything even more nerve racking. I heed and hawed enough to waste time waiting for some movement of any sort; I had vengeance to deliver, some hot tropical guys to hit up for food and to somehow make my way to Philly by tonight.

I forced my legs back underneath me, rather than continue down the waterside boardwalk I opted to wedge back up towards the back of the buildings, the foliage was pissing me off with each thin branch that whipped me in the face, the ones that connected flat stung and made me more and more angry with each one. I could feel the raised whip marks on my face that itched and stung from whatever was on some of the leaves and by the halfway point between buildings I was ready to quit and just go to the beach.

The paint chips fell to my feet as I brushed up against the wooden walls making my way slowly towards the back. I found a small narrow drive that looped around to the back of the shops, probably a small delivery drive. Most of the buildings had an abandoned appeal to them, real ghost-town like and it was unsettling. I couldn't see any reason for the lack of people, I was beginning to put two and two together that perhaps this whole cove was overrun by scumbags or that maybe anyone smart enough knew better than to come around the area. My heart began to pound in my ears again, I found myself scanning everything around me over and over and straining to listen for noises as I made my way towards the yellow building. Szeda was telling me when I had his nuts tied to a floaty buoy as I dragged it behind the boat that the building was dark and filled with things stored inside, a good place to hide girls while arranging for them to be sold off elsewhere.

I crept low and knelt down beside the back corner to try and listen for any movement inside, I didn't want to go stick my ear to the dirty window and risk being seen from the inside so I just hugged the wall. I heard a motor from down the road a little and quickly crawled backwards to hide from view. I laid as flat as I could among the thorn ridden shrubs next to the building, squeezing in closely in the long black coat. I heard some men shouting from a drab green Jeep that eased passed me and I froze hoping to blend in enough with the ground to keep from being spotted. I heard three men's voices and strained, hoping to hear the name Tarak to confirm that I found the man that I had come for. I tried to let my brown hair hide my white skin against the ground; with the long black coat on I had some camouflage help already. The back door was a garage style door and the front was a standard door that looked like a closed business, both looked tough enough that I wouldn't be able to get in silently to take a look around. With the gunmen Irena described that Szeda kept around inside, I sure as hell wasn't going in all General Custer style, nor willing to end up the same way. I had it in my mind that I didn't want that prick to rape my dead corpse.

As I breathed in some of the earth lying face down I caught the glimpse of cement floor through a mouse hole or rotten spot at the base of the wall. The wood was soft near the ground, the moist dirt had softened the base of the wall and with a wriggling finger I was able to make the hole larger and larger. With my face shoved against the dirt and looking up I could see some metal racks with boxes and crates on them, behind the racks, the men that arrived had some guns slung around their shoulders and they were wearing splotchy camo fatigues with berets. There was no denying I'm in deep shit. I could see three rather dark skinned men; they looked like Bahamian military, if there is such a thing.

I poked and pulled at more of the rotten base boards as carefully as I could until I could almost fit my face in while the men talked and clanged metal boxes together. The half rotten particle boards at the base of the wall was soft a mushy, not to mention rife with bugs and gooey stuff I kept putting my hand into, it was cold and slimy and I did my best not to think about what it could have been. The clangs and clinks seemed to echo in the building, I couldn't hear any whimpering or signs that I was in the right place so I continued to doubt myself. I couldn't see any tall cement columns like the ones that Irena described being tied to or any other hint that there were girls being laundered through the area before being shipped all over the world, but I couldn't leave without being sure. I had an inkling that maybe Szeda may have been full of shit and lied to me, maybe to figure out a way to escape but with the risk of losing his nuts I couldn't imagine he'd lie to me, it'd be pretty impressive if he had.

I carefully pried more and more of the baseboards back, cautious not to pop a board off a nail and make enough noise to alert the guards. I wondered for a short while as to why these guys had machine guns and what they may have been doing that was so special that they needed heavy automatic weapons. I tried to think about what I was doing rather than what I was going to do; my stomach grew woozy at the thought of trying to sneak up on someone, especially if they had a machine gun. The thought of getting shot paralyzed me with fear; it has always stopped me in my tracks for that extra second. I could shake off the fear but there was always that extra second of pause that could get me killed some day. I practiced gun disarming in my training, over and over again I grabbed a rubber shotgun and turned it on my aggressor or the same with spinning a pistol around and retaking the upper hand but these assholes have machine guns, the equation changes significantly.

I had a boot knife tucked into my sleeve and was beavering my way through a soft rotted baseboard of a Caribbean building for something or another. On the inside of the building are three men in fatigues carrying very scary machine guns, my heart was in my throat and I had to keep lowering my head onto the ground for small pauses to rest and keep my eyes from seeing spot. I tugged and cut away at enough of the soft wood to wedge my chest in, each time I heard a sudden stop in the voices I held my breath and stopped moving. The three men casually walked around and hardly bothered to look beyond some of the tall metal racks lining the walls, right where I was hiding. I weighed shoving the racks over onto the three men and hauling tits at them full bore before they might notice me, or maybe I could pin them under one of the metal racks and get a gun from them but this wasn't *Missing in Action*. Even if the machine guns only shot a dozen or so bullets a minute, there were still a lot more bullets than I was willing to dance with, it was all so scary and it made my hands shake.

The three men grew quiet as they moved around in the building, when they were at their most quiet I froze but when their talking resumed I let out all of my breath to squeeze myself the rest of the way through the small hole. The dirt on my hands was gooey and it left splotches down my chest and on my thighs, bummer was that it didn't mask the urine stink of the long coat I borrowed from Szeda, it just mixed with the rotten earthy poo smell. The building stank of dust and cigar smoke grime. Inside was poorly lit and I could hardly see much of the floor beneath me. I felt dirt and bits of grit under my hands and slowly pulled myself through the small hole.

Jagged pieces of wood caught on my waist and hips as I wriggled like a seal on ice, I was terrified that I would be heard and each small noise blared in my ears. I pulled myself along the floor between the rack and the wall, I was pretty certain half of the dirt I was crawling in was actually mouse turds but I couldn't see all that well so I pretended it wasn't. I kept inching slowly as I headed to the front of the room to investigate further. At the back was the garage door that the men entered through, towards the front was nearer the waterfront so it was my first choice of places to go to get back to the boat but everything was frightening and I wanted to just go home. In the streams of light that beamed around me showing flecks of airborne dust prancing around one another, I made out wooden rafters, some of them had boxes or things stacked on top. The voices I crawled towards were muffled and hushed but I had to know what was going on.

My mouth was dry and it was difficult to swallow, it was probably for the better as I was probably breathing in dried mouse crap anyways. The warehouse was dark as hell, it was hot and muggy and I was in riding gear plus a piss stained long coat and here I am, laying on the dirty floor of a foreign building in a foreign land and I couldn't figure out how I was in the position I was in, fearing that any one of the three big guys with guns might find me and that be the end of me. Jackasses say that "night is the darkest before the dawn," that's ridiculous, it's darkest at the apex of the night, the midpoint between sunset and sunrise because before dawn there is still enough light waves refracting off of the atmosphere, it's a simple concept and if I live through whatever it was I was doing, I promise to stop using that phrase. The warehouse was crazy dark in the corners but that was where I was laying and it masked me well, the shadows once again were my ally.

I wondered if the breathed in mouse turds would give me some herpa-syphill-aid cancer or other kind of respiratory STD. I really don't make all the best decisions for myself I revisited in my mind over and over, even before getting thrown into prison I often found myself in one sticky situation or another. One time in school I was being mocked for being a gym rat, of course I was proud of it but his girl Catie began rambling on that I was turning tricks in the locker-room. I'm usually one to keep my temper and even Tyler told me to brush it off but one day when I was already agitated she started in in the hallway, it only took one punch to the side of her head to send her to the floor crying. I wasn't necessarily proud that I jacked Catie but I certainly wasn't ashamed either. My forehead was sweating profusely, sweat ran down from my arm pits and I could feel it soaking my shirt below me causing it to stick to my skin.

The first few days in prison I was pretty concerned about a lot of things, I knew very little Spanish because I got around on English and with bilingual people when I needed them. The prison was large like a mountain of cement and steel that rose up from the ground. First processing sucked, me and three other inmates, dudes no less, had to stand in the middle of a room a few feet apart and strip down to the bare essentials (nothing). One inmate to my left was a fairly ripped guy with greasy hair that hung down to his chin and a wiry chinstrap beard underneath. The other guy was a darker tanned older guy with a round hairy belly and faded crappy tattoos on his arms. There were three guards in front of us and three behind us, lucky me only one of the six guards was a girl while the other five eyed me like a steak.

I spent months modeling before I missed wrenching on bikes for fun and began working at the shop I was busted in. Modeling was fun getting to wear all the newest gear, getting an assistant to dote on me and make sure I was eating healthy while staying in hot shape. I liked the attention of modeling, sure there were plenty of pervy creeps and having to smile while they wrapped their arms around me for pictures was sometimes miserable to just chew through but it was a good time nonetheless. Modeling was all glamorous and full of champagne parties and wild clubs for a while, I knew that it wasn't my life nor something I wanted to do for long but I can at least say I did it when my body was at the peak of youth and toned shape and totally rocking. Being a hot gringo helped me along to start modeling, it began with just riding around to some of the bike stores in my bikini tops solo, no dudes had to show me how to ride and then a few guys took interest and that was how it started.

I was grunted at and had batons waved at me to instruct me to slowly remove my clothes one piece at a time, I fought to keep from breaking my teeth as I clenched my jaw so tightly from the anxiety of the situation. I felt ashamed; the guards were as cold and emotionless as the cement walls around me as they stood like gargoyles glaring at me. The guards smirked and raised eyebrows at me the entire time eyeing me up and down in the most humiliating ways possible. Standing in a skimpy bikini modeling biking gear or even just laying out on a nice sunny Mexican beach nude to tan evenly with crowds around me doing the same never made me feel small, but that processing room changed everything. The male guards looked me up and down, I have never been all that chesty and I was ok with it but the eyes pinpointed on me began to make me feel self-conscious and I hated it.

I thought about Pickle, I can't tell you how many times growing up the large man would don his American flag board shorts and plop onto a floaty chair at any and every pool gathering he was invited to. Pickle would rub his hands on his stomach as he floated around the pool, he wasn't in the best of shape, nor the best shape he had ever been in for that matter, but he was proud of himself. I thought about what Pickle must have felt like when he first looked in the mirror to see the blistered skin and divots that he was left with after the gas he was caught up in that burned him a little, I suppose anyone would dislike a sudden change in appearance but in all honestly, everyone has their changes and everyone adapts to them, acceptance is the difference in being happy with yourself or being your own worst enemy. Pickle was never one to hide himself away, each time Chips would shout to Pickle about "all that sexiness" trying to persuade him to wear a shirt, Pickle would respond with "more sexy than you'll ever get" and his self-assured attitude would not waver.

Pickle once told me that each day was a countdown to the last and eventually you'll run out of tomorrows, I try not to sit and stew on the philosophies of it all but I also can't walk past someone being bullied or feeling tortured and pretend I didn't notice. All of my friends and club members all signed the contract with the military to serve their country, come hell or high water, they all took their oath and were willing to risk their life so that strangers could continue to enjoy peace, and in Marc's case, he did in fact give his life. I was honor bound to Tallia, Irena, Kelsa and countless other girls that had become sex slaves to these pigs. The animosity against women around the world was endless and fueled by ignorance and there aren't enough people that have the ability to do anything about it, but I am here, and I will.

I caught a glimpse of one of the military men standing with his back to the shelf in front of me in the grungy tropical warehouse. I couldn't see the other two men so I might have found a small window of even playing ground if I took them out one at a time or got his gun from him. I rose up to kneeling and eyed between the man's legs, an ideal place to jerk the blade of my knife to sever his femoral artery and let him bleed out silently and quickly while his two buddies were across the way and speaking to a man I couldn't see, I thought that maybe if I could reach around him fast enough I could hold his gun with one arm and choke him into silence with the other but wearing two jackets and fighting dehydration might slow me down a lot.

The man closest to me had his back leaning against the shelf; I sized up his body and made a map of his torso in my mind. My nerves were unraveling, once I kicked off this small rumble by sneaking up and slicing him or shoving my blade in between his ribs so he couldn't suck in a breath of air to scream then there was no telling how it might end, my suspicion was: *bloody* and I was terrified. The man leaned his head down to light a cigarette, with his head down I stood up and eased a bit closer, so close I could smell him, that oniony sweat odor wafting from his pores, it was thick. My stomach tightened with anticipation. I rubbed my sweaty palms on the legs of my coat and slowly pulled my knife from the sleeve while the man puffed his cigarette and shifted his weight.

The man I shadowed carried his gun slung over his left shoulder with his arm resting on top of it; his hand was nowhere near the trigger so the thought of him getting off some shots to alert his pals to my being there wasn't likely to happen. I still faced the fear of one of his pals hearing a bit of commotion or even just seeing the movement. In the movies the moment you slit someone's throat or shoot them, they're dead and stop moving but that myth is a major movie flaw, they can squirm or fight back for days. From the stories of Dexa and his time storming doors I had plenty of stories told to me about post death kicks and spasms. One time Dexa barged into a door to come face to face with a man holding a large knife looking to put it into Dexa. Dexa had his flak jacket but the man was wildly swinging the blade and all Dexa could do was jump to tackle the man, pinning him against the wall and then falling to the floor with him.

Dexa clobbered the man with the weight of himself and full gear, Dexa pushed the blade away and got in closely to the man to inhibit his free swinging hand. Dexa grabbed the blade and eased it slowly into the wild man's neck while bashing his forehead into the man's face to subdue him. The man kicked and grunted for nearly five minutes with Dexa sprawled out on top of him face to face waiting for life, and threat, to leave his body. I convinced myself that if I had to take someone's life that it would be for good reason, I fought off thinking about the lives I had already taken and there was justification behind them, these army guys were very armed and I was a bit scared but I thought about how Dexa must have felt and how bravely he acted despite being scared.

I worried that if I reached around and slit this man's throat if I would have an army on me or maybe I wouldn't do it right or maybe he'd overpower me and then all of my problems would get worse in a hurry. I continued to scan the room, I wanted to make sure that if I did anything that it was going to be planned out and not get me killed, my hands trembled a little as I gripped my knife. "Syon" I heard a voice speak out, suddenly breaking up the near silence. The man standing right in front of me pushed forward off the rack to gain momentum to head in to meet with his buddies. As the man pushed off the rack to get moving I sunk back down to a squat, hoping my knees wouldn't pop under the stress and blow my cover. The sudden startle made my throat dry up and my eyes begin to tear up a bit, I was so close to getting ready to jump the man and the rapid pounding in my chest was causing my adrenaline to surge through my veins like an untamed river bursting through a damn. The man sauntered as he made his way to the other room, as he opened it I saw what I needed, an older tan man with speckles of gray hair speaking to the other two military men.

I leaned in to watch as the men took money from the fourth man, all three officers thumbed through their wads of cash and chatted back and forth. I hunkered down and waited for the men to move about more, seeing inside the room was hard and there wasn't much I could make out just past the door other than the lighter skinned man. My leg muscles spasmed and throbbed but I held tight, I tried to keep my head down to let my brown hair fall over and hide my lighter face in the dark while I waited. After a few minutes of standing with the door open the three men stopped milling around and began to make their way back to their green jeep they drove in on, leaving me and the fourth man alone. I ducked down to hide in the shadow of the corner as the three uniformed men walked past the metal racks and left. My heart was racing and my temples throbbed as I waited for them to leave. Each crick and creek of the back garage door or floor boards set my blood on fire with nervous anxiety and impatience. I was alone and scared but determined to find out what was going on and put a stop to it.

My chest burned as I struggled to keep my breathing silent and under control, I thought back to my in processing into the prison. I filled with rage and felt the tips of my ears grow hot as guard snickered and sneered as I stood naked with two other inmates in the middle of the room. The older of the two inmates just stared forward while his arms hung to his side and his ass hung behind him while the younger one with the longer hair and cheesy chinstrap style beard kept wanting to turn his head toward me. The middle guard in front of us barked orders at the younger man each time he swayed to begin to turn towards me. The younger inmate's eyes would begin to drift towards me and then the guard would bark, just pulling the leash enough to keep him in line.

The large inmate dropped to a squat and coughed really hard with his arms raised out in front of him, the stern guard with the beady eyes then shook his baton at the younger inmate next to me and he followed suit. I could hear a guard walking really close behind me as the other two inmates squatted; the guards behind us had stepped up good and intimately close behind us while our backs were turned. I had seen enough prison movies to know that the squat and cough is supposed to release anything you may have stashed within yourself, it's also endlessly embarrassing and disgusting, I didn't want my hoo-ha that close to the nasty floor, oh it was so gross. If I was going to ever catch hepatitis C; that was the moment.

Squatting down in front of one prison guard while facing three others was about as nerve racking as I had ever experienced in my life, you can't be much more vulnerable than to be naked and squatting down with your arms held out in front of you, it was complete exposure, and degrading. I had sparred plenty in my kick-boxing years, I brawled and squabbled a little in school and since then but the most concerned I ever been for myself was at that moment. I was stark naked, in a room with seven other guys, two of them convicts and already naked, I wanted to explode from the floor and begin doling out ass whippings except with each guard armed I didn't want to quickly end up beaten within an inch of my life, especially because no one knew where I was.

As I squatted the smirks on the guards in the front of the room began to crack. I felt the body heat of the guard behind me and the foul breath on the back of my neck. As my butt neared the floor I struggled to keep my balance, holding my breath was a challenge. The guard in front of me mumbled something so I began to raise my arms out in front of me just like the other two felons. As my arms neared parallel with the floor I felt the cold hard baton begin to trace up and down my sides. I closed my eyes as hard as I could as the baton nudged against my ribs and towards my breast. The baton moved from the outside of my breast towards the front and back down to my hip. I had to bite my lip to keep it from quivering as I fought to focus on being anywhere else than in that room at that moment.

I heard more jeering from the guards at the front of the room as they chuckled a little, their boots made tapping noises as they shifted their bodies back and forth a bit laughing at me. Under my bare bottom I could feel the cold from the floor; my feet were already freezing and numb. The baton was scary because I had no padding and any hit from it to my body would have surely broken something. There was a slight air below my rear from the movements of the guard behind me; each step they took made my body tense up in nervousness. I fought to keep my eyes closed as some of the murmurs turned to cackles and laughter. I dug down deep to hold in every ounce of scared emotion that ran through me. The room fell silent for a moment, I held my breath as long as I could without passing out and as I began to slowly exhale through my nose *boop* I felt the baton tap, *me*.

I hopped at the disturbing feeling, the baton was almost aligned with me down there and as my nerves and anxiety peaked I hadn't expected the touch and it almost sent me overboard. My body jolted and my eyes almost popped out of my head. I was appalled that the baton hit me in my private area, I was already frightened and nearly ready to be raped or to try to fight off a rapist but it didn't really expect any of this, I was terrified. Once the baton hit me where it did my body jerked and as I was on my way to standing and clenching my fists, one of the guards shouted something. My eyes burst open but were white with rage for a moment. I turned my head to prepare to fight whoever connected me with the baton and I was ready to shove it inside of them: sideways. As I turned to face off with the female guard wearing bright red lipstick and a grand smile shock hit me before I was nudged to follow the other inmate towards my clothes.

I heard the jeep peel out and pepper the back garage door with pebbles and gravel on their way passed and I took the sign that I was clear to figure out if Tarak was in the other room or not. I kept my knife clenched in my hand and stepped lightly towards the door. The door looked like your normal office door but what else that might have been on the other side had me extremely curious, and pretty concerned. The wall went all the way to the ceiling, there was no way to climb up or to gain any sort of surprise so I had to just go at it as I was, exposed and raw. I searched some of the shelves for other things I could use to my advantage, I had a feeling that if homeboy inside was in fact a human trafficking sadistic freak, then he would probably be guarded and ready for anything at any time, and I wouldn't be the stronger of the two of us. I found a handful of tools and spare boat parts on the shelves, not really much of anything I could put use to but I had to come up with something, and fast.

I grabbed a handful of dirty oily rags from a milk crate and searched for hoses or belts, anything that was rubbery or old. I tried to be quiet as I shook some metal tins for any form of fuel I could use for an ignition source. Tallia popped into my head, the tall dame with the rocking body and pissed off attitude set Davor's place on fire, I think she was on to something. I found some old fan belts on the bottom shelf and began to wedge some into a chunk of sticky radiator hose, not many things that would normally be all that flammable but wedging some of the oily rags into the open end would give me some form of wick to work with. I had a small half ass concocted, fire ball thing, I tried to find a paint thinner or fuel but only had some axle grease on one of the rags, not so much luck.

I moved slowly back to the corner I was hiding in as I used the grease on the rag to coat one side of the chunk of hose; I needed it to be real sticky. I used my knife to shave some wood shavings off the wall and pile on top of the rags stuffed into the rubber hose I held onto. I used my knife blade to also shave some rust pieces off the bottom of the shelf that sat on the floor, I was hoping to make the fireball burn really hot and quickly by using whatever solvents on the rags with the rust shavings (a part of gun powder and smoke bombs) to make a really smoky and stinky distraction. Pickle once had a list of chemist's notes about things you can add to other things to get smoke bombs or sparklers or things like that so I searched my brain to recall what was on that list while wishing I paid closer attention in chemistry. I didn't have much in regards to flammable or explosive fluids but with simple ingredients I could figure something out.

I used a hand full of rust mixed with some oily residue on a rag and began to rub it really hard against my knife blade while keeping an eye on the office door. The friction grew on in my hand and I just continued to rub faster and faster. After half a minute the rust and solvent mix began to get really hot and started to smoke. I thought back to many of the stern warnings in auto shop about how important it was to put dirty rags into a metal container to keep them from combusting, well I'm combusting now. The rag let out a small spark and then continued to smoke. The strong smell of the rag stank in my hand but as I transferred it onto my knife blade I continued to stoke it by blowing on the smoking part. The rag began to flame and I had what I needed: fire on an oily rag coated with grease. I caressed the rag and nursed the flames as I tiptoed across the floor with the half greased rubber tube in my free hand. I pressed the rubber hose to the door below the handle and set the burning rag across the top and then began to wait.

The rag slowly caught the hose on fire and the door began to char above it, I regretted not knocking but as the flames licked up the door and handle it began to burn the upper door frame. I continued to search for a pipe or wrench or anything I could use in my free hand as a weapon to get the upper hand. The room filled with dark black smoke, the hose continued to burn after the grease warmed up and slid down the door, the grease caught fire and continued to burn on the door. I heard a noise beyond the crackle of the small fire, the rubber melted into a pile and burned hot at the base of the door, the chemical smell began to burn my eyes. I began to regret not checking for a side door on the far side of the building, the thought that maybe he just slipped out made me feel really stupid but I continued to hope.

I slowly began to stand up and then the door burst open, my heart stopped and I froze for a moment. When the man pulled the door open a large cloud of black smoke swirled in the air and wafted into the office, engulfing him in black tarry soot. The man began to stomp at the fire with his feet as he raised his shirt up around his face. I tucked my face into my sweat soaked shirt and set my right foot behind me. As the man danced and stomped around on the small pile of fire the hot melted rubber began to catch his feet on fire, which made him move faster and faster frantically. I tucked my knife between my teeth with my shirt and slid off Szeda's jacket. I held up the black jacket and used it to shield me from the eye burning smoke that billowed from my small fire ball on the ground. The man was too busy turning in circles to notice me and my black shroud sprinting towards him. The man was wearing dark reddish pants and jacket, I scanned him for a gun but couldn't spot one as I decided to leap over the small fire and tackle him before he caught sight of me rushing at him from across the flames.

Whomp I leapt over the small flames and engulfed the man with my jacket before landing on him on the ground. The man's body was limp after landing on him; I quickly looked around in the other room to see if there was anyone and was quickly grasping the knife from my mouth to ready for a fight. I reached my foot over to the door and swung it closed with my foot before the rest of the room filled with dark black smoke. The room was wood paneled and disarming; it looked just like an ordinary office, desk covered with papers and paperwork, a few random pictures on the walls and now a thinning black cloud of smoke hovering near the ceiling light. I pounced back from on top of the man and dragged the long jacket with me. I pulled the door open and used the jacket to cover over the fire to extinguish it while keeping an eye on the man on the floor, who just stared up at me.

I felt a small pit in my stomach, what if I had the wrong guy, what if I set fire to the wrong building, what if the fire didn't go completely out under the jacket and because of the hot burning rubber and grease it flickered flames then caught fire again trapping me inside? As dread began to fill me I asked him his name. The man just stared up at me from the floor; his expression was both confused and angry. The man's eyebrows clenched together and his jaw muscles bulged as he flared his nostrils with his heavy breathing. I held my knife tightly in my left hand as I kept my right readied for some surprise attempt from the man still silent on the floor. I began to nervously take steps back and forth across the small doorway, the pit in my stomach began to knot up and ache with regret. "Roll over weak stream" I instructed as I cleared a pile of papers off of the man's desk by wiping my outstretched arm across the top. The man kept his left hand opened at me in a defensive stance then began to use his right arm to sit up a little and roll himself over. I made the mistake of moving slowly towards the far side of the desk from him when the spry bastard popped up from the floor and began sprinting towards a small brown door nestled in the back wall.

I banged my way around the desk and hurried to catch up with the man before he made it to the door. I reached my hands out to tug on the man's jacket as I neared him, he stopped to push the door open as I caught him and then he turned. I was quickly face to face with the man as he turned to face me; I brought up my right hand to defend myself as the man spun at me with a closed fist. I felt the man hit the padding in the forearm of my jacket as I began tussling with him. I was too busy using my hands to deflect his attempt to hit me as we stood almost nose to nose exchanging hits and body blows. I kept pace defending myself from the man trying to hit me, my bout felt like a mix of Jet Li and Jackie Chan flicks and with each block we were both able to squeak in a shot or two, I held my knife backwards and as I punched I turned my fists out to slice across his suit coat, hoping to draw blood each time.

The man began to slow at his attempts to fight me off and I took over with dominance and began hand boxing. As the man raised his arms to block his head from my punches I began to work my knees up into his ribcage; feeling each slamming knee sink into his bony ribs. The man slowly curled more and more after a few hard knee to his sides and he began to slump. I upper cut with all of my anger and rage, catching him in the throat, feeling my hand sink into the soft tissue brought me a feeling of relief that maybe I was winning. On the second time he had ducked his chin, I felt like I punched a brick wall when I connected with his chin and my winning feeling was gone. The sharp pain in my hand was slow to register as I was systematically punching as hard and fast as I could, knowing that my life depended on it. The man slumped towards me but in my wild rage I hardly noticed, I just pivoted and continued to punch and kick to keep him from doing so to me as I kept him pinned against the wall.

I contemplated the man's fighting style; his wild punches weren't very well coordinated nor showed of any style of organized fighting. The man I fought with landed limp wristed punches mostly to my forearms in blocks, the man didn't turn his waist to square up or give me a smaller target. He didn't block punched very well or even punch with much force, he was a sloppy fighter. Not many people can fight for crap at first; it takes a few decent fights to learn to control your adrenaline enough to even register what's going on. After a few fights you can almost think about what is going on but in all reality, it's all still going so quickly that you can't make sense of much, you need more fights for that. It's not until after a dozen or two fights that you can think back to your training and observe your opponent while fighting; my observation was that this guy can't fight for shit.

The man thudded onto the floor and groaned, my arms were numb and my chest burned from the smoke and exertion but I wasn't ready to stop fighting for my life. The man hid his swollen face behind his hands as he lay on the floor by my feet. As my adrenaline surged through me all I could do was shout and scream at him for making me get into a fight which I didn't want to do. I quick stepped my feet to keep from kicking him while he was on the floor. "Who are you I shouted" while staring down at the floor. "Who are you" the man responded. The burning rubber smoke was thick in the air and smelled of noxious gas. I quickly searched around in the office for signs of the human trading the man did but was simply seeing papers with bank or account numbers on them or knick-knacks on the shelves. Worry welled up in my throat that I may have screwed up, that I may have almost killed an innocent man or that Szeda had bullshitted me the entire way or even that everything was a trap and maybe I was on the verge of an ambush.

I began to stress about the armed men coming back and catching me, I don't know how many holes they might shoot into me but didn't want to find out. I grew louder and louder shouting that he needed to answer me but he cowered behind his hands and kept his body curled up on the floor. I kicked at the man to get his cooperation, I was still amped up after my fight and needed a little more physical outlet so I paced while searching more of the office around me, being sure to keep the man at arm's reach this time. The man failed to answer me so I looked around to find a way to help him volunteer to cooperate with me. I flashed back to "Tango and Cash", one of Pickles' favorite movies, and then I had an idea. I hurried around the desk and dragged the chair from behind it and got into position. The chair had the five points under it rather than the four which I could have used from the movie but I was going to make due.

The man hardly moved from his fetal position, his legs straightened slightly when I stepped a few feet away, telling me that his defensive position was just that, defensive. I tugged open the top desk drawer looking for any sort of gun or other looming threat that he might have tucked away but there was nothing but more papers. The urgency to get my ass moving and clear from where the men stood armed with assault rifles a few minutes before was hanging over my head, my pulse raced and beat in my ears but I had to know for sure. I dragged the chair over to the man on the floor and just looked down on him then began smiling. I found a sliver of pleasure in the rush as I had been dreary and tired for four days and with all the running I still needed to eat more clean meals before I was going to feel one-hundred percent.

The man was wearing burned and melted loafers; I couldn't find any laces so I was out of luck to tie him up. I snagged Szeda's jacket and laid it on top of him before setting the chair on his chest, making sure one of the outstretched legs was resting the wheel on his neck. I leaned and pushed down on the chair to apply pressure and I returned to asking questions, this time with a little more persuasion.

A few unsuccessful minutes of interrogation passed before I even got a peep out of the man. I explained about Davor dying painfully and about Irena rooting through the slum-bag Carl with a rolled up magazine, I even warned him about how close Szeda was to losing both his nuts to infection and atrophy if he didn't hurry up but he just stared blankly at the ceiling. *Bam Bam Bam* I heard a banging at the back door causing my heart to jump up into my throat. I felt my face turn pale with dread as I was totally busted. I kicked the chair backwards towards the desk and kicked the man over onto his stomach onto the jacket I covered him the rest of the way with and then zipped the coat up. The man kept his hands on his chest so I tied the arms of the sleeves tightly around the back of the man and then dragged him from the floor. I pushed and shoved the man towards the back door he was attempting to escape from as I barged through the door. I thought the door lead to a bathroom but what I found resembled what it was I was looking for.

Setting eyes on the inside of the questionable room made me furious. I looked quickly to find several pairs of shackles chained to metal panel lined walls, there were a few measly tattered blankets thrown on the ground and that wasn't It, one toilet in the near corner that could be seen from the door looked putrid and at the base of it were several pairs of what looked like underwear, girly underwear of course. Some of the tattered rags were stained and looked spotted with dried blood, the floor was also covered in dirt and filthy, it was more than obvious that people had slept there at one time or another.

My fists clenched and if the back door hadn't been banged on again I might have hauled off and returned to beating the man mercilessly. The second round of door banging set me in motion to find an escape route and fast so I began charging through the door and back into the office where the man was still on the floor. I grabbed the man up and hurried to push and coerce him towards the front windows which were mostly painted black on the inside. I shouldered into the man to keep him moving but he pushed back against me which further pissed me off. I grabbed the chair with my right arm and hoisted it up from behind me and then hurled it towards the window.

The glass shattered; spilling shards everywhere, I watched as the glass broke into thousands of pieces and then bounced around on the ground sending small sparkling pieces dropping around the now large opening in the wall. The man stopped pushing back for a moment as the glass made the wretched sound as it exploded all over while the chair bounced off the window frame before landing back on the floor. I felt the man ease up pushing back against me for enough of a moment that I decided to jump up and double kick him as hard as I could with both feet in the back, sending the man hurtling towards the now broken open window and then over the ledge. I landed on my bruised butt cheek after the kick but the dread of armed soldiers storming in on me was enough to encourage me to my feet and to dive out the window. I felt glass in my hands and in my hair as I tumbled out of the window and towards the boardwalk. The man was still doubled over on the wood plank lined walkway but I didn't have time for lounging about and soaking up sun just yet, it was time to go.

I stumbled a little trying to race to my feet and then towards the boat a few docks down while jerking the pud up and then dragging him with me. The man all but refused to get up and go with me without using all of my might to force him up, I guess he wasn't fond of getting kicked through a window but some guys have smaller nuts than others. The man refused to stand up as I jerked on his collar so next I grabbed his ear and nearly tore it off hurrying him up from the dock. My finger slipped at the last moment on his greasy skin and I almost punched myself in the face. I frantically looked around waiting for the sight of machine gun barrels to appear out of nowhere. I was already beat up, tired, and pissed off at the world, not to mention on a deadline to get the hell back to the States where I was being chased by two dick-bags rather than a bunch of commandos carrying big ass guns.

I grabbed the man's ears from behind him and kneed him as hard as I could in the back, making his ribs pop and snap against my force. The man leaned forward with anguish and I used his momentum to scoop under his arms and begin to drag him down the walkway. Hurry, panic, fear, all of my emotions were coursing with urgency and my eyes began to sting as they started to well up. Each step was labored, each sway to half carry half drag this heavy old man back to my boat and away from any prying eyes was a fight to get to the boat. I focused on getting back to what I came for and figured that I would keep him subdued and drive out to the open water for some peace and quiet to get back to asking the man what was going on. I still wasn't certain that I had Tarak but paying off soldiers definitely made him suspicious.

My legs burned and my body ached but I mustered enough pissed off to hip toss the man into the back of my boat, I almost couldn't get my hands free from under his armpit and was almost pulled over the edge of the boat. I had no one in view as light smoke seeped out from the broken window of the building I had escaped from. I searched between all the buildings and tried to look in through the foliage that grew in the small gaps in between but I couldn't spot anybody yet. I jerked at the knots that tied the boat off and threw them into the boat. I was in a hurry to get the hell out of the docks and out into open water but I knew that if I hurried I might forget something and screw myself over. I needed the safety of the open ocean because in the small cove I could be easily taken over, plus I needed to be in international waters.

I quickly untied the ship and slowly eased out of the dock and back through the cove. I was fast to shed my riding jacket after I was burning up and pouring sweat, plus it still smelled a bit like Szeda's piss and I wanted to be able to defend myself with hand to hand if either of my buddies tried anything while I was distracted. My body was shaking with adrenaline and I panicked while I tried to carefully but quickly get my ass out of the cove. As I backed up I caught sight of a man in fatigues standing at the broken out window of the building, waving his arms. I coasted backwards enough to clear the dock but not by much as I shoved the throttle forward began to make my way out of the area. The tall stone wave break wall was the only thing between me and safe open water but even in my hurry I fretted going too fast and tearing apart the motor or catching the propeller on something in the water in the shallower depths of the cove.

I thought back to when I got to drive a small Checkmate speed boat in school with friends. We spent a week camping and ample time lounging on the front part of the boat, quietly laying on our towels evening up our tans as best as we could while our friend Sandy's dad Rick just kept casting lines off the back of the boat. I wasn't that big of a fan of fishing and didn't find the taste very appealing until I got a little older but something as simple as fishing sounded lovely right now, I'd setter for anything instead of out running military goons in foreign territory. The four of us would lie on our belly's and tuck the backs of our suits in to expose more of our skin to the sun, (spanky's leave terrible tan lines) and Rick would keep his back to us and then announce "cover up" to make sure we had time to make ourselves respectable before he stood up and caught a full glimpse of a bunch of teenaged girls, his interest was in the fishing.

During our week of camping and boating we each got a simple coarse on boats and boats safety. We got to go tubing for hours on end and Rick would let us each take turns just towing a raft with the rest of us dangling out the back to cruise the big lake. I liked driving, the girls on the back hooted and hollered for faster but even with them wearing life jackets, I was afraid to go to fast. Risk kept his feet up on the seat at the front of the boat and just held his hand up to flick his fingers in one direction or the other when we were supposed to turn. Rick was a funny guy; he kept his white beard trimmed and his khaki bucket hat pulled down near his eyes. Sandy wasn't embarrassed by Rick when he would raise his hands to cover his eyes if one of the girls didn't tug their suit out of their backside fast enough, he would just apologize and say "oh god, did I just see my little baby girls butt? It's weird without a diaper on it, I might still have one" or something along those lines.

I remember one hot summer day when most of us girls were at cheer practice, Sandy was a cute girl with chestnut colored hair that she kept cut in a slanted bob that was very short in the back, she was very cute. Sandy thought that practice would be a good idea on a blistering ninety plus degree day, despite everyone else's objections and complaints. We spent hours in the hot sun practicing and even then I wasn't nearly as sweaty as I was backing that boat out of the cove from my nerves and panic.

The motor began to roar and as I motored faster than the "no wake" signs suggested, I was on my way back to water closer to home.

I was just passing the large rocks the bordered the cove when I noticed I had two problems; One was there was a boat backing out from a dock behind me, my palms were sweaty and my armpits leaked down my sides as I tried to watch where I was going and to what was going on behind me. The second problem was the older man; he was fumbling and flopping on the floor trying to wriggle free from the coat I had wrapped him in and tied around him. The motion of the boat rocking up and down kept his balance off and kept him from being able to fully stand up but that wasn't going to last for long. I tried to keep my back to the side of the boat to steer and keep my newest bestest friend from trying to get away. I tried to jerk the throttle or steering wheel a few times as the man tried to stand in order to keep him off balance, causing him to topple over a few times.

The man had melted shoes and bits of fabric burned to his legs from my small ding dong ditch fire, he was groaning and fussing as he tried to rock himself to his knees or feet and he continued to gravel. Each time my buddy tried to make it up to his knees all I could do was kick him back down and then get back to the wheel to get through the cove to get out. I was scared and certain that I was going to crash the boat or get caught. My blood pressure was sky high and I was many miles from safety, I was on my own and there was no help coming for me. "Dallas girl, you sure did it this time."

The sounds of the water splashing up the sides of the ship masked some of the motion from Tarak, his body moved and worked to easily free himself from the coat once he put some coordination into his escape attempts. Tarak tried to roll over to begin to crawl away from me and towards the door of the cabin. With panic as my conscience all I could do was think to raise up one of the small metal tool boxes and smash him in the head cartoon style like I did to Szeda. I tugged a metal box from under the bench and sure enough it felt heavy enough to do the job. Wrenches spilled all over the floor after the "clank" of the small toolbox meeting with the back of Tarak's head, leaving him to collapse to the floor. I feared turning my back on such a nasty man but I was also frantically trying to get away from the docks and the billowing smoke that was rising higher and higher into the sky from the shop I "borrowed" Tarak from.

I kept watch behind me as I passed the large wave break stones that lined the inlet to the cove when suddenly there it was, the yellow boat that backed out from the docks a few moments after I did. With my heart thumping wildly in my ears I felt my pupils dilate with adrenaline as I frantically watched behind me and ahead of me, alternating with a wild head whipping back and forth out the windows. The faded yellow boat followed me out of the small cove inlet, the canvas colored top hid the passengers away but I felt my temples bulge at the thought of soldiers filling the ship and then following me out into open waters where I would be easily rundown and then overtaken.

I watched as the larger ocean waves crashed against the large rocks that stood as large silent gargoyles in the water, I could tell that the yellow boat was gaining speed and so was my heartbeat. I have fought in prison, I have fought in gyms, dojos, and studios, I have taken on multiple enemies or fellow contenders at once, but I have absolutely no idea how to fight with a boat. I couldn't find myself with any other options but to haul ass so I shoved the throttle down and followed the little compass on the dash westward.

I thought back to some of my high school tussles, this girl Brenda thought that I had some interest in her man and his dangly bits so she convinced herself that she was going to beat me up. I did spend more time trying to talk myself out of fights than actually fighting, it was the right thing to do and I was raised that way, or at least I tried. Brenda tried to reach for a handful of my hair from behind me and as soon as I felt her grip, I turned to punch her in the tit as hard as I could; most of the time punching someone in the face hurts your hand so I aimed for the softer tissue of the breast. The scrap with Brenda resulted in us slipping and sliding on the tile floor from some spilled water or something, it sucked being wet but it was also nerve wracking trying not to slip and break your neck while defending yourself, this might totally suck.

The waves made the boat rise up and then drop, my stomach bounced between my butt and my throat in the water when "whomp" I heard another noise on the boat. Tarak was still motionless on the floor, his body jostled a little as the boat dropped off of some of the choppy waves but he wasn't moving. I eyed the cabin trying to find the source and when I looked up, the yellow boat following me had veered off to another direction. My heart nearly fell out of my chest with relief that the boat hadn't been chasing me; I felt my eyes begin to well up and my knees feel weak with relief. I was so relieved that a few small tears dribbled from under my eyelids and my hands slightly trembled as I slowed the speed of the boat. I kept enough speed to motor up and down the choppy waves until I got to the larger ones of the deeper water in the distance I could see the larger waves giving way to deeper troughs in the water but it didn't matter. "Thump" another noise banged from inside the cabin, this time I was certain it wasn't a wave slapping the side of the boat but something inside that wasn't there before.

I let go of the steering wheel and took one step towards the bed when it happened again. I was startled and jumped a bit, landing in a defensive stance and ready to punch something if I had to. At first I thought maybe a critter or something might have crawled aboard while I was face down in the dirt and I was ready to punch an animal to keep from getting attacked if I had to. I shook off the idea of a small animal and then thought what if a kid was playing on the boat and then freaked when I started dragging Tarak down the dock and hid. There was a slight sting in the back of my eyes at the thought of a small child being scared and hiding and then me having rushed on to the boat and then take off like mad. Awww I began to feel terrible as I reached towards the bed to lift it up and help the poor child.

Boom I began to lift the mattress of the bed when it exploded upwards and the board the mattress sat on slammed up and against the far wall. Szeda flung himself upward and began to lunge from the cavity beneath the bed. I was stunned with shock for the moment, I completely forgot he was under the bed in the cubby hole and the bastard finally freed himself. I stumbled back a little after nearly tripping on Tarak as he laid on the floor. Szeda had a look of fury on him as he reached his arms out for me; his hairy hands were shaking with rage. I slammed backward into the work bench covered with odds and ends, the bruise on my left side hip flamed back to life, causing me to wince and lose strength in my leg. I struggled to keep my eyes open against the pain as Szeda stammered to climb out of the small box that bed sat on to come at me.

"You bitch, you almost ripped off my balls, I'll cut off you tits and feed them to you" Szeda spat out his vulgarities through his clenched teeth while struggling to free himself from the wood bed frame. Szeda lunged at me again with his hands headed for my neck as I fought to remain standing against the wooden bench.

Pain shot down my left leg and it hurt too much to even stand on, I felt my chest tighten and fear began to flood over me. I couldn't keep my mouth closed as I gasped for breath. My left arm caught Szeda's right hand but my right caught his shirt at his chest while his left hand found my throat. Szeda had longer arms than I did; his strength began to crush down on me. I twisted and turned to try to break from his grasp but failed as his thumb dug deeper into my neck. I felt his strength start to get the upper hand on me as I fumbled for my footing on the rocking ship. I couldn't get enough of an angle or any leverage to take away his advantage over me and I began to sink towards the floor.

I began to fall lower on my sore leg as it buckled under the pressure of Szeda pushing down on me. I knew that if he got much more of an advantage then he would surely kill me. Szeda let his spit bubble at the corners of his mouth as he continued to struggle to squeeze harder around my neck. I fought back with all of my might but just couldn't get free. I began to feel a headache as he continued to clamp down on my neck, I had only moments before I passed out and then the foreskin would win and I would die.

Szeda was straddled over top of Tarak on the floor, he was getting taller and taller overtop of me as I got closer and closer to the floor under his weight which he was now forcing down on me from behind his straightened arm that grasped around my throat. I frantically moved my right hand trying to claw and rip at his forearm but couldn't find the right pressure point to break his hold; his adrenaline had shut off his ability to feel my scratching. The floor was crowded so I couldn't intentionally drop and take away his superiority, I was running out of options to break his hold and I was also running out of oxygen.

As I slid down pressed against the work bench my head bumped against the corner on my way to the floor. I was running out of time and was beginning to see spots indicating that I was beginning to lose consciousness. I fought to hold myself up on my right leg and raised my left to kick with all of my might to his closest knee, thwack...thwack...thwack. It took two hard kicks to his knee before he loosened his grip just a little, on the third kick he began to topple to the side as his knee began to buckle and the boat teetered a little. I swung my right arm under his hand and back over top to trap it in my arm pit and take the control back and get a moment to take in a breath. My throat burned and it felt like I was trying to swallow a soccer ball but I kept his hand clamped in my right armpit and used my left hand to push against him, tripping him over Tarak.

Szeda and I shouted and screamed back and forth as we struggled against each other. "I want to shove my knife where your thighs touch you whore" he growled, I swore back threatening his pathetic life but with my scratchy voice barely squeaking out my aggression, I was barely heard. My anger was the only thing keeping me going, my vision was still blurry in my left eye and my ears felt like they wanted to burst into flames but I fought. Szeda grit his teeth, jarring them together as he fell to the floor. I repeatedly jammed my knees into the man's sides as our arms were locked in a struggle for dominance over the other. With several dozen knee thrusts I felt his right hand that was grabbing at handfuls of skin and clothing on my side begin to loosen up.

I broke Szeda's hold and forced his hand across his body to finally take away his leverage. I forced Szeda's arms crossed and worked to pin him down with his elbows in the corner of floor and bed. Szeda was indeed stronger than me but I had trained to deal with such deficits and my time spent training gave me abilities to overcome my opponent. Szeda began to weaken his grip; I thrusted forward with both of my outstretched arms to further bind him into the corner. I kept his right arm twisted across his body and struggled to wedge my thumb and forefinger under the crook of his elbow and pinned it into his jugular veins as I forced all of my body weight down onto him. Szeda spit at me while, his muttered words slurred as his face grew red. Szeda was jammed into a small corner and with my hand closing off his already restricted windpipe I waited for him to black out and completely stop fighting. My legs were tangled up with his and I couldn't get enough traction to completely lean over top but I made sure my face was near his as his eyes slowly rolled into the back of his head before his arms finally went limp.

In some of my martial arts training we practiced choke holds, in the movies people pass out and are out for many minutes, which isn't the real case. I was sparring with a thin beautiful black girl that had a long lean body; she had long hair like Laila Ali and also an extremely mean jab. The girls name was Maggie Keller or "Killer Keller" because she was fatally precise with each long legged kick and punch. Killer Keller guarded her inside tightly and wouldn't let in punches, she was just amazing to watch fight but she was also impossible to beat as an opponent. Maggie ran track and kept her long frame nimble with dance and yoga, she was also super sweet outside of the gym. I enjoyed training with Maggie because she executed each move perfectly and even when you knew what she was doing, it was always a second faster than what you could block or anticipate. After a few months of getting tired of Maggie handing me my ass I learned to overcome. Maggie had a long sweeping right kick and rather than take the full force it was easier to rush into her kick and leap into her body and begin to Royce Gracie grapple her.

The first time I choked out Maggie she came too within a few seconds, she was spun and disoriented but she still had enough wherewithal to come up swinging while I was still straddling her. The second time I learned to roll her a bit so when she came too I was out of eyesight but it was difficult to wrap tight enough and keep enough momentum and placement to make it to the floor in order to hang on enough to cut off her air. One of the times I tried the same move with Maggie she dropped her leg to the floor to steady herself and caught me, caught me like I weighed nothing, which did not end well for me after I was swung to the floor knocking the wind out of me for what felt like the rest of the week. One of our instructors was always present when we did more than shadow spar with one another and each time, I was being tapped to move off once her hands went limp. It took several months of getting owned by Killer Keller before I learned to adapt and finally overcame, she was so proud of me she even smiled and hugged me after the first time, she was such a gracious sparring partner.

I held tightly to Szeda until my awareness kicked in, I may have hung onto his throat a bit longer than I should have before I realized how long it had been but the prick deserved it. My adrenaline burned in my veins, my chest heaved up and down and I began to untangle myself from the man in dark pants and dress shirt, both covered in piss on the floor of the cabin. My feet were tangled up pretty good in Tarak and Szeda on the floor. I knelt forward and had to climb onto Szeda to untangle our legs from the fall over Tarak's body. I was a little uneasy as I knee crawled up Szeda to the bed, my hands moved quickly but the rest of me felt like I was wearing wet clothes. I tried to ignore the fact that I was probably half covered in his urine as I gave myself a bit of space from the two bad guys on the floor.

I sat on the edge of the bed for a moment and rested my heavy feet on the pile of body parts below me. My head hurt and throbbed for a moment from dehydration before it set in that we were still adrift in the water. I located my roll of trusty tape on the floor; it probably fell from the commotion but luckily didn't go far. It was urgent that I bind Szeda up again; his mouth was still red from being taped once already but so what, with all the excruciating brutality he's inflicted on who knows how many young women so I had no feelings against his suffering. I hurried to wrap his wrists and once again put a strip across his potty mouth. I secured Tarak's hands behind him as he began to move a little on the floor as well. I had two grown men, err scumbags, on the floor of a boat that I probably shouldn't have been in, out in an ocean I had no familiarity with, beyond the water borders of my country that may prove to be a safe haven for me, all I could think was "Dallas girl, what the hell did you get yourself into?"

BRRRRRUHM the motor revved up as I pushed the throttle forward to get myself and my makeshift crew on our way back to somewhere safer..ish. The boat bounced up and down waves as I followed the wavy flinging compass to the west, I felt my body grow tired and weary while standing at the wheel but I had to get back or I was certainly making more enemies than I needed. Szeda came to, aggressively, his feet kicked and twitched as he fixed his eyes back onto me. Tarak struggled to try and pry his hands free from his tape but it ultimately just lead to him wriggling and grunting also. I cleared the horizon of the island that I left behind before I felt safe enough to slow down the ship again. I had some questions I needed answered. The first idea I had about tying a buoy to Szeda's prickly haired pair of dice seemed to work well enough, and for these two faux alpha macho super guys, I suspected they were very attached to their balls.

The horizon was clear in all directions so I felt it was safe enough to begin my work. I thought about Irena and Tallia and what they had put up with, my stomach crawled at the notion of having to get buck naked with Carl to earn rent for Davor, frankly it all made me nauseas. I was raised that everyone had their civil liberties and that they should be respected, that was why most of my biker brothers' served their country; to protect those liberties and freedoms for others'. The two men I had flopping on the boat deck like a pair of caught marlins were two bastards that stole the lives of many girls, I had nothing but contempt for such pieces of garbage and my ability to restrain my loathing fury seemed to have gone from me.

"To take a girl to bed by force or against her will in any way is rape" I began to tell my two pals as they tried to fight me off from taking their pants down while dragging them towards the back of the boat a bit. With a pair of half-naked dudes lying on the floor of the boat I found two of the floating pool like buoys I needed and began tying them with some string and fishing line. Szeda already got to experience this once and his balls still looked a pretty purplish blue and sickly. Tarak tried to fight and jerk back and forth while his pal Szeda just whimpered and tried to roll away each time I stepped near him. Fittingly for what I thought was suitable for Tarak I made a small noose out of fishing line and dropped his T- Cruise and his giblets through the hole and cinched it up fairly tight. As I affixed Tarak with his little pecker neck tie I watched as his eyes grew very large yet again while he stared at me, I blew him a kiss to show how terrifying it is to be the victim of anything that was against his will, a misfortune he dealt out regularly.

I had both of my guys laced up pretty good when I removed their mouth tape to let them begin to frantically lose their minds. Szeda had a sullen tone when he spoke, I prodded him if the man next to him was in fact Tarak, he dropped his head which told me that it was but his mouth just murmured "just do what you are going to do." Tarak was losing his mind with anticipation, his body twitched like a squished spider and he nearly knocked me over a few times as I stepped around him to work. Tarak refused to answer me if he was in fact Tarak, slipping his little Jonah Hills into a fishing line noose wasn't convincing enough so I let him watch me throw the blue and white buoy over my shoulder and into the water behind me. I looked at Szeda and squinted while nodding, he knew what Tarak was in for but still refused to encourage him to be forthcoming with what I needed; confirmation of his name.

Tarak grew more frantic, his questions about what was going on and who I was became strewn together into ramblings of a mad man. My anxiety was at its' peak, my chest was tight and I was struggling to breath but I wouldn't let my captives see it. I did feel a little guilty for what needed to be done, I wasn't some emotionless psycho or much of a vigilante but the risk of letting these bastards live was a greater pain than I could handle living with. The few lives I had taken since I got out of prison were mere scum, no different than bleaching microorganisms on a counter top but they were still lives nonetheless and I wasn't raised as some gibberish chanting terrorist, I knew that most life was supposed to be cherished. I felt the tension in my chest clench my heart; what would my father, or mother, or Pickle truly think of all this?

Chips would give me a high-five for having the inner sense of utilitarianism (for the greater good) but it doesn't mean that it is all that easy to deal with. I stepped into the cabin, my emotions had welled up and my eyes began to water as I took a harsh look at what I was doing, who I had become and where I was. I was alone, I was abandoned, I had turned away from my friends and family chasing my sense of duty and honor to other girls that had truly been ripped from their homes and sold off around the world. My eyes stung as they poured meager tears down my cheeks for the moment. I was scared but I had much more important things to deal with than just being a little frightened, I think about all of the soldiers that have to strap their boots on and head out around the world to fight in real battles, not knowing if they'd ever return, and many don't. I took a few deep breathes to calm down, a good cry sometimes does fix some things but I often prefer to hold them off until I have a few quiet moments to do it alone.

I felt *MegaDeath* begin to fill my veins, the heart pounding power chords I used to work out too now put my head back on my shoulders and reminded me that I am a strong, proud girl and I do indeed make good decisions for myself. It was time to kick some dick and go home and have a grilled chicken salad, and maybe finish my massage that was so rudely interrupted the yesterday. I stormed back out of the cabin while finishing wiping my eyes and trying to hide my sniffles. Neither man bothered to move much in the few moments I was out of their peripheral view. I was reignited with anger and I felt restored with vigor. The sun was warm on my body, my tattoos looked fresh under a slight layer of moisture of sweat and with one buoy already bobbing in the water behind the boat it was time for Szeda to head into round two of the bobbing-ballsack game. I wondered who would last.

I don't believe in the devil, nor any other imaginary hoop-la, I grew up around many men that had seen the absolute worst in people and what those people were capable of and each one found their place in the world as they worked. I didn't feel myself as evil but I, like everyone else, was certainly capable of evil things. Szeda sold women and ran them around the world for the pleasurable company of the highest bidder, even letting that fat pudgy man Terry and his man boobies lay with that innocent young Asian girl for a few dollars. Tarak was the one on the ground that I abhorred; his mere breathing filled me with hate. The flash back thoughts of Tarak raping Kelsa with his knife and coring her made my gag reflex act up; all I could think about was *that poor girl*.

I stepped up and onto Tarak's chest each time I had to pass him, I made the short conversations longer by stepping onto him over and over heading to the back set of benches to sit so they could see me and then around behind them to keep them to leave them guessing what I was up too. I inched the throttle forward and watched as both men really came to life squirming. I don't think I could have gotten either man to move so much unless I had probed their prostates with jumper cables. I walked back to the deck as Tarak was beginning plead to stop. "Yes you dumb whore" he kept shrieking over and over. The high pitch in his voice made me wonder if testes were really associated with the pitch of a man's voice. Szeda squirmed in silence; I couldn't figure out if he just accepted his fate or didn't want to appear to be the traitor to the other man.

As the boat bobbed up and down the waves I let Tarak continue to berate me, the man called me names in more than one language, it was actually impressive that he knew several languages that he could call me names in from what I could tell. Tarak shouted that he loved to cut girls; it enticed his manliness to make girls cry, especially while raping them. Tarak forced hundreds of girls to lay still while he inserted knives or whatever he could find *entertaining* into them. Tarak liked to take girls by the breasts and lift them up then cut them. That which made a girl a girl, he liked to destroy to remind them that they were for a man to own and to do what they wanted with them. Tarak spoke about how his "god" gave him all the women around him to take; they are all his property; "bequeathed unto me from the almighty." I felt my left eye twitch at all the ignorance spewing from the scraggly unshaven mouth of the man still cursing and spitting at me as he reminded me that because I had a slit between my legs, that it was only a matter of time before I was to be "condemned to hell and to spend eternity being raped by goats." I don't know why goats, why is it always goats? they have funny eyes and they're adorable.

My patience grew extremely thin very fast with my empty belly, I was super hungry and getting tired of hearing the same old rhetoric so I smiled and excused myself from my guests to duck back into the cabin for a moment to keep some of my composure, I didn't want to give Tarak any form of enjoyment that he was getting to me. I had control of my power and I wasn't going to let that scum bag enjoy my displeasure. As I stepped back into the cabin the boat swayed a little, my body lurched a little and I nearly tripped over that damned tool box, again. I braced myself against the small tool bench in the cabin and hated that damned stupid tool box. I reached down to pick that stupid tool box up to throw it in the water, except I was struck with an idea again. I searched the cabin for a moment but couldn't find any rope so I had to improvise; I grabbed the sheet off the bed.

I stood over Tarak and Szeda with the heavy metal tool box in my left hand, a stained bed sheet in my right, and a Harley Quinn smile on my face. Tarak squirmed and fought as I stood all Captain Morgan like with my left foot on him, Szeda on the other hand was a beaten man. I tore the bed sheet as best as I could down the center and began to twist and twirl the sheet tightly, I kept my eyes locked onto Tarak the whole time. Tarak held a look behind his eyes that was half dead half psychotic sadist, he had a long life of sick twisted fantasies, but it was about to be over.

Tarak was a monster that took pleasure in causing other people pain; from where I was standing he wasn't looking very delighted at the notion of his own pain. The buoy had Tarak's nuts pulled rather taught and his knees were buckled attempting to release some of the pressure from the string tugging on him. Tarak shuffled his legs in a desperate attempt to keep moving to keep from getting pinned down; he certainly was a squirmy bastard.

I tied the bed sheet rope in a large X around Tarak's body and through the handle of that stupid tool box while I fought against him to sit up, his fighting became more violent and chaotic when he realized I was tying him to a weight. I knelt down to be beside the terror, his breath was hot as he leaned up to curse at me while I worked. I braced my body against his and dug my boots into the deck and shoved the man closer to the back of the boat. Tarak grunted and threw his head back violently trying to head-butt me; his resilience was slightly admirable but frustrating. I commended Tarak for his steadfast hold on being a jerk and refusing to just give up, but it was pissing me off. The slew of berating phrases and filthy names that poured from his mouth were vulgar and downright nasty, it was clear that the upbringing that this man had was as dejected as he was.

As I began to pry the man from the ground it hit me, "Oh wait" I blurted out while dropping Tarak back to the deck of the boat. Tarak let his tense body release as I dropped him back to the deck. "I almost made a huge mistake" I surprised Tarak; this moment of pause came as I was nearly ready to hurl his body over the back railing of the boat and into the ocean. Tarak fell silent for a moment but it was over in an instant as he returned back to cursing me and my "womanly vagina of ill sins" and so on. "My vagina isn't any of your concern Tarak, my vagina isn't the one that dropped you out into this world making you the mean nasty vile piece of Y-chromosome you are" I spoke clearly to him as I opened the tool box I had tied to him. Tarak kept wriggling and trying to fight me as I kept knelt down behind him and pushed against him with my shoulder. Tarak was a terrible person, he was a tough bastard and was giving me all sorts of hell but I can't admit to having expected as much but I was weary and worn out from everything.

Tarak paused for a moment as I relocked the toolbox full of sockets and wrenches. I nearly forgot to remove the disposable cell phone I had called Carol on, she might want to hear from me soon because it was later in the day and I was still half a country and some ocean away from Philadelphia and where I'm supposed to meet her. The second time I squatted down to hoist under Tarak he really began to fight back, his back arched and it made him nearly impossible to get moving, the stubborn bastard was really struggling to stay on the boat even though his balls were pulling into the drink. I fought with the stubborn ass to get him rolled up onto the back bench, Szeda began to shout a little more while Tarak chanted over and over that I was going to burn for what I was doing. I used to find it remarkable that there were such ignorant people out there that believed such horseshit but it wasn't something on my mind at the time. I braced my arms under the older man, his graying short scraggly beard blurred as his head whipped side to side as he neared the back rail. I watched the surface of the water cap white as the tips of the waves splashed against the boat sending water several feet up into the air.

Tarak kicked as hard as he could, his burned shoes and pant legs flung wildly as I tipped him over the railing, letting his weight finish taking him to the water below. There was a moment of remorse, each anger fueled time I took someone's life I felt like I inched closer to being someone I didn't know, someone like these monsters that did what they did, and further from being the innocent little girl I remembered being. I leaned towards the back of the boat with my hands on the rail as I watched the white bed sheet pull the man below the surface, the boat rose up onto the large waves and when it sunk back down again there was no more Tarak in sight. My body was tired and I knew there was still a very long day to go, I couldn't help but to just stare into the water; what have I done?

I felt a twinge of something, it wasn't guilt nor joy for what I had done, the little scared girl inside of me just wanted to go home and cry, there was still a sense of feeling lost in me but there was also the pride in myself about the overall sense of justice that I held dearly. I felt some of the tension that gripped my lungs let up, the salty air that whirled around me seemed lighter, the breeze cooled my skin finally and I felt solemn. I couldn't find a complete sense of equality, I felt a bit angry for having gotten into many of the situations I had been in, I felt a bit disappointed in myself for not having walked away but it was tainted with new found self-assurance for who I was and pride for liking myself again. It was hard to know I was doing a wrong thing that was so incredibly right, I was taking a man's life but I did it to save the lives of countless others' and it was bittersweet. Tarak was holed up in a country that would never prosecute him if he was caught, he knew his loopholes and that was what made it my job to take him out.

As the boat drifted idly in the water while the swirl patterns in the water seemed to touch me, I was out in such a beautiful ocean and even though I was out for bad reasons it seemed good, I still felt torn. I was proud that I was serving justice to some bad people that might not ever get it had they not crossed my path and maybe this was my destiny but with each time I let my anger, my hate, my rage or my snap decisions take hold of me, I stepped closer to being one of the bad people I was trying to stop. I justified each of my actions but I wondered how long I would travel down that slippery slope before there was no turning back or heaven forbid, I begin to find actual enjoyment in the hurting of other's rather than pride for stopping the hurting of others. Dexa used to tell me: "evil is hardly the intent, just most often the result" and suddenly I felt that heaviness in my chest.

The notion that a woman shares her body with anyone else is the way it goes, but as it is her body a woman should have complete control over herself. I used to think I had a good handle on the world around me when I was a teen; I knew how the club worked, I knew how many of the other biker clubs worked and who to avoid. I thought that because I wasn't some naïve spoiled teen girly girl that I had a better grasp of the world, and especially my own body. The last few days have really kicked my butt not just physically but emotionally as well. I reflected plenty in prison and took a giant step back and looked at myself and my life from a third person point of view. I still have pride in myself but I wonder if I'm heading in the right direction for myself.

The swishing of the water was loud, my stomach had been empty and I was beyond parched after having sweat out every last drop of water my body contained, I was desperate for a smoothie and a facial and some time for more deep reflecting: I need a vacation. Szeda still wriggled and cursed me from the floor but in all honesty it was all white noise by this point. I wanted to wrap my arms around my tucked up knees and rest my head for just a moment, I just wanted a few quiet minutes to listen to the waves splash and squish along the boat but I knew if I took my eyes off Szeda for even a moment that he would like bite me or do something stupid.

I want a large plate of black beans and pineapple bits that had all been roasted over a fire with colorful peppers and some light airy music to play, I want to veer south and go to Cuba to live, far from people chasing me, far from wherever in life I was truly running from and far from myself.

I stood up after watching Tarak and all of his depraved notions sink below the surface of the ocean, there was a final sense of absolution in me. The water gave way to deep blue down below and finally the sun felt good as it kissed my skin again. I turned to look back at Szeda, his pants still around his ankles and the floating buoy in the water behind me still tethered to his bits. Out of the corner of my eye I notice a large boat barreling right towards me. I had about two hundred yards between myself and a very large boat suddenly zooming at me by the way it was cutting up the waves. I felt a knot in my stomach; it was time to go. I jumped over Szeda on my way back to the cabin and shoved the throttle forward to get going.

I held on tight to the steering wheel to brace against the thrust of the motor and in the same instance, Szeda began to howl in pain. "Shit" it hit me that his balls were still tied to the buoy, or at least they *were*. Szeda made his bed, I had my own ass to save and a very menacing looking boat coming at me with a severe amount of pissed off driving it. I throttled up as fast as I could and then scrambled to make sure I was going in the right direction to get back into the United States coastal waters according to the compass pointing west. The large boat coming at me was black and the water was white as rushed down the sides of the ship while it barreled right at me. I steered with both of my hands and kept my right foot braced behind me to fight the inertia of the boat. My stomach was twisting in my belly and my head pounded as I rushed. The humming from the engine out-roared the panicked pain shrieks of Szeda as I could see a bit of his body rolling around on the back deck.

The large ship slowly closed the gap behind me, as it neared I could see that it had a very large gun on the front as well as some men lining the side railing holding on and all staring at my boat. Sweat poured down my forehead, down my sides and down the rest of my body too. My heart was in my throat for a very long while as I kept my fingers crossed and I did my best to get as close to the safer waters of the U.S. as I could. The boat bounced up some of the waves and slapped the water pretty hard as it came down some off the others; the beating was rippling through my already fatigued body. I fumbled with the temporary cell phone I shoved into the waist of my riding pants as I hoisted Tarak over the railing to his death and began to dial while I waited for it to power on.

The phone continued to beep at me that it was out of range and anxiety screamed through me. My fingers ached, my thumbs shook and hitting redial was nearly impossible as the boat shook beneath me. I was frightened that the boat chasing me was going to deep fry my ass when it caught up with me, never mind frightened; I was *certain*. I was angry that I couldn't catch a twenty minute break to pee and also that my hands shook so badly that I almost couldn't grip the steering wheel. The adrenaline surged through me but it didn't do me any favors, it just dried my mouth out and made me want to cry. My eyes burned with fear as I frantically whipped my head around, I tapped on the GPS but it was all blue, no sign of land, no bearings to learn from, nothing. I tried to hold the dying cell phone in different positions hoping to find any sort of service to be able to call for help, but there was nothing.

I was running out of options as the boat slowly drew near. I could see enough to tell that the men lining the side rail were in fact wearing the same fatigues that the three soldiers in Tarak's warehouse were; I was certainly going to get deep fried in all of this mess. I wondered if they were coming for Tarak, which I didn't have, or if it was because I was fleeing their waters leaving behind a smoking building on their shoreline? I gasped to breathe as I tried to finagle a plan, I certainly didn't want to end up in prison again but I had a sneaking suspicion that if I was caught I'd end up right next to Tarak, oh man I kinda hope for prison. Each time I redialed that damn cheap phone it beeped "No signal" and with each squawk, I felt less and less hopeful. I was straining to think of something, anything to get out of this bind, I need like a rescue chopper or the coast guard to get out of this bind, but we are the only two boats I can see.

As the boat behind me gained ground, err water, my outlook grew more and more dim, I had no options as far as blowing up the boat behind me or anything like, I didn't have a flare gun, or a real gun, or a bazooka, I wanted a bazooka. I was frantic and alone and shit out of luck and panicked so I couldn't come up with much else I could do. The boat tailing me was still fifty or sixty yards behind but catching up, I had a small window of wiggle room for something if it were clever enough. I thought about the first time I evenly matched with Maggie, I took some body blows and even though I didn't physically feel like the winner. I knew that earning the win was going to take some body blows and some abuse, nothing in life is easy, except a reality show hoe (snicker). I ducked to stay out of sight of the ship behind me as best as I could when I had to move around, for all they knew I had a boat full of people with guns trained on me. I grabbed a bloodied and still writhing Szeda by the collar and dragged him into the cabin from the deck. I searched through as much as I possibly could in the cabin, any sort of spear gun or something projectile. I wished for some of the greasy oily rags from the warehouse, I needed to make something as smoky as possible to block their view but once again luck wasn't in stock for me.

I found some honing oil but still lacked much of anything else I needed so I broke apart the hand-held part of one of the communicating radios on the dash; I needed the wires to strip them of their plastic sheath. With a bite from my teeth I had some exposed wires so I looked around and the best option I had at the moment was to take the mattress and pour some of the honing oil on the corner. I was pushing my luck trying to outrun one boat while trying to set fire to the one I was steering. I suddenly felt like any number of crazy 80's action movie buffs that always have some Wyle E Coyote like ideas but still work out, except this isn't scripted and I didn't have a stunt double. I pushed some of the radio wired into the small stain of oil and as I flicked the talk button, I dragged the other wires around hoping for any sign of a spark of something to get hot enough to ignite that bastard by shorting out the bare wires across each other. Szeda was growling and letting out spit bubbles on the floor, he was in bad shape and bleeding pretty badly but I wasn't going to administer any sort of aid to him.

As the boat gained on me I was failing to start a small fire, the grungy mattress would surely smoke as the foam burned but I was having a panic attack rather than a bon fire. I looked around until I found a small circular piece of metal shard, it was a sharp bastard so I wedged it into the mattress as best as I could and began winding the small copper wire strands around it as fast as possible. I pulled more wires from the chord and continued to wrap it all around the metal coil, sort of like steel wool and a battery to light a cigarette prison style. Small orange embers started two glow bright around the edges of the metal so I gently tried to hold my breath long enough to blow a little oxygen onto the embers until they birthed out a flame. I rolled the mattress over the hot and burning oil and duck walked to the back of the ship. The mattress smoked as the small fire burned in the middle of the rolled up mattress. I had a small tail of smoke following me as I continued to barrel to the U.S. as fast as I could make the boat go.

I picked up my riding jacket, it was still brand new with the exception of the mods I made to the inner lining of the forearms but it was done serving a purpose. I turned the arms inside out and pulled the last bit of money I had left. I stripped my shirt off and tossed it out onto the mattress for more to burn. I tucked the bit of cash I had left after buying a bike and sending money out to Lu into my bikini top. I had to wriggle and adjust my top to hold the money against me tightly; I wanted to make sure that it was certain to stay put. My roll of tape still around my left wrist was all but gone, if I was lucky I only had a few feet left but something would have to do. One of my only options now was to expect some swim time, which I couldn't do in my riding gear, the other was to hide away and claim that Szeda kidnapped me but with his balls missing and life still in is body; that option wasn't in my favor.

I stripped off my new cute boots and then tugged down my pants. I was often willing to strip down with friends and go swimming in my undies in school but now with a castrated Szeda writhing on the floor next to me, I felt my skinny dipping times might be behind me. There's no difference between underwear and a swimsuit anyways but once I started riding more frequently I learned you wear through normal undies from all the sitting pretty quickly so when I was younger I started wearing bathing suit bottoms under my clothes almost full time, wow was it paying off. My toes gripped the carpet now that I didn't have riding boots to protect them from whatever I might step on on the floor.

Szeda was still moaning and groaning on the floor as I stepped around small puddles of his blood. I was losing my gap in front of the boat behind me and it was time to make something desperate happen. I tried one last time to get an idea of how far I was from U.S waters and that sliver of hope to wake up alive. The small GPS indicator showed a partial black line in the blue water but I had no idea what the squiggle represented and in my hurried frustration I wasn't going to read the owner's manual. "Connecting" my fate seemed to have changed for the moment as my phone began to ring. The phone dialed Carol but I didn't have any time left for talking. I dropped the phone and began to pick up Szeda. I used my riding pants to tie Szeda to the steering wheel, he slumped forward and being in only my bikini, feeling his warm bare legs on mine totally was gross.

As the mattress began to spit flames into the open air I used my riding pants to lash Szeda to the steering wheel. I imagined gunships popping holes through the boat like the movies and I didn't want to be the target standing at the helm if that happened. Szeda remained slumped over the top of the steering wheel as I continued to barrel towards the U.S. waters. I was out of options and out of room and all while my heart was in my throat, I was screwed. The only thing I could think to do was to send my pursuers on a wild goose chase to try and get more distance. I felt like I was slowly burning each piece of wood I was floating on in the sense that I was destroying each item at my disposal, it was only a matter of time before I was completely out of resources.

I thought about taping Szeda to the wheel so that when he fell the boat would turn but too tight of circles and it would be obvious, I needed one northern turn so that I could jump to the water. The boat was speeding along and the impact would probably hit me like a train, I felt sick to my stomach. I had a knot in my gut at the speed of the water rushing past the boat, I had known guys in high school including Mark that liked to wake board and often times he mentioned that hitting the water was very similar to hitting cement at the same speeds. I began to tie off a wad of my tape to the steering wheel and unravel it from the wad around my wrist. Lightning struck my brain; I remembered that I hadn't gotten my bike keys from my pants pocket so I panicked. I shuffled to Szeda and began to feel for my keys in the pockets while trying to keep an eye out for the boat trying to run me down behind me. I found my bike keys and decided to tie the key ring in the strap of my bikini tie and then tuck them into my other bra cup to keep them from flying off and told myself it was time.

I mentioned laying a bike down when I was younger, well here's what happened: I was just learning to ride an old Honda that Lu had gotten for me. The rules state that for a certain amount of time I was supposed to ride with an experienced rider blah blah blah but it didn't say what role the experienced rider was supposed to have, meaning I sometimes left that rider at home. I mostly rode the streets of town at slower speeds until leaning into the turns became second nature. All the nuances of a new bike are all different and could only really be learned from practice and time, neither of which I had patience for. One night I pushed my bike down the driveway, down the street and finally far enough that I thought I was free to find my way once I fired it up away from anyone that might catch and then stop me. I headed out on my bike for a Friday night ride, I could have easily asked any number of the guys from Car13 to go with me but I wanted my own freedom, the same as any other real rider.

I made it past the limits of Waylon, I thought about heading up to see my dad but going to a federal correctional facility with only a learners permit was tempting more fate than my little ass could risk. I had a few nights of riding under my belt, nights of staying out under the stars and sleeping next to a bike, it was an easy way to spend the night and plenty cheap enough so I wasn't all that worried about getting back in any hurry, I was free. Lu was working the bar so it was only the neighbors that kept an ear out for me that I had to sneak past, I was sure that when Lu got home my ass was going to get hided but that was a problem for the next morning, not that night. I cruised around some of the roads for a while, riding solo was a very nice contrast rather than have each and every turn scrutinized by Lu or Chips when I rode with them. Dexa was a fairly laid back rider but because he was so timid he didn't want to take on the responsibility of being an overseer of me and my still developing riding skills.

Lu had given me pointers as to how to lay down a bike and to let your body slide on your elbow pads to salvage your skin and bones, I practiced it in my mind well enough but as I had learned plenty of times in kick-boxing, mental practicing equals a hand full of steamy crap in comparison to a real world application. I was swerving from white line to white line on a wide open and docile road, I wasn't sure where I wanted to go but I knew I loved being out and free. As the night passed on I found myself in New Mexico, not all that far but regardless, I was a state over and all by my pretty lonesome. I wasn't far from a small town called Zoelle when a few racing trucks barreled down the highway. Big rigs are intimidating because of the wind wash that sends your butt scooting left and right when they pass but pick-up trucks aren't much to worry about so long as there isn't a dickhead behind the wheel.

I watched in my rear-view as headlights rushed up behind me on the highway, two sets rode side by side and flew up on me rather fast. I felt my hands clench tightly onto my handles and my ass clamped down onto my seat as best as I could as the trucks drew near. The truck in the left lane roared past me while the one right behind my drove uncomfortably close to my back wheel. The dickhead in the following truck revved and roared his engine at me and it made me super nervous. I wasn't all that comfortable or steady at sixty or faster on my bike yet so I couldn't really speed up, the severed foreskin driving behind me continued to play with my nerves from behind the wheel of his big shitty truck. After a mile or two of the truck trying to become my thong they finally decided to slowly pass me. Hanging from the passenger side of the truck was a scraggly skinny teen with a lame trucker hat on and splotchy pubes sticking out of his face from what I could see in the dark. The boy shouted to me several times but as the genius couldn't really figure out, it was hard to hear him over my exhaust.

I fought to keep my handle bars straight as I rode, it took a few tries but the dark haired kid looked to be in his upper teens and wearing a ripped up sleeveless shirt while his lighter haired buddy with a giant wad of dip pushing his lower lip out drove, they both kept looking over at me and from the corner of my eye I could see strange and random motions. The driver must have seen my long blonde hair flailing from the back of me and decided to mess with me that night. The driver hooted and hollered while the passenger held out a beer bottle trying to insist that I take it from him, I was too scared to release either of my hands at the higher speed. I was white-knuckled on my throttle and couldn't imagine letting go to grab hold of a beer but he continued to wave it towards my face. The duck-butter driving began to swerve at me and that was when my nerves really began to unravel. I felt a knot in my stomach and I began to ease back on the throttle to slow down but so did the truck and two boys in it. The truck kept pace with me and as I finally got down to under forty miles an hour the passenger began ripping his shirt off and trying to impress me with his Bugs Bunny like torso.

The passenger kept most of his body hanging in the open side window of the truck trying to show off as the driver still easily swerved towards me on my bike. The passenger stripped down and was mostly nude while hanging out of the window grabbing *himself* in the late evening as I was trying to keep from wrecking my bike. The passenger had his left leg in the window and his left arm holding the handle but was kicking his right leg out and his right arm doing a number of things to gain my attention to... *him*. As I continued to slow down the passenger made wilder and wilder motions, his legs kicked out and his hand mimicked that of a monkey at the zoo with all the self-tugging he was doing. The passenger kept kicking his leg out and trying to tap my helmet with his bare foot, it was hard to keep my nerves even at the slower speeds and not get kicked in the head or handle bars causing me to swerve right into them and crashing.

The boy had his naked ass straddling the window of the truck and facing sideways, his legs continued to swing at me and each time it nearly hit me in the face or head, it almost sent me into the ditch. The boy was waving his foot in my face when I reached and grabbed it with my left hand, I didn't want to wreck but I had a knot in my stomach and no other options. I jammed my foot down on my brake as I held on tightly to the boy's leg and fought with all of my death gripped right hand to hold my handle bars as straight as possible. I figured if I was going to get wrecked by some dude being a dick then I was going to squish his grapes in the process. The boy's legs ripped from my hands as they kept driving buy I could tell he was pulled hard and violently into the window sill as I stopped while riding. My bike skidded forward for a foot or two before my body slammed into the tail of the truck.

Time stopped, *THOOMB THOOMB* my heart pounded in my ear as my thighs clamped down onto my bike and my right arm fought to keep the braking bike forward. The bike began to turn as the truck sped on and my tires screeched out into the darkness like a ferocious eagle. My left arm reached for the grip to help keep my front tire straight when I hit the carcass of a dead animal and the front tire popped up a little. My butt bounced at the same moment that the handle bars ripped from my grip, signaling the start of a bad set of events. My butt didn't return to the seat, the bike fell from beneath me while the rest of me followed my path of momentum. *THOOMB THOOMB* my heart beat pounded loudly in my ears while my body just floated, I watched the headlight of my bike flash along the ground as it laid flat to its side and then begin to leave a trail of sparks behind it as it began to slide along the dark pavement. My body was weightless; I thought that if I could just work my arms to spread out that maybe I could just fly home or even just glide slowly to the ground. The night was silent, there was a random flash of the white headlight and the occasional orange sparks flying into the air against the bleak pavement as my bike continued to slide.

I watched as I floated overtop of the pavement, the yellow painted slots in the middle of the road went by me, two, three, maybe even four long yellow painted lines striped paste below me before I realized I was in some weird time vacuum. The tall lights of the truck in front of me continued on down the long darkening road as I tried to tuck my arms around me. As I continued to float I started to tuck my head a little and I tried to roll into the air kind of like cats do when they fall. I turned my head as hard as I could towards the sky. The sliver of horizon to my right was a medium blaze orange and as I turned to face the sky I began to make out stars from the horizon to my left. I felt myself smile at the notion that I was flying towards the stars, up, up, and away. I felt as motionless as the night air filled my clothes and made me feel even light... *THOOMB THOOMB* my heart beat twice more before the evil prick gravity reached into the night and volleyball spiked me to the pavement.

I hit with a heavy *THUDD* and I tried my best to tuck to roll or to slide without flailing too much and risk taking an arm off. There was moment of what sounded like splashing as I rolled and flopped against the ground along the pavement. I watched as the dark pavement and the lighter sky took turns spinning in my view for a moment before I felt enough ground below me to jam by heels and elbows out a little to slide on rather than just continue to roll out of control. The stars didn't move above me but I felt that I slid for a few more feet before I felt myself come to a stop. I smelled of burnt hair and hot leather when I laid there and took mental stock of my body. There was an entire numbness that washed over me, I couldn't tell if I had entered that seven minutes of brain activity they say occurs once you die or what was going on.

I didn't feel hot, I didn't feel cold, I didn't even feel the hard ground below me, I felt the pressure of the asphalt but it was sort of removed, like when a dentist drills your numb tooth, you're sure it would hurt but the pain is blocked, that was all I felt, that numb pressure. I flexed each finger to my thumbs and counted each one out loud; ten individual fingers. I tapped each toe to the soul of each boot and counted again. I didn't feel insane pains shoot up my body, I felt the muscles in my legs tighten as I flexed them on my mental mapping of my body looking for injuries. I rolled my head slightly and then moved my toes again to make sure that I wasn't risking suffering any spinal injuries and then I continued to feel out my body, like I was in a dream of sorts. My heart pounded so fast I couldn't hear, I rose up my head and couldn't find a sign of the truck I tangled with just moments before.

I turned to see that my bike was almost forty feet behind me and almost completely off the edge of the road. As I sat up I looked at my hands to visually see them, I clicked my toes together and watched them work as instructed. I began to cry uncontrollably at the near death run in I had just had, I knew I was scared, frightened, relieved, just all of it but I was still a little numb too. I found myself in the deepest pile of crap imaginable (at the time) I was out of state after having snuck out and had just nearly died on a long road alone, there was no stopping the tears as they poured down my face. My mind blanked and all I could do was bow my head and keep on pouring out the tears. I was so grateful to be alive that there was no punishment Lu could have doled out that I wouldn't happily accept. After my nose was filled with snot bubbles and my shirt soaked with tears on my chest was when I caught enough of my breath to start piecing myself back together.

My front tire hadn't stopped spinning as I approached it, my body felt turgid like I had just finished working out and it was full of blood pumping into all of my muscles. As I bent over to begin to stand up my bike I felt the sting in my back, the tinge wasn't in the spine but it quickly jolted across my back like lightning. Reaching my hand behind me I felt what filled me with dread. My back burned and my fingers felt gravel filled ooze. I must have slid more than I thought, In the light of my headlight I looked at my hand covered with blood and clear ooze and grit. I was road rashed. I felt my lower lip begin to quiver with the pain that seared through me, I knew that I had to hurry and do something while I still had enough adrenaline surging through me to numb my pain.

I grunted and pried my still hot bike from the sand filled ditch. My bike wasn't all that mangled but scraped all over, the exhaust had a bend on the side and the front fender was twisted. It took a jolt of my strength to get my engine turned over and every fiber in my back was beginning to burn like it was on fire. I stood my bike up and rode like a forest fire home. I spent the longest most miserable hours riding home, my jacket and shirt flapped against my injured back and it would take some steel wool type of scrubbing to get all of the dirt out before I could get patched up. It was hard to make the ride home, I was desperate for Lu's comforting despite how mad I knew she'd be, My body wanted to keep giving up to fall over and die from the pain but I was too stubborn to die.

The sick feeling that filled me when I knew I was going to wreck myself and my bike was coming back as I stared at the water as it rushed by. I didn't have any padding or any ability to slow the boat down to soften my landing. I was wearing my two piece bikini and was about to fling myself from a very fast moving boat, ugh I felt like an asshole for what I was about to do to myself. The mattress spewed thick gray smoke from the back of the boat and it obscured being able to see my newest stalkers which hopefully meant that they couldn't see me either. I had a small window and nerves or not, I had to make a move. I backed out of the cabin door while holding onto the end of my tape rope tied to the steering wheel; I bent my legs a little and began to clench my teeth in anticipation. My chest muscles all tightened up, my knees felt weak and my stomach was feeling very icky. Looking towards the west I could see what appeared to be something that resembled the coast, I couldn't tell you how far but at least I knew what direction I needed to go.

I clenched my left arm across my chest to hold my keys in my bra and my cash also. I waited until I jumped as high as I possibly could and jerked the tape tether. The boat swerved from underneath me and once again: my body floated as everything happened to nearly stop before easing into slow motion. I watched as the blood covered deck of the boat coasted beneath me, I watched without control as my heels dragged through the air and hit against the side railing, sending my legs upward towards the rest of my body. The silver railing on the side of the boat clipped both of my heels, it wasn't a painful hit but rather a hard nudge which then sent my feet coming up at me and rolling me backward towards the water. I tucked as best as I could but as the boat turned I was flung outward toward the water. I was worried about coming down on the edge of the boat but the outward force propelled me out enough to clear most of the boat but my ups did not. I felt like a cartoon, there was no grace to my uncontrolled spiraling and back summersaulting towards the water.

I tumbled through the air and into a rising wave and then into the water, the wet engulfing ocean was a shock to feel as I plunged deep into the water. I kept my arm clutched to my chest as my right arm began to wave chaotically to make sense of what direction I was swimming towards as I rolled over and over under the surface. I kicked and kicked but couldn't stop tumbling in the water long enough to get my bearings, I felt like I was trapped in an undercurrent like you see happens to surfers that just get rolled around and around or bashed onto reefs and shredded to pieces. The hard smack to the water stole most of the wind from me and with the hit, I was a little stunned before being able to get to swimming. The water was chilly, my petite body felt like a leaf in the fall wind except I was in the ocean.

My eyes burned in the salt water but once I got close to the surface I wanted to burst upward all Little Mermaid style for breath but I quickly remembered in my panic that I was running from a boat full of killers so I rose slowly to look out for the ship that was following me on the boat. I searched for the trail of smoke and sure enough the black boat was gaining on the burning ship. The water splashed and tossed me around, I tried to keep my legs crossed after I jumped but everything happened so fast I hadn't notice for a moment that my top had become misaligned I nearly freaked after part of me fell out of my top and I was terrified that I lost my keys or my money. I treaded water for a moment and watched as the black boat sped away after the one I left Szeda tied to. I felt around to make sure that my cash was still in my hand and cupped to me and used my free right hand to put my top back on in place and tuck my keys still tied to my string back into my right side bra cup so they would stay in place while I swam. I heard some popping noises from the distance, they were hard to tell what they were as the water splashed my face but I wasn't going to wait around to find out if they were gun shots so I began swimming.

It was pretty dark when I hauled my water logged carcass onto the dry beach. I fought to keep the *Jaws* music out of my head for about two minutes and each time I felt myself grow tired of all the swimming I imagined something had just touched my foot and my energy was instantly renewed to keep swimming, just like Dory. I felt bloated and tired and just weak from the exertion. I floated plenty but as the sun set while dog paddling the concern of making it to shore in the dark freaked me out, I was worried about getting disorientated in the night and then just finally giving in and drowning so close. I had hours to swim and think about how I got into the situation I was in: swimming for my life after having run for my life after having killed for my life after having had to bargain for my life. I realized I was gambling way too much with my life for people that I hardly knew, with my one and only life. I was more tired of running to save my ass than I was tired from swimming, maybe it was equal.

As the sky darkened I kept my eyes locked on some of the lights in the distance and hoped I was swimming towards buildings on land and not some cruise liner floating away. My right shoulder was knotted and stressed, my left ass cheek was a giant knot, my back was torqued and my head was throbbing with a migraine from being dehydrated and my body was so utterly drained of energy that the thought of merely slipping beneath the waves and letting it all finally end grew to be more and more tempting each time a wave slapped me in the face. I tried to think about how my dad spent his long days dealing with the pain of his badly burned arm in the hot desert sun and the sand grinding away at his open would. I thought back to the hours of riding I had to do after I wrecked my bike and how terrible it was to try to get it scrubbed out. I still think about how the scars have faded and lightened and even though I hardly think about them, I still remember so much of the pain and the torture of healing afterwards.

As I kicked my legs and struggled to keep up my swimming water continued to wash into my mouth, the salty bitterness kept me fairly angry and kicking my feet. I swam for hours until I could actually see beyond the shoreline to visibly spot buildings in the distance, a sight that renewed my hope, even though very little. I kept my eyes closed for most of my swim to picture being in a swimming pool or hot tub, many of my thoughts reverted back to *Deep Blue Sea* where sharks made a mess of Sam Jackson. I bargained and pleaded that if I was going to get mauled by a pissed off monster that I didn't want to see it coming and I hoped that it would be fast. I love animal planet but when a seal rips apart a penguin or a shark chews the shit out of a seal, I never wanted to find out how they felt.

Once I felt my feet kick sand beneath me I tried to stand to walk towards the beach, the density of the water washed me back and forth with the waves and after my third stumble and fall back into the water I tried to get back to half swimming half trudging through the water. The water temperatures climbed a little as I neared the beach but the air was getting very cold on my wet body. My jaw shook with my body shiver and even the warmth of the sand couldn't stop the whole body convulsing shiver from taking over me. My vision was blurry, I felt light headed and I worried that if I got any more dehydrated that I might pass out and then succumb to kidney failure from all the saltwater exposure. I remember from biology that salt water dehydrates you and that is why saltwater animals don't drink the water but get it from the food they eat, I had to pee the whole swim but I held it to keep my body from losing the rest of the water that might be in it through osmosis to the ocean I was swimming in.

I dropped to my ass in the sand after crawling a bit away from the waterline. My head hurt, my entire body ached and there I was, finally sitting on the beach like I wanted. I had been in Florida and ocean adjacent for a few days and only after having been flung from a speeding boat and then having swam a few miles to shore did I finally got to sit on my ass in the sand and look around for a bit. I watched as the sky shut away the last few bits of orange, I was missing another looming deadline to meet this Carol lady but I was too tired to care. Carol threatened to mess with my dad in prison and my family back in Waylon but each one of them are smart, militarily trained, and far enough from me that their repercussions of knowing me should have minimal blow back. The beach was pretty empty for being a pleasant evening, I have absolutely no idea where I am and for the first time in days I have time to myself so I don't give a rat's ass.

I pulled my cash out of my bra top and counted out six hundred bucks. Stabbing my right breast are the keys to my motorcycle that was still parked in the South Pointe marina parking lot, and I had nothing left to give and no way to give it if I did. My aching back and muscles wanted to be cradled by the sand, so much of me wanted to just lay back and wake up in the morning somewhere that didn't matter, like I once did in Mexico, but a girl passed out in the sand in a bikini will either end up robbed, raped, or in jail; none of which had my vote.

I felt like throwing in the towel in prison, I felt like letting myself drown in the ocean, I felt like lying beside the road in Atlanta after leaping from a moving truck, but something inside of me just hated the idea of giving up. I felt sick, all the time spent in the water wore me out and I knew it was dangerous to go so long without water or food and out in the sun and so on. I felt my body shiver keep surging through me and I worried that it was a sign of hypothermia getting a stronger grip on me. I needed to get into a warm bath and let the water soak back into me and hope that I don't pass out in it and drown. Man it would suck to swim miles and miles in the ocean only to drown in a friggin bath tub an hour later.

My body refused to cooperate as I tried to roll over. I felt like a walrus in the beach as I heaved back and forth and rolled and heaved to try and get my body up and underneath me. Each step was a struggle, the sand shifted under my weight and I seemed to stumble and fall every other step I took. After my third or fourth fall I just began to cry again. I was so tired and had no will to continue any more, my body was so dehydrated that I couldn't even tear up, but I sobbed anyway. Down on all fours I just sat there, my butt wanted to fall back and rest on my heels but my head just couldn't let it happen even though it just hung off of my neck, my hair brushing lightly on the sand. If I rolled to my side I might just stop breathing and die from exhaustion. My chest seized, I tried to fight for breath but I couldn't keep from crying enough to take a full breath and suck it up. There was thirty more yards of sand until I reached some shrubs and then what looked like was a hotel. I couldn't find the strength or coordination to stand so I just crawled, slowly and painfully, I crawled.

When I lifted up my bike after wrecking it several years ago my body also fought what I needed it to do. The pain in my lower back burned as I inched my bike from the ground, I had leg pressed weights for months to strengthen them under Lu's suggestion for just that reason but it didn't make it any easier. I had no way of knowing how bad my injuries were but I was miles from any sort of help and the journey to get it seemed impossibly long. Digger told me that after he pulled the man from the fire that he spent days wandering the desert like Moses before he could get his arm medically treated, there was one evac chopper for the accident and he knew there were men much more hurt than him that needed the medical attention so he hid his injuries and made his way back later on. I imagined how bad Digger must have felt dealing with a burned arm in long sleeves in the hot desert, my scraped up back shouldn't have been so much to complain about.

I rode for over two hours to get back to Car13 as the wind whipping up my back caused the burning sting of the road rash to remain sharp for the entire ride. I forgot about my wrecked bike and the bent handle bars; I focused on keeping my back still so it didn't burn with each bump along my ride. I pulled up to the bar to tell Lu what I had done and hoped that she would take me to the hospital, my concern for being in trouble fell to the wayside of just wanting to hug her after my brush with death and the fear of never seeing her again. The emotions that filled me after my wreck made me a sobbing blubbering mess for a few minutes of post-accident adrenaline but when I got to Lu at the bar, that was when my emotions over took me. Lu had no idea why I moseyed into the bar or a real certainty how I got there but as soon as I saw her standing behind the bar chatting with Pickle I began crying. Lu could tell something big happened and she began welling up immediately when she saw me crying at the door.

I cried too hard to speak as Lu rushed to me, the look on my face was probably poor and pathetic but Lu sprinted to me worried that maybe I got a phone call that something terrible had happened to Digger in prison. I sobbed and blubbered for minutes before I caught enough of a breath to start apologizing to her. Lu wrapped her arms around me and as she held me tightly the searing pain caused my entire body to spasm and contract. After a few painful seconds I gathered enough strength to push back from Lu enough to catch my breath and begin to explain that I was injured. Lu had some oozy gravel on her hand from my jacket and didn't realize what had happened yet, I nearly stood on my tippy toes from the pain while hugging Lu but it didn't matter, I needed my mommy to hold me.

I hugged Lu with all of my might; I buried my face in her shoulder and felt forever grateful that she was there for me. I nearly hit the ceiling when Cheryl reached forward to lift my jacket and revealed that I was grated like hamburger underneath my jacket. Lu went from loving to concerned instantly as Cheryl yelped out that I was a bloody mess before she began ordering Chips to pillage the first aid kit and quickly. Most of the guys milling around the bar were hollering about my first lay down rash, Lu swatted most of the guys off that hooted as Cheryl lifted up my jacket and the back of my shirt to inspect the damage. "Dirty old goats" Lu barked before threatening to make it last call if they didn't settle down. Cheryl and Lu lead me into one of the back rooms while the other bartender Steve took over. Lu had enough reserve not to pepper me with questions until she was sure I was ok but I could tell by the reddened look on her face she was in need of knowing.

Chips and Lu helped me to get my jacket of while Cheryl dug through the first aid kit like a puppy in the trash. Chips took a seat across a small table from me to stare me in the face, I assumed to keep my attention. Lu flipped a chair around for me to sit in backwards and Chips held out his hands. "I don't see a crystal ball buddy" I snarked to Chips joking that he was getting ready to play gypsy palm reader. I had a pretty bad feeling in my stomach over what was going to happen but if the three of them said it had to happen, there was no getting out of it. Lu nodded to take a seat and Cheryl warned me she'd need to clean the grit and crap out of my back (not a thrilling notion) and that it was going to hurt like childbirth. I put my smaller hands into Chips' meaty palms and grabbed on as tightly as I could and closed my eyes.

After an hour of what sounded like steel wool rubbing against a rusty tail pipe and a whole lot of bellowing howls on my behalf Cheryl scrubbed and cleaned the dirt out of my road rashed back. The blood permanently stained my panties and my shirt was ruined but the half chewed through portion of my riding jacket was fairly bad ass though. As a girl it sucks to try and sleep on your chest, I couldn't sleep for the first few nights from the pain even with an anesthetic spray let alone sleep on my side for weeks until I was healed over. I wasn't insecure about my gnarly rash scar because all the guys at the bar or bike clubs were all high-fiving the badge of tough chick honor but when it comes down to it, I knew that there was nothing to be ashamed of. I walked away from an accident and got to tell my side of it and that was bad ass.

Once Cheryl was done scrubbing away at the majority of my back Lu stood me up and together they bent me over the table to reach the lower injury; "Look, Cheryl, I don't know how you and Chips get down but I ain't in to it" I tried desperately to joke to mentally take myself anywhere else but bent over that table like I was about to get whipped. "Relax Dollar" Cheryl tried to coax me as she tugged down my riding pants to get the waist below the injury. I felt the top half of my ass hit the bare air and the chill was different than I had expected but made much worse as Cheryl dabbed some peroxide on me, the wet made it much colder. Chips kept his eyes deadlocked on mine and remained seated at eye level with me, he kept a stern face but the uplift in his eyebrows showed more sympathy for me than he'd ever admit. "Slap that ass woman" Chips muttered to Cheryl as he winked at me. Cheryl got back to work scrubbing all of the sand, dirt, and grit from my gooey oozing open back wound, Lu and Cheryl worked while Chips did his best to hold my hands and let me squeeze as the pain seared through me, he really helped me to hold back the tears.

Chips let his voice turn soft as I gritted down and bore through what sounded like to rocks being rubbed together as Cheryl removed dirt. Chips repeated over and over that he was proud of me for toughing it out and that I was going to be ok, it was strange seeing him so supportive when the basic nature of our relationship mirrored that of thirteen year old boys. I remember the euphoria that filled e once an anesthetic spray was applied and Cheryl was done scraping away my skin. After bandaging was applied I didn't even care than half of my ass swung out in the air, I wanted to collapse down onto that cold table and immediately pass out knowing it was finally over. The cold table top felt amazing to my warm cheeks, it was comforting that Chips held my hands but as I let all of the air out of my chest and all of my muscles loosen up with relief: *SMACK* Cheryl gave my good right butt cheek a mild slap to throw me off guard and to lighten the mood.

I reached the luscious green grass after the journey across Florida's piece of the Gobi desert; it was soft under my hands, even after the gritty sand wore down my fingerprints as I crawled. I stopped weeping and began to chuckle that it had only been a day and a half since I had fallen out of a window and down onto grass that seemed to be as hard as rock and nearly broke my ass and here I am nearly making love to grass because it was so soft and welcoming. My arms quivered beneath me as they wanted to lower me to the ground for a moment, just a short, slight, restful, moment, but I knew if I did then I would be waking up sometime the next day, if I woke up at all. I rocked forward and backward for a moment rife with indecision. I knew my mind was as tired as my body but that my body would power through if my mind convinced it too but I was losing my ability to keep a straight thought, I just continued to weep.

I had no idea of where the hell I was, I had six hundred bucks and a pair of motorcycle keys tucked into the top of my bathing suit to my name, no identification or proof that I was a legal person or anything, I had my two piece bikini and that was it, I had absolutely nothing else. It had been a few days since I left prison, which I did with more clothing that I currently had on, and I lost count of how many times I had gotten my ass kicked. I felt like hammered dogshit. I had been slapped and punched by Putty Nuts in a box truck, nearly blew out my eardrums in New Orleans, Body dropped a gas station robber in Texas, almost blew up an international airport, fell from a third story window, kidnapped one man and went out into international waters to kidnap and kill another man and now I swam like five ocean miles to collapse on the stupid beach in the penis tip of Florida I hope. I miss Melanie, I miss Shay, I miss a green smoothie, I miss a Tuna pineapple salad with extra greens and I miss my home.

The air didn't replenish my energy as I huffed and puffed, I spent all of my energy swimming and there was absolutely nothing left in me. I was certain that I had enough heat stroke from the sun on my face swimming that if I hid under the shrubs that I'd certainly die and quickly, but the grass is so soft. I remained on all fours for one more half thrust forward until I felt myself slide into a downward dog pose. My hands wouldn't move forward and once my face touched the soft sand filled grass, my butt dropped down and everything went black.

www.ingramcontent.com/pod-product-compliance
Lightning Source LLC
Chambersburg PA
CBHW021958170626
46808CB00001B/211